THE KURDISH EPISODE

A different kind
of story!
Enjoy!
Joe

Publications by the author:

Short stories

A Family Matter
Too-late Dowry
Egyptian Pounds
So White plus Seven
The Metzes
A Subtle Play
Novice Bank Robber
Pretend Love
Cousin Paul
We, The ROTC Cadets
The Snow Queen Contest
Henri Rochemont

Hardback books

Three-Phase Electrical Power

This book is a fictional work that in no manner is intended to represent any actual events or persons, dead or alive.

ISBN: 978-1-5323-9859-9

Edition 2

Printed in the United States of America

THE KURDISH EPISODE

A Novel

Joseph E. Fleckenstein

CONTENTS

Chapter - Title - Page

Chapter – Title – Page

1

A Government Man Comes Calling

THE driver asked his companion, "You sure we're on the right road?"

The man next to him responded, "Yeah, the GPS says we are. And the sign back a ways said Barlow so we can't be far wrong. The place should be another half mile or so."

They continued along in silence. As they came up behind a farmer driving a corn harvester, the driver accelerated and quickly pulled past the slow moving contraption. His companion pointed ahead while declaring, "There it is: McDougal's Firearms. Looks like it was a gas station at one time–Esso, I think, from the shape of the sign. What a hell of a place for a firearms store. So far away from people and houses."

"Yeah. Maybe the guy doesn't know much about business. I'll pull in. Let's get this over with."

Sean McDougal sat on a stool behind the counter, cleaning a new Beretta shotgun that the UPS deliveryman had brought to his shop that morning. Before he could show it to an interested customer, he needed to remove the protective coatings of grease the manufacturer had applied. When the opening of the front door activated a duck call, Sean looked up to see a serious-looking man enter. At a distance of ten feet in front of the counter he called out, "Good morning, sir." The visitor was dressed in a dark blue business suit, tie, and white shirt. A man of a serious demeanor and a type that did not often visit gun shops. Sean wondered *What the hell could this guy want?*

Although the visitor was dressed in the old style of a salesman, he did not appear to be a typical salesman. He lacked the forced smile and superficial glad-to-see-you air. Robbers, especially those on drugs, often targeted gun stores. Unregistered guns of all types can easily be sold in back alleys, and they command a good price. Was this man intending to exit the shop with an armful of guns that he hadn't paid for, leaving the shopkeeper dead on the floor?

Sean set the shotgun on the rack behind the counter and moved to a position near the cash register. There, on a lower shelf, he kept a loaded 9 mm Glock. He asked, "What can I do for you, sir?"

The man glanced right and left while he kept his hands at his sides and in clear view.

"Mr. McDougal, I have an important matter I would like to discuss with you. Do you have time? I suggest we speak alone. Just the two of us."

A man out to rob a shop would prefer to know if he had to contend with more than one person. Sean shifted his right hand to the shelf below the cash register.

"We're alone here. Go ahead and say what's on your mind."

The man nodded politely. "Sir, I should perhaps mention I know about your past and your background. I'm an employee of the federal government, and I had access to your army records as well as other government documents. I also spoke with active army personnel who knew you during your days in the service. There's more, of course, but it's not relevant at the moment. Is this a convenient time for us to talk?"

"Sure," he replied. The stranger's words piqued Sean's interest. Nevertheless, he didn't relinquish his grip on the 9 mm.

"My name is Jason Wagner."

The visitor reached into a trouser pocket and withdrew a card. Sean gave the man points for not having reached into a jacket pocket for the name card. Without looking at the card, Sean placed it near the cash register. The visitor continued.

"We are searching for a special kind of gun dealer. More to the point, we need a gun dealer with a federal firearms license and one who has a proven record as a loyal American. A man who knows firearms and who has military experience. A man who can take care of himself under challenging circumstances. We think you are the right man for the assignment. If you are interested, and I have reason to believe you will be, you would go abroad for a month or two. You would coordinate delivery of a large shipment of guns and associated munitions. This is a clandestine operation, and it might involve serious dangers. Of course, we expect to pay you well for your efforts."

What the stranger had to say was interesting. Running the business has been a hell of a lot better than doing carpentry work. No question about it. On the other hand, a chance for adventure is entirely something else. Despite a developing interest, Sean preferred to keep a poker face.

Sean stared at the stranger.

"Let me get this straight, Mr. Wagner," he said in an even tone, "You want me to be a gunrunner? Is my understanding correct?"

The visitor winced slightly. "I would not say 'gun-runner.' That term suggests selfish and nefarious motives. To the contrary, we hope to help thousands of needy and desperate people. These are people who, without our help, might be enslaved or killed. People who are friendly to America and who identify with our values. Mr. McDougal, you need not say yes or no today. We understand that you would need time to think about our offer. If you have any questions or if you would like to have more information, I suggest you speak to one of our high-level officers in Fairfax."

Sean looked at the wall to his right to emphasize his reluctance. "I might be interested. Of course, I would need to know more."

"Naturally. Here is what I propose: Call our headquarters anytime during working hours and ask for Matthew Barton. Mr. Barton will no doubt invite you to DC for a visit. I'm sorry. I cannot tell you more than that. I traveled here today for the sole purpose of making contact with you and to personally extend our invitation to you."

The visitor slid a folded piece of paper across the counter toward Sean. "This is the number at the agency headquarters," he said. "Mr. Barton will be expecting your call."

Sean said, "I'll think about it. No promises."

"Fine. We hope to hear from you. Please understand our need is an urgent. Could you call within two days' time?"

"Sure. I'll call one way or the other tomorrow afternoon."

"Excellent! Thank you for your time."

The man turned and went straight to the black SUV parked at the front of the building. When he opened the passenger's door, Sean saw a second man, dressed in an identical suit, in the driver's seat. He wondered if the two also had matching ties and shoes. In a few seconds, the SUV was on the road and soon disappeared out of sight.

Sean retrieved the hoagie that he had brought to the shop earlier in the day and laid it on the counter beside the cash register. He unwrapped the wax paper, folded the loose onions back into place, and took a bite. Chewing, he stared up at the mounted head of a ten-point buck on the far wall. The deer's glass eyes seemed to be questioning Sean as in the vain of, "How about that guy, Sean? You don't see visitors like that every day. Do you think he is legit and really has something of interest?"

The stranger's visit stirred memories, sending Sean's thoughts drifting off to past adventures. To times when enemy combatants were firing bullets and mortar rounds at him and his fellow soldiers. When sudden death was a distinct possibility. He appreciated he was living a comfortable and safe life. Yet, he had to acknowledge that, all things considered, he preferred an exciting life to a boring one. He missed the adrenalin rush, the comradeships, the challenges. With the first bite he told himself he wasn't that hungry after all. A mixture of thoughts ran through his head as he folded the wax paper around the remainder of the hoagie. He carried it to the small refrigerator he kept in the corner office. Maybe he would take it with him that evening when he went home to think about the unusual invitation.

2

Taking Care of Business

EXCEPT for Saturdays, Sean saw the most traffic on Fridays. A number of the locals were off work Fridays and a few of them came to his shop. Many were merely browsing or dreaming with no serious intent. Others were truly in the market for a gun. Their reasons varied. Hunters wanted the best gun they could afford to help them bag game afield. Others used guns for shooting at inanimate targets. A few prospective customers were looking for a handgun to carry or keep at home for unwelcome visitors.

As Sean entered the shop Friday, he knew he was going to call the agency. He had promised he would, and he always strove to be a man of his word. At the same time, he did not wish to seem too eager about participating in the government's "project." Before striking a bargain, whether buying a used gun or an automobile, he had learned to seem only a little interested, almost disinterested. Play the cards close to the vest. Keep your counterpart wondering. Go to the brink.

As he walked to put the overhead lights on and unlock the front door, Sean noticed a Lincoln sedan pull into the parking lot. The model and year suggested the owner would most likely be the type who would be in the market for a new gun and perhaps one of the more expensive models. The driver, a middle-aged man, pushed through the front door and looked around the shop. He was wearing a pair of jeans, a western shirt, and hiking boots. He sported a slender mustache. As the man strolled toward the counter, he surveyed the assembly of long guns against the rear wall. His gaze settled on the group of shotguns behind the counter. Sean realized he must stop thinking of the so-called project the government man had mentioned and slip into salesman mode. "In the market for a gun, sir?" he asked.

"Why, yes. I see you have a good selection."

"The best for miles around. I have handguns, rifles, shotguns, smoke poles. You name it. Either we have it or we will get it for you. Do you have a specific gun in mind?"

"Maybe. I do a little small-game hunting on my brother's farm, and my sixteen-year-old daughter expressed an interest in hunting with me."

"Good for her. I like to hear about women taking up hunting, especially young women. The outdoor sports offer a wonderful chance for youngsters to experience nature and wildlife with friends or family, and it's a great way for family members to build memories. Would you be hunting rabbits or birds?"

"Both, I would say. Mostly birds. My uncle has a few quail and lots of pheasants. He told me he would like to see us shoot all the pheasants we can use because they pick out and eat the corn sprouts by the hundreds. On occasion we can expect to chase out a rabbit or two."

"May I ask the young lady's height and build?"

"She is average-sized for her age. I guess around five foot-four and slender."

"From what you tell me, I believe a 20-gauge should be just right. The twenties are smaller overall than the 12-gauge guns yet plenty good enough for what you have in mind. I believe your daughter might like a Remington Model 1100 auto. The autos kick less than, say, a double or an over-under, and you get three quick shots. Plus, the autos are less expensive than other types. If she is just starting, you might not care to buy one of the more expensive guns. You know: See if she takes a genuine interest in the sport."

Sean stepped to the gun rack behind the counter and selected a shiny new shotgun. He handed the gun to the visitor. "I would recommend one like this."

Hesitating, the man asked, "How much?"

"Let me check." Sean flipped through some papers he kept near the cash register and pushed buttons on a calculator. "That one is $650."

"Is that your best price?"

"Yes, sir. I'm sorry. The Remingtons command very little markup because a lot of dealers sell them."

Sean wanted to give the man a chance to think about his price. Besides, he never wanted to be seen as pressuring someone to buy. He extended his hand. "By the way, I'm Sean McDougal."

They shook hands.

"Jim Hanson. Pleased to meet you."

Mr. Hanson walked around the shop floor, lifting the shotgun to feel its weight and balance. Sean could tell the man knew guns to some extent.

He paused and nodded to Sean, "Okay, I'll take it. It's going to be a birthday gift. I'll need shells too, say number five shot."

"I believe she will be pleased with the gun. If you bag more rabbits than you can eat, I could help you there."

"I'll keep you in mind. No promises though."

Sean completed the mandatory state forms and in a few minutes gave the man his purchased items.

The moment Sean's customer left the gun shop, Sean's thoughts returned to the visit by the government man and the standing invitation to adventure. He should call to see if the man's proposition merited further time and evaluation.

Seated at the desk in the small office, Sean dialed the number that Jason Wagner had given him the previous day. A live person answered on the second ring.

Sean swallowed. He hoped to have the proper voice for the occasion. "Good morning. I would like to speak with Mr. Matthew Barton."

The operator said, "One moment, please."

Sean heard the rustling of paper. The operator advised, "Mr. Barton is at Extension 570. You may wish to make a note. I'll transfer you."

On the second ring a man answered. "Hello, this is Matthew."

Sean answered in like manner. "Good morning, Mr. Barton, this is Sean McDougal."

"Good morning, sir. We hoped you would call. Mr. McDougal, if you are available, I would like to meet with you to discuss our project. How about we get together for lunch?"

Sean grew suspicious. As yet he had no proof these people were actually representative of the US Government.

"Why don't I come right to your office?" he asked

"There are certain protocols we are obliged to follow. I'll explain later. I suggest we meet at the Saigon Restaurant on 15th Street in D.C. We can have a relaxing lunch while we talk about our mutual interests. I'll be with another agent. If all goes as expected, we will drive you to our offices here in Fairfax for a tour of our facilities. You may leave your car at the restaurant. We will have a driver return you to your car afterwards. Would Monday at noon be convenient?"

The roundabout procedures described by the stranger seemed odd to Sean. At the same time, he realized he was dealing with intelligence officers who, by practice, would be circumspect.

"Sure, noon will be fine," he answered.

"At the restaurant ask for me."

Sean replaced the receiver, and continued staring at the telephone. *Are these guys legit? Or is this so-called project some kind of illicit and perhaps illegal operation? What about the hazards Jason Wagner mentioned? Is my bent away from the mundane in reality foolhardy and perhaps even drawing me into grave danger?*

3

A Neighbor's Visit

SEAN continued to think about the coming meeting with the government agent. He wondered what they might have in mind for him. What about the gun shop? Who would manage it while he was off tending to the government's business and perhaps contending with people of questionable character and dubious intent?

The sign on the front door of the shop stated that the shop was open from noon to seven, Tuesday through Saturday. From experience, Sean had found his current hours to be the best for business and best for him. A visit to D.C. on a Monday would work well, since he would have the shop closed that day.

As closing time approached, he was looking forward to settling in at home with a beer to stimulate the thinking process. He had turned off the parking lot lights when, a few minutes past seven, the front door opened and Wally Woodrow entered.

Wally lived at a farm a mile away from the shop. His uncle owned the property and let Wally live in the coach house behind the main house. Wally had been living at his uncle's place for several years before Sean moved to the area. In exchange for the free rent, Wally took care of his uncle's two horses and helped with chores around the property. The uncle either liked his nephew or felt sorry for him. Maybe a little of both. Wally did not own an automobile and usually used his bike to go buy groceries in Barlow. On occasion he would ride one of the horses to town. One afternoon, Wally had stopped by McDougal's Firearms for a firsthand inspection of the new business in the area. More visits followed, and over time he and Sean became friends.

Wally and Sean had a common need, namely another person to talk with at times. Wally was one of those types who projected a misleading image. The clothes he wore appeared to be an inheritance that he might have received from a larger father many years in the past. The colors never matched. Wally was small in stature and meek. His glasses were too large for his face, and he seemed gullible. However, Wally proved looks could be deceiving. In fact, he was well versed on a wide range of topics. He rarely lost an argument, and almost always had a quick and solid comeback.

Sean was always glad to see Wally. On his own initiative, Wally started helping Sean at the shop. He would sweep the floor, clean the windows, and otherwise help with odd jobs. Wally never asked for the greenback cash Sean gave him. Wally had made it clear that under no circumstance did he want Sean making a paper record of payments. He explained that he lived off a government check and did not care to have any interference with the regular delivery of those checks. The payments he received were not large. On the other hand, Wally said he didn't need much.

"Evening, Wally. I was just closing. How's it going?"

"Good."

Without needing to be asked, Wally pushed the deadbolt on the front door. Sean waved him into the small office in the back where he withdrew two Budweiser longnecks from the small refridge. He twisted the caps from the bottles, handed one to Wally, and asked, "How did you get here today? By bike, horse, or shoe leather?"

Wally took hold of his beer and sat in the recliner across from Sean's desk. "I don't ride the horses at night. The car lights hurt their night vision. I walked. Cheers."

Wally took a swig and asked, "Any sales today?"

"Yeah, a few. Maybe enough to pay the electric bill."

"Aw, Sean, don't give me your Pennsylvania poor-mouth speech. You got plenty in the bank."

"How would you know?"

"I have my ways."

"Baloney. You're bulling me again."

"Really?" Wally leaned forward toward his friend. "I can tell you two weeks ago you had over twelve thousand in your bank account. Maybe the amount changed since the last time I looked."

Sean frowned. "You know a clerk at the bank? An employee who shouldn't be talking about customers' private information?"

"No, nothing like that. I've never been in the bank where you have your account, and I don't know any of the tellers who work there. You forget I spent time at the Defense Intelligence Agency, where I learned how to hack into things online. Don't worry though. I didn't transfer any money out of your account, but I could have. I was just curious."

Sean didn't know whether he felt more shocked, amazed, or angry. "Damn, that pisses me off. I would think the bank would be more careful with those things."

"Sean, it's a way of life today. Live with it and be thankful I'm not a thief."

"Don't you worry about federal or state cops backtracking to catch you? I mean, doing the things you are doing?"

Wally shrugged. "It's not going to happen. I operate out of an old cabin near the farm. It's on a piece of land that nobody wants. The property is landlocked, and that's probably why nobody claimed it. I think the sheriff took ownership. I put the internet service to the cabin in the name of a fictitious person, a James Schultz. Once a year I visit the cable company to pay the annual bill. I find a guy in the line, somebody who doesn't know me, and I give him cash to pay my bill, plus a few extra bucks. I tell him I have a medical problem and can't stand on my feet long. I sit outside and wait for the man to bring the bill stamped 'paid.' The cable company doesn't care who pays the bill as long as they get their money. If someday, someone traces my activities to that cabin they still wouldn't know who operates the computer that is connected to the cable. I use a laptop that I never leave in the cabin. When I leave, the laptop goes with me."

Sean grinned. "Wally, you surprise me. I never thought you could be so clever with computers, let alone so devious."

Wally laughed. "The feds taught me all that. I was a good student."

Both men took a draw on their beer and were silent for a spell, savoring the taste and Wally's recent disclosure.

"I think your business will pick up pretty soon. Hunting season is not that far away," Wally said.

Sean took another draw on his Bud. "Yes, I'm sure the hunters will start coming around. They'll be looking forward to the small game season and maybe thinking of a new gun."

Sean set his beer on the desk. "A strange thing happened yesterday. A man came by the shop and invited me to be a gunrunner for Uncle Sam. My guess is that the project would bring me back to the Middle East."

"That's some kind of an invitation."

"I haven't heard all the details yet, so I may or may not be interested. I don't know what I would do with the shop. Let me ask you: Do you think you could run it for a spell until I return? Of course I would pay you for your time."

Wally finished his beer and dropped the bottle in the waste can.

"Yeah, I could do that provided you pay me the regular way."

"Sure, Wally, I'm sure we could find an arrangement to your liking."

After Wally took off down the road, Sean checked the doors before stepping out to the parking lot. The evening air had cooled, and a breeze was rolling fall leaves across the parking lot. Standing outside the shop door, Sean paused to listen. In the distance, an owl was calling. The bird's call seemed forlorn, and he wondered why the bird was calling in the first place. Why would it care to announce its presence? Was it seeking a mate? It sounded lonely, much as Sean. He waited until the bird stopped calling before going to this car.

4

A Trip to Washington

SINCE Sean expected the agents in D.C. to be dressed in suits and ties, he did not care to have them peering down their collective noses at him in his flannel shirt and jeans. He would be comparably dressed. Sunday he drove to a nearby town where he bought a dark grey suit, the first he had ever owned. He also brought home a white shirt, tie, shiny black shoes, and one pair of black socks.

Once home, Sean thought he should try on his new purchases. First, he tried the shirt and tie. The tie became a problem. Having never worn a tie around his neck, he didn't know how to proceed. He visited YouTube, and on his fifth attempt was able to make a reasonable Windsor knot. Slipping into the suit jacket, he went to the bathroom to check himself in the mirror. The reflection caused him to chuckle: Sean McDougal, native of downtown Donora, Pennsylvania, former carpenter and ex-army corporal, dressed in a fancy business suit! Smiling, he wet a comb and ran it through his wavy black hair. As usual, he patted the hair in an effort to keep it close to the top of his head. Pleased with the reflection in the mirror, he stood back and saluted. He was prepared for the big city and the people who live there.

Sean's dark black hair and heavy eyebrows probably came from his Irish ancestors. Likewise the blue eyes. People always noticed the eyes which seemed to speak a language of their own. They conveyed friendliness, compassion, perhaps a little devilishness. Sean was of average height and slender. He lacked what could be called classical movie-star looks. He was somewhere around a seven, yet he did all right with the ladies. His easy and relaxed style compensated for other shortcomings. Although he could be charming if he wanted, he could be tough too. Donora had taught him toughness, and he'd learned well. To stay fit, he visited a gym several times a week. He also ran the roads near the trailer park to keep his wind up.

Sean had grown up in Donora, a small Pennsylvania town where steel mills once provided work for the men and money that kept the town alive. In recent years, though, the boarded-up shops and abandoned buildings attested to the adversity experienced by the families that stayed. The demise of the steel industry brought particular angst to Sean's mother. Abandoned by her unemployed husband and alone, she had struggled to raise three boys and a girl in a small apartment two blocks from the Monongahela River.

Sean was able to take care of himself and his younger brothers in a rough neighborhood. One particular incident in Donora had given Sean's fellow high school students reason to show him respect. Sean's first day at high school, the class bully intended to let Sean know who was king of the roost. To intimidate Sean, he told some of Sean's friends that Sean's mother put a red light in the window when she needed money. Sean told the bully to stop the slander or he would make him stop. The bully threw a sucker punch that Sean had anticipated. He blocked the punch and followed up with a left jab that the bully later told friends seemed to come from nowhere. The next day the bully, displaying a shiner, came looking for Sean with two of his bigger friends. The friends grabbed Sean while the bully approached to "even the score." As the bully prepared to throw a punch, Sean kicked the boy in the gut with both feet, knocking the wind out of him. The boys were holding Sean by the biceps, which allowed Sean's hands to be free. He used his right hand to pull up on a finger of the boy holding his left arm. At the sound of a crack, the boy released his hold and jumped back, howling and shaking the hand with the broken finger. With his freed left arm, Sean swung a fist into the face of the boy holding his right arm, giving him a bloody nose. Once free, Sean went to the bully who was still gasping for air, grabbed him by the shirt, and blackened the unblackened eye. That day Sean won respect that lasted to graduation day and beyond.

Sean's first job out of high school was doing carpentry with a house builder. A large part of his paycheck went to pay the rent and his mother's grocery bills. For several years, he had enjoyed working outdoors and building houses. The physical activity kept him in shape, and he liked breathing the outdoor air. However, in time he found the work repetitive and boring. He also began to resent his foreman, a rude man who played favorites. Sean had been thinking of the army for a while. The military way of life, new experiences, and a chance to leave Donora all seemed to call to him. As the months ticked by, the whisper in his head became a shout: Join the army, get out of Donora. Do it! One bitter-cold winter day Sean didn't go to work. Instead, he visited the local US Army recruiting office. The sergeant had all the right words for an attentive young man and a potential soldier. Sean enlisted in the infantry, hoping to see combat in the near future. The army did not disappoint him.

Sean spent most of his active duty overseas, living in tents in hot, dusty, and hostile foreign lands. His company commander had often sent Sean's squad on excursions into dangerous territory where he had become engaged in firefights. On more than one excursion, Sean saw buddies take bullets and shrapnel. The army returned some of them in wooden boxes to grieving parents, and some were returned with missing body parts. At the end of a six-year tour of duty and two minor wounds, Sean concluded he had had enough excitement for a while and did not reenlist. Because he had spent most of his tour in the Middle East, he had few opportunities to spend his pay. As a result, he had accumulated a sizable bank balance that was waiting for him the day of his discharge. Sean had used part of his army pay to start the gun business.

A short time after his discharge, Sean drove to the town of Barlow, Pennsylvania where one of his army buddies, Mason Keller, was buried. Sean and Mason were together the day Mason took a bullet, and Sean had driven to Barlow to visit with Mason's parents.

Traveling on the main road out of Barlow, Sean passed an old Esso service station with a "For Sale" sign posted out near the road's edge. He had been thinking of starting a gun shop, and the sign caught his attention. He recognized the area as rural and different from what he knew in Donora. No doubt, he thought, there would be an ample supply of people in the area interested in buying guns. Sean turned his car around and went back for a second look. Paint was peeling off the building and litter was strewn about the property. The concrete bases where the pumps once stood were still in place. Because of the building's dilapidated condition, Sean guessed he might be able to buy it at a good price. He called the real estate agent and inquired. Sean submitted a low bid and the owner came back with a counteroffer. Eventually they agreed on a price and Sean had the beginnings of a gun shop.

McDougal's Firearms provided Sean with an income, albeit a meager one. Nevertheless, he preferred the smaller income and the independence to a higher income and the routine of punching a clock in someone's business. Every time he considered working for someone, he remembered the supervisor he had at his first job out of high school. His independent spirit told him he would have trouble working for that type of person again. Besides, he knew guns and enjoyed dealing with people who had an interest in hunting or shooting. In a good year he made enough to pay the bills and a little more. Living in a trailer also helped to keep expenses down. For a while, he told himself he was content with his new rural way of life. Gradually he became accustomed to his quiet and isolated days in Barlow. Living near Barlow was different from the army or the urban setting of Donora. He realized a problem, though. There was no woman in his life, and the prospects in Barlow seemed bleak.

***

Sean had no trouble finding the Saigon Restaurant in the Capitol. He whipped his fifteen-year-old Toyota into a lot behind the building and parked. Standing beside the auto, he slipped into the new suit jacket and wiggled the shirt collar with the uncomfortable Windsor knot. Following a walkway that led around the building to the front of the restaurant, he encountered a man standing in his path. Dressed in tattered clothes, the stranger extended a hand toward Sean.

"Buddy, can you spare five dollars for a meal?"

The message as well as the threat was implied. *Here we are outside this fancy restaurant. If you can afford to eat in a place like this, you are very lucky. I have had neither luck nor money. I'm sure you would not miss a mere five dollars. And if you do not come across with a bill or two, I might get upset. Street people like me are quick to get upset, you know. Violent, at times. No five dollars –no guarantees!*

To Sean's way of thinking, an able-bodied man in need of money should seek employment somewhere. He should go find a job and work for compensation and pride. Besides, he resented threats or attempts at intimidation. According to Sean's creed, he showed respect and he expected respect in return. The man blocking his path showed no respect. A quick assessment suggested the potential threat was not up to Sean's boxing or karate abilities. Actually, he might enjoy a little tussle if it were not for the new suit. Sean stepped close to the man to show he had no fear and whispered, "Get out of my way, you ugly son of a bitch. If you want to eat, go sweep floors or do dishes somewhere. Go to a soup kitchen."

With clenched jaw, the panhandler stepped aside to allow Sean to pass. Sean winked at the man as he stepped by, continuing to watch his back.

Inside the restaurant the hostess, a young Vietnamese in a tight-fitting dress with slits to the top of her thighs, greeted Sean.

"Are you alone, sir?" she asked.

Sean responded, "Yes, all alone. Story of my life. All the girls I liked didn't like me, and the ones who liked me I didn't like. What's a guy to do?"

The hostess blinked a few times, not certain how to reply. "Let's hope, sir, your luck will change in the near future. For today, would you prefer a booth or a table?"

"I was invited here to have lunch with two gentlemen. I believe they might already be in one of your private rooms."

"Yes sir, you are correct. Your friends asked me to watch for you. Follow me, please."

With heels clicking against the masonry floor, she led the way to the rear of the establishment. Following several feet behind her, Sean considered the parade-of-one. His judgment was no doubt the same as the many men who had witnessed the same exhibition: *Great curves, a practiced swing.* The hostess stopped at a small room and tapped on the door. A voice from within said, "Come in." She handed Sean a menu and told him, "Enjoy your lunch, sir. A waitress will be here shortly." The sound of heels announced to all within earshot that the restaurant's hostess was returning to her station near the front door. Observations welcome!

Sean entered the room, allowing the door to remain open. Inside, two men sat next to a table that had been arranged with a linen tablecloth and two place settings. Linen napkins and wine glasses complemented the genuine china dinner plates. The men stood as Sean entered. The elder of the two, dressed in a government-standard dark blue suit, approached Sean with extended right hand.

"Mr. McDougal, I'm Matthew Barton. I am pleased to make your acquaintance."

"Sean McDougal. How do you do, sir?"

Gesturing toward the second man, Barton said, "And my associate here is Stan Patkowski."

At six-feet-five, the man was a full head taller than Sean, and his shoulders seemed as wide as the doorway. The big man approached Sean and thrust forward a huge, calloused hand. Sean shook hands with the giant. Matthew gestured toward the table.

"Please have a seat, Sean."

Matthew nodded to Patkowski, who promptly told Sean, "Excuse me, Mr. McDougal. I'll be waiting in the car. Enjoy your lunch, sir." He gently closed the door behind him on his way out.

Matthew sat across from Sean at the table. "Sean, we appreciate your taking time to come down for a chat," he said.

"No harm in talking."

"Right you are."

In response to a gentle knock on the door, Matthew said, "Come in."

A waitress, dressed entirely in black, entered. "Excuse me, gentlemen, would you like an aperitif?"

Matthew told Sean, "Please order whatever you wish."

Sean asked the waitress, "How about a bottle of Pinot Grigio?"

"Yes, sir. We have two grades. Would you prefer the top grade or the less expensive one?"

Barton said, "Yes, the better grade."

As the waitress exited, Barton reached into his breast pocket, withdrew a business card, and handed it to Sean.

Sean took the card, and placed it in his shirt pocket. Matthew continued.

"Before we get down to business, tell me about yourself. We already know a lot, but I would like to hear it from you and in your words."

"Okay." Sean took a breath. "I was born in western Pennsylvania. Never knew my dad. He abandoned the family when I was three. Mother still lives in Donora. I own a gun store in Barlow. It keeps me in beer money, groceries, gas for an old car, and only a little more than that. You know about my service in the infantry. I don't do drugs and I have no police record–which you probably already know. I have neither a wife nor a girlfriend. That's me in a nutshell."

Matthew pursed his lips as he listened intently to Sean's self-portrait. It was a life very different from his.

5

Friends in Need

AS Matthew Barton and Sean waited for the waitress to bring the wine, Barton said, "This is what I can tell you today. As you are no doubt aware, the Middle East is experiencing a lot of turmoil. The United States has interests there that must be protected. Otherwise, our adversaries will step in where we should be. Our friends in the region need our help. I'm talking about arms, ammunition, supplies. That's where you and I come into the picture. One of our immediate goals is to deliver an assortment of supplies to our friends so they can take on our mutual enemy. The shipment will consist of rifles, mortars and some other items needed by combat troops to wage a good fight. These are brave fighters who are desperate for help and who are fighting a cause that deserves our support."

Sean nodded, suggesting agreement with Matthew's line of reasoning.

"Your role would be to coordinate delivery of the arms," Matthew continued. "If you take the assignment, you will go to France and make contact there with their representative. Our friends have told us they prefer to deal with a flesh-and-blood contact, a person who has authority to do whatever is required. They say it's their accepted way of doing business. They don't believe in making deals over a telephone, by emails or through a third party. I would be remiss if I did not tell you this is a dangerous assignment. Our enemies have spies, and of course, so do we. In fact, we assume certain enemy agents will do whatever they can to prevent delivery of our shipment. I'm referring to possible sabotage, armed intervention, perhaps attempts at assassination. That's the picture in a nutshell. Sound interesting?"

With a tilt of his head, Sean remarked, "I might be interested."

"Good! Of course, we will compensate you well for your trouble. We would consider you a contractor to the federal government. The first payment we would make is a three-hundred thousand dollar signing bonus payable upon your staying with the project to the end–successful or otherwise. The pay is forty thousand a month. We will make the payments to a Swiss bank account of your choice. If you die in the line of duty, we would pay an additional five-hundred thousand dollars to your estate."

Barton's mention of the large sums of money caught Sean's attention, and he tried his best to appear nonplused.

"One other thing," Barton said. "The Agency will deny any affiliation with you. As far as we are concerned, you are a freelance gun dealer. You are not to mention the method of payment for the weapons to anyone. Nevertheless, we intend to have the people we are helping know it is America that is helping. The arms, of course, are made here, and that fact is stamped on every weapon. Outside of the people we are aiding, we would like the role of our government to be ambiguous and seemingly unofficial. Deniable, you might say. One-way or the other, the objective is to help our friends help America. The best way to do that is to provide those people with the means to fight our mutual enemies."

The waitress arrived with a bottle of Pinot Grigio in a bucket of ice. She removed the cork and bent forward to pour a sample into Matthew's glass, thereby allowing the men a view of her fetching cleavage. Matthew confirmed that the wine was satisfactory, and she filled both glasses. She followed her exhibition with a broad smile that implied, *There, gentlemen, I hope you enjoyed the peep? If so, a few more dollars added to the tip would be appreciated.*

The men waited in silence. Sean wondered how she would be in bed. Would she be a giggler or a moaner? Would she like to romp around a bit or would she merely prefer to remain still on her backside and let the man has his way? Standing back from the table, she asked if the "gentlemen" had decided on their orders. Sean said he would have the beef and lettuce curry. Matthew chose the crepes with shrimp and bean sprouts.

Matthew's brief description of the government's project had captured Sean's imagination. He felt it drawing him like steel to a magnet. Yet, he rarely would jump to an agreement of any type. That would not be his style. He said, "What you described sounds like a worthwhile project. I can understand why the government would want to help our friends, and I'm sure I could handle the operation. On the other hand, I have this business venture up in Pennsylvania. It would be hard for me to get away. I don't know…"

Matthew interrupted Sean, "Sean, I have authority to change the terms somewhat. We think you are the perfect man for the assignment, and we would like to sign you up. What if I raise the sign-on fee by forty big ones and the monthly rate by five? What do you say to that?"

Sean paused, waiting for the waitress to exit. At the sound of the door closing behind her, he lifted his glass in a toast. "Count me in. Here's to the project."

Matthew lifted his glass, and the two came together with a "clink."

"Glad to have you aboard," Matthew said. "You'll start by going to Paris. You can rent an apartment online in advance of your traveling there. Because we want this operation to have the smell of your interests and activities, we thought it would be best if you rent the apartment. Paris will be the starting point, and that is where you will make initial contact with our friends. As we speak, our goods are packaged and ready for shipment. The rifles are the latest Model M-16 manufactured by Colt Industries. The shipment also includes an assortment of .50-cal sniper rifles, handguns, mortars, M1 meals, and medical kits.

"We arranged payment for the shipment through a Swiss account. The various suppliers do not know who paid for the orders, and we presume none of them really cares. Delivery of the weapons and other materials will occur at a time and place selected by our friends. For the present, we are pretending that the export documents were forged. Our enemies are aware that an arms shipment is on the way to our friends, and they may have an inkling our government is the source. Yet they do not know with certainty, and they do not know how, when or by whom. If you haven't guessed by now, I will tell you the weapons are intended for the Kurds."

Sean did not wish to appear surprised by any of Matthew's disclosures. He didn't listen to the evening news or follow America's dealings with foreign wars. Nevertheless, he had learned about the Kurds and their plight during his tour of duty with the US Army in Iraq.

To acknowledge what Matthew had told him, Sean said, "Okay."

"I might add," Matthew continued, "that, as Americans, we have considerable sympathy for the Kurds, their plight and their cause. I don't know how much you know about them. The Kurds are neither Arabs nor Turks. To the east they have the Arabs and to the west the Turks. Those neighbors have treated the Kurds poorly for centuries. Today the Kurds are fighting ISIS, our mutual and mortal enemy. They are desperate to keep ISIS from overrunning their lands and enslaving them. In our opinion that is reason enough for us to aid them. They have volunteered to provide the blood. The least we can do is to supply them with material support. Frankly, it's a messy situation. Alliances in the area seem to shift from year to year and for a variety of reasons. Nevertheless, we believe the Kurds will remain our good friends well into future years, and we are determined to proceed full speed with our project.

"We have been in direct contact with the Kurds, and I should add we also have independent sources in the area. The ISIS operatives may have learned of our plans to ship the arms. In the Middle East it is impossible to know with certainty who is a true friend, who is on the other side, or who might be a freelancer playing both sides. Money often determines alliances."

Matthew continued advising Sean on the logistics of the project. Sean tried to pay attention while a thousand thoughts buzzed around in the back of his head. During their meals, the men ate in silence. Both men had considerations to evaluate, and neither felt obligated to make conversation. When they were finished eating, Matthew sat back and said, "We will send you a contract that repeats the terms we discussed. The period of the contract will be for three months, which means we will pay you the monthly rate for three months. If you finish in one month and return home, no problem. We will still pay you for three months. Just don't sign another contract for services with another party during the period of the contract, because you supposedly will be our man during that time. The contract consists of two copies, namely an original and a copy for you. Sign each one and return the original to us. That will make all things legal and proper. I suggest you keep your copy in a safe deposit box at a bank."

Sean responded, "Yes, sir. I'll be certain to promptly return a signed copy of the contract."

"Okay. I would like to take you to our facilities to finalize a few details. You may leave your car here. Stan will drive us to headquarters and later he will bring you back here to your car. Sound good?"

"Fine, let's do it."

Barton paid the bill, leaving a generous tip for the pretty waitress, Sean noticed. Outside, Stan Patkowski was waiting in a black sedan with a license plate that was stamped "U.S. Government." As Sean and Matthew approached, he climbed out to hold a car door open for them to enter. On the way to Fairfax, Stan remained silent while Sean and Matthew, seated in the back of the sedan, exchanged small talk. Upon their arrival at an entrance gate to the agency, a uniformed guard approached the sedan to check credentials. Patkowski drove his passengers to the front door of the building and stepped out to hold the door again for the men. He said, "Mr. McDougal, I'll wait for you in the lobby. When you are finished with your business, you can find me there."

Matthew led Sean into the lobby, where one of the guards gave Sean a pass with his photograph and name clearly visible. Sean studied the pass, wondering where they had obtained his photograph. They went by elevator up to the fourth floor and then down a corridor to a door marked "Director." Matthew invited Sean in and gestured to a chair near his desk. Reaching into a desk drawer, he withdrew a pouch and handed it to Sean.

Barton said, "Here's a thousand dollars equivalent in euros and a thousand dollars in Iraqi dinars. You will need to pay for miscellaneous items once you arrive abroad. Your contact in Paris will be one Azad Jibril at the Sirnak Restaurant. Here's the password. After you have memorized it, burn the piece of paper. It's one of our rules."

Matthew handed Sean a folded piece of paper and continued to outline details of the mission. He pushed back from his desk and rose. "If you don't have any questions, I'll bring you down to Stan."

Sean expected the walk-through of the building that Barton had mentioned earlier. Yet, he was entirely willing to forego the experience. He didn't think he would enjoy walking around a government building peering at whatever sights they might have, so he took care to avoid mentioning the subject.

Barton stood, more or less indicating the conference was at an end. As he walked toward Sean, he asked, "By the way, I meant to ask you. You have a gun shop and, I'm sure, you know guns very well. What would you say is a good pistol for a person to carry for protection? One that would not be too heavy and conspicuous and, yet one that would do the job. What would be your preference?"

"I like the Walther ppk in .380. It's light, easy to conceal and double action. That means if you are in a hurry, you don't have to fiddle around with a safety. While it's not the most powerful gun around, it's adequate. I sell them in my shop. They're very popular with people who know guns."

"Thanks for the professional advice. I'll make a note."

Sean wasn't sure what Barton intended by "make a note." Barton placed a hand on Sean's shoulder, and said, "Let's go down to the lobby."

Stan Patkowski was seated and reading a magazine. Barton shook Sean's hands and said, "If you have any more questions, please call. And, Sean, be careful. Watch your back."

Patkowski dropped Sean in front of the Saigon Restaurant, and Sean walked around the building to the parking lot behind the building. The panhandler who had approached him earlier was sitting on a patch of grass near the parking lot. He pretended he didn't see Sean while he kept busy scratching the back of his hand. Sean concluded the guy was waiting for easy prey and wouldn't trouble him again. Safe inside his Toyota, he removed the bothersome tie. He placed both hands on the steering wheel and took a deep breath, his thoughts wandering. The sight of the restaurant reminded him of the waitress.

That was one cute chick. I can picture her wearing only a thin pink panty and stretched out on a bed. Or with nothing at all? Say, nude. No, on second thought I think she would be more appealing with the pink panty. Like a chocolate bar wrapped in silver paper, waiting to be unwrapped. No doubt the big cities have a better crop. What do I have up in the Pennsylvania wilderness? Wide bottomed country bumpkins whose reading interests are limited to the Farmer's Almanac. Time to go, Sean. Forget the girls. You have things to do.

***

Matthew Barton went to check in with the department super. He proudly announced, "The McDougal guy said he will take the assignment."

"Good. Do you think he can handle it?"

"I do. He seemed sharper than the last few we used."

"Is he aware of the dangers involved?"

"He'll learn those in due time. I just hope he's a quick learner."

6

Sunni Precautions

BASHIR Masri considered himself a true believer, a follower of the Prophet Mohammed, Peace Be upon Him. Likewise, his parents, their parents, and ancestors as far back as anyone remembered had all lived their lives as devout Muslims. In his prayers, he often thanked Allah for his religion. Over the years, he had witnessed the self-serving and corrupt behaviors of the politicians who ruled the countries in the region. As many of his countrymen, he became convinced the promises of ISIS offered the only worthwhile future for him and his children. A caliphate without country distinctions. An area of the globe where laws are based on sharia, Allah's dictates. His convictions and his hope for a better future led Bashir to volunteer his services to the Islamists. He believed his contacts, influence, and financing would be of value to the cause, and those with authority within the organization had given him an important assignment.

Bashir was carrying a bag of groceries as he walked along a street in the town of Haditha in western Iraq. He intended the groceries to disguise the true purpose of his travels, to suggest he was shopping. No one could be trusted, not even friends from years ago. The turmoil of the land had bred a plethora of alliances and loyalties. Near the Great Mosque, Bashir turned onto Al Jamal Street. In the distance, a dust devil appeared in the middle of the street. As it moved toward Bashir, its twisting and swirling movement suggested the embodiment of a supernatural spirit. Bashir stopped to watch the form wind a circuitous course toward him before it collapsed into a pile of dust. He proceeded to the third house from the corner, the stately home of Marwazi Alwan, a high-level ISIS operative. Bashir knocked on the front door and waited. Slowly, someone cracked open the heavy wooden door. The man behind the door did not speak as he expected the visitor to state the purpose of his visit.

Bashir softly said, “My name is Bashir Masri. I have information for Mr. Alwan.”

The man, a revolver in his right hand, slowly pulled the door open and stood aside. “Please come in, sir.”

Inside the house, the guard invited Bashir to have a seat in the outer room. Plush oriental carpets on the floors and polished furniture suggested the presence of wealth. The guard's eyes shifted to the bag in the visitor's hand.

"I see you have found a source for groceries."

The guard had politely expressed his concerns about the bag and he waited for a response. They mutually understood the bag could conceivably contain explosives or weapons. Marwazi Alwan had numerous enemies. To allay the guard's suspicions, Bashir told the guard, "I found a delicious cheese today. Let me see if I can find it."

Bashir pretended to be looking for a package of cheese as he withdrew every item from the bag and placed each on the small coffee table. The guard sat nearby, watching, with his right hand still gripping the pistol in his pocket.

When Bashir came to the cheese, he held it high. "Here it is. A Labneh cheese. Delicious and difficult to find these days."

The guard said, "With circumstances as they are, you were lucky to find all those groceries."

One by one, Bashir returned the items to the bag, and both men took comfortable seats across from one another. In time the guard spoke.

"Sir, Mr. Alwan is saying his noon prayers. At the lunch hour he will be entertaining visitors from out of town. May I get you tea while you wait?"

Bashir thanked the guard for his offer and responded that yes, tea would be fine. In twenty minutes the guard returned with a tray, a cup of tea, and a dish of cookies. He sat the tray on the table near Bashir, and excused himself before he disappeared behind an interior door.

Mid-afternoon three men, escorted by the guard, emerged from the inner quarters of the mansion and exited through the front door. Bashir noticed all three wore the traditional Arab kufiyah. The design and coloring of the head covering suggested the men might be businessmen from Qatar who were possibly negotiating the sale of the oil that would provide ISIS with cash to pay its bills and its fighters. The guard secured the front door, and turned to Bashir. "Sir, Mr. Alwan will see you now. If you will follow me, please."

The guard led him through hallways to a large room where Marwazi Alwan sat behind a large oaken desk. Alwan presented a combination of contrasts. He wore the Arab head dress, much as those worn by his recent visitors. Otherwise, he appeared unlike an Arab. His skin was as light as a European one might see on the streets of France or Spain. As Bashir entered, Alwan stood. He was tall and erect and his eyes seemed to pierce Bashir's soul to question his honesty.

"Ah, Mr. Masri, I am delighted to see you again. I hope you are in good health and prospering these days."

Bashir lowered his head in respect before answering. "All is well, thank you, Mr. Alwan. Allah be praised. I hope you are living well too, despite the trying times."

The two men were ardent followers of the Wahhabi version of Islam. Often in the past years they had met to pray and discuss verses of the Koran. They had long believed a primary tenet of the faith was there for all to see, the Prophet's words plainly stated in the fifth verse of the ninth sura: *Slay the idolaters wherever you find them.* Together, they had often shown disdain for those who did not believe the Wahhabi interpretation of the Koran. How, they had often asked, could supposedly good Muslims not believe what Mohammad clearly intended? Their belief was also a bond they shared with the ISIS fighters who were fighting for the faith on the battlefields of the Middle East. They intended to do what they could to support the young and brave soldiers in their fight against the infidels.

Bashir knew that Marwazi Alwan was a busy man, and to talk excessively about inconsequential topics might be considered presumptuous or impolite. Having asked about Alwan's health, he shifted promptly to the business at hand.

"I heard from our contact in Paris. As you might remember, he has the friendship of a man within the Kurdish circle who talks freely with him. Our man reports that the Kurds are expecting a large shipment of rifles and other arms from the Americans. The

Kurds have become jubilant over the promise of arms from abroad. A man from America is expected to arrive soon to coordinate the delivery."

Marwazi Alwan said, "We were developing big plans for the Kurds, and we hoped to trample them in the near future. We know they are growing short of supplies, including food, ammunition, rifles, everything. May I assume we will be taking action to intervene? Who is this man who provided this information? Can we depend on him?"

Bashir's gaze shifted to the floor. "I am sorry for delivering this disappointing news. I merely intended to keep you informed."

Marwazi Alwan moved around his desk toward his visitor. Coming near, he said, "Please do not misunderstand me, Mr. Masri. Of course we are grateful for your assistance and your valuable contributions."

"The American has not yet arrived," Bashir responded, "but he is expected any day. I promised to keep the informant's name a secret. I can tell you, though, that his mother was a Kurd and his father an Arab. His father's relatives approached him to seek his help. In response, he agreed to provide information only if we pay him well for his services. It seems he has divided loyalties. He said he was equally partial to the Kurds and their problems, as well as the Arabs and their grand vision. I must say I was obliged to pay him more than he deserved."

Marwazi Alwan played with a pencil on his desk. "You say the Americans are about to send arms to the Kurds. I wonder. If we were to learn more, perhaps we could have our soldiers intercept the shipment. We would put those arms to good use."

"You are correct. We shall try to learn what we may of the shipment. What you suggest is possible."

Marwazi Alwan's glance at the door suggested to Bashir that their discussion had come to an end. As Bashir placed his hand on the door handle, he said, "I will keep you informed."

Marwazi Alwan said, "As-salaam. Do what you find necessary. Let me know if you require support of any kind."

Bashir touched his forehead. "As-salaam."

7

A Trip to Paris

IN the days following the meeting with Matthew Barton, Sean scurried around in preparation for his departure overseas. He bought some additional clothes of the type he would need on his adventure and a carry-on suitcase. At the gun shop he spent an hour with Wally going over inventory and the accounts. He gave Wally a key to his trailer and asked him to check on it occasionally. He showed Wally the satellite telephone he had rented for the trip and gave Wally the phone number.

The next day, Sean packed his belongings and boarded an Air France plane to Paris. In past years he had spent time in Paris and was looking forward to the City of Light. He was moderately proficient in French, and he liked the city.

From the airport, Sean traveled by bus to the Place Charles de Gaulle and from there by Metro to the Eleventh Arrondissement. He brought along only one carry-on suitcase with its contents. From his trailer he had paid the rent online and in advance for the Parisian apartment.

Sean's interest in things French originated with one Marielle Duprée, a nurse with Medécins Sans Frontières, a French organization that provides medical care to the many victims of strife in the broken countries of the Middle East. Sean and Marielle met at one of the social get-togethers sponsored by the organization. The events were called "teas," although most attendees preferred the stronger beverages that were also available. The group held the socials in order to give their volunteers a respite from the human tragedies they encountered daily at the clinic. The hospital also invited a few men and women from various nearby organizations to the socials. The weekend that Sean met Marielle, his commanding officer had selected him and his squad to go to the social. The officer intended the treat to help the men forget their recent and traumatic experience up one of the ravines north of the American post.

Marielle and Sean became good friends, and soon more than good friends, spending time together on the days they were both off duty. Months later, when Marielle returned to Paris, Sean took a month of R&R and flew to Paris to be with her. Marielle had completed her stint in the Middle East and returned to her job as a nurse at the Hôpital Saint-Antoine. She worked during the day, but the two got together most evenings and every weekend. With time, though, they realized they could not share a future together. Marielle was caring for an aging and ill mother, and Sean knew he would be unable to earn a worthwhile living in France. They parted with expressions of regret. For a time, they corresponded, but gaps between letters gradually grew longer. Eventually Sean stopped writing altogether, since he didn't wish Marielle to think that that he might return to France.

As a consequence to the affair with Marielle, Sean started taking French lessons, if for no other reason than as a way of remembering Marielle. During his tour of duty in Iraq he took online courses by using one of the computers in the company's rec room. The programs offered a good way to fill his time in the evenings and weekends. When he returned to the States, he continued his French studies and soon became moderately proficient in the language.

Traveling the Metro in Paris, Sean wondered if Marielle still lived on Rue Caulaincourt with her mother. He still remembered the street number and the apartment despite the years that had passed since his last visit there. A part of him longed to see her again. Yet, he was facing a challenging assignment, a treacherous adversary. Perhaps, he thought, the present situation didn't favor a renewed romance. He had to keep his mind clear and focused on the project if he intended to stay alive. A wandering mind would not benefit that end.

Sean had no trouble finding the building at 35 Rue Traversière where he had rented an apartment. A small sign near the front door stated that the manager's office was down a set of stairs. In the basement, Sean found a plump, balding man behind a dilapidated desk. The man was tinkering with a door lock that was probably from one of the apartments in the building and was in need of repair. The smell of alcohol filled the air.

Sean said, "I believe I have a reservation for an apartment. The name is Sean McDougal."

The man said his name was "Claud" as he searched a board against the back wall that held a number of keys. He selected one and, handing it to Sean, said the apartment was on the fourth floor. He added that Mr. McDougal should let him know if he needed anything–that he was capable of procuring all sorts of things. Sean stared at the man without saying a word. Clearing his throat, Claud added, "Away from home, men sometimes become lonely." As he returned to the malfunctioning door lock, he said, "Enjoy your stay, Monsieur."

When Sean turned to exit the room, Claud interrupted him. "Oh, monsieur, I almost forgot. Somebody sent you a package." The rotund man stumbled from behind his desk and rummaged through a mixture of items until he produced a small carton that was labeled "Sean McDougal." The package had no return address.

As he climbed the four flights of stairs to his home away from home, each leg felt like a fifty-pound bag of potatoes. Jet lag was having its effects. Once in the apartment, he decided the package could wait. He left it on a table near the only window in the apartment, and crawled between the sheets of the small bed.

Sean slept until six in the evening. When he awoke, he was rested and hungry. Except for a sandwich at Kennedy Airport, he hadn't eaten in twenty-four hours. He immediately thought of the Kurdish restaurant. According to Matthew Barton's suggestion, Sean should eat at the Restaurant Sirnak, a restaurant also in the Eleventh Arrondissement. Matthew had told him to pretend to be an American businessman on a trip to Paris. The Kurds would be in touch with him.

Sean slipped into a jacket, donned a Yankees baseball cap, and started for the restaurant, a mere four blocks away. He knew the restaurant had an even number, so he crossed over to the sidewalk that ran in front of the odd numbers. That would afford him an opportunity to see the place from across the street without appearing too conspicuous.

As Sean walked along the sidewalk across the street from the restaurant, he could see it was a working man's establishment. Its menu most likely appealed to a small fraction of Parisians interested in trying foreign cuisine or to homesick Kurds living in

Paris. Through the front window, he saw two couples seated at a table with a bottle of wine between them.

That evening, Sean planned to try a restaurant other than the Sirnak. He believed he owed himself a relaxing meal. Business and contact with the Kurds at the Sirnak could wait. Two blocks beyond the Sirnak, he spotted an interesting-looking restaurant, the Restaurant Les Relais d'Alsace. The menu in the window listed Alsatian *choucroute garnie*–Alsatian-style sauerkraut with sausages. Sean didn't read any farther. He entered, and a waiter directed him to a seat at the rear of the room.

The restaurant did not disappoint. Sean enjoyed a delicious meal and two glasses of a white Alsatian wine. He paid the bill and returned to his apartment building. As he approached the fourth-floor landing, he first noticed an attractive foot wearing high heels near his door. Taking a second look, he saw a pair of shapely legs, crossed. An attractive, middle-aged woman was sitting on a chair outside the door to his apartment.

"Good evening, sir. I trust you have been enjoying the sights of Paris. It's certainly a pleasant evening for strolling about."

She rose as Sean approached. Sean knew the purpose of her visit, but he asked anyhow. "May I be of assistance?"

"Now, that's an interesting question and one I don't hear often. Why, yes, perhaps we can talk. That is, if you would be inclined to invite me into your apartment?"

Sean's first inclination was to be brusque with the *fille de joie* and shoo her away. He was about to speak when a thought occurred to him. "Sure, let's talk. Come in and I'll offer you an after-dinner drink. What's your name?"

"That is very courteous of you. I can tell you are a true gentleman. My name is Hélène."

In the apartment, Sean half filled two wine glasses from a bottle of Dubonnet the landlord had provided. Sean handed one to his guest and wished her *sante*. The two exchanged casual observations for several minutes. When the drinks were finished, Sean withdrew a fifty-euro bill from his wallet and pressed it into Hélène's hand.

"Here, this is for your time. If you will tell me your telephone number, I may call you if I have need of your services. Now, I'm tired from traveling and the change of hours. I will say goodnight so that you may run along."

Hélène, with a puzzled shrug, leaned forward as she stood to allow her ample and braless frontal parts to shift around. "Thank you, sir, for the generous gift." She gave Sean her telephone number and departed. Sean climbed into bed, tired and alone.

8

A Visit to the Kurdish Restaurant

ON Sean's second day in Paris, he slept late. His body wanted more rest, yet duty called. He shaved, washed, and while dressing remembered the mysterious package the apartment manager had given him on his arrival. Retrieving his pocketknife, he slit the edges of the cardboard box. Inside, wrapped in crinkled newspaper, he found a Walther ppk in .380 caliber and a box of bullets. Sean stopped, thinking. *It was Matthew who asked what my preference would be for a handgun. I guess he didn't want it to be known that he provided an illegal weapon to a person in France.* He would give more thought to the implications that he needed a pistol. At the moment, his pressing need was for a cup of coffee. He shoved the box and contents under his bed, exited the building and headed for the bistro at the end of the block. At the bar, he ordered a *café au lait* and a *croissant.* Then one more of each.

Midday, Sean walked the streets of Paris and visited a few of the famous sights, many of which he had seen in prior years while accompanied by his French lady friend. He noticed the landmarks held less attraction than they had on those earlier outings. Back then, he and Marielle held hands and shared laughs. On occasion Sean would steal a kiss. Memories of Marielle continued returning. He wondered if she still lived with her mother or if she had married. No matter! Regardless, he was not going to contact her. He resolved he would visit the Restaurant Sirnak that evening. No doubt, the Kurds were anxious to meet with him to speed delivery of the arms. He ordered himself to stop thinking of Marielle.

In the evening, Sean once more strolled past the Kurdish restaurant in the guise of a lone businessman searching for an interesting place to eat. He could see the restaurant had two waiters serving the patrons. One was relatively dark-skinned, the other was of a lighter tone. He turned about, crossed the street, and entered the restaurant. The darker waiter met Sean near the front door and invited him to a table near the front window before passing through a swinging door to the kitchen. Sean reviewed the menu, and when the waiter returned, he ordered Kurdish beef kabobs and mineral water. He knew the Kurds were Muslims who did not imbibe wine, so they might naturally have become leery of a person who drank wine. Matthew had told Sean a dark-skinned waiter at the restaurant by the name of Azad Jibril had connections with cognizant persons in the Kurdish armed forces. Matthew had said the man could be trusted.

As the waiter placed Sean's order in front of him, Sean asked him, "Are you by chance Mr. Jibril?"

The waiter stepped back, surprised by the question. "Yes, sir. I am Azad Jibril."

Sean said, "I was merely wondering. A friend of mine told me you are an excellent waiter."

Appearing surprised, the waiter said, "Thank you, sir, for the compliment. I try to do my best."

Sean beckoned Jibril closer. "I hear the Kurdish beef is best in Erbil. I thought I would like to go to Erbil one day. I've been told Erbil, with its river, is very pretty."

Azad responded with the agreed-upon password recognition. "Erbil is a pretty town, but I believe Kirkuk is more exciting."

Sean finished his meal, and the waiter brought his check, telling him, "Sir, you should plan on coming here tomorrow. The cook is going to prepare *kofta.* If you want Kurdish cuisine that is the real thing. The dish is lamb mixed with onions and our special spices. It comes with rice, our vegetable of the day, and a salad."

"It sounds appetizing," Sean said. "I will make it a point to come back tomorrow."

Sean started to return to his apartment. The evening air seemed to invite him to experience the sights and sounds of Paris. Soon the cold winter air would be moving in. He thought he would stroll the city's streets and continue to take in its sights and sounds. He took a few steps before changing his mind about the direction. As he turned about, away from the apartment, he almost collided with a young couple who had been walking behind him. The woman was clinging to her beau's arm as though she feared he might try to escape. The man apologized first.

"Sorry, sir."

Sean responded, "My fault."

The couple maneuvered around Sean and continued on their way. Sean, envious of the man, resumed his stroll, remembering how it felt to stroll with a lady friend on the streets of Paris. Feelings of loneliness started drifting back. In the next block Sean spotted a bistro. Three men sat at the bar and a couple occupied one of the tables. Sean took a seat at a table nearby and ordered a cognac. Many years had gone by since he had sipped a cognac in France.

During his second drink, Sean considered a visit to the street where he knew Marielle had lived–to see it one more time. Perhaps for the last time. At the Voltaire Station, he took the Metro Number Two line and in twenty minutes was in the Eighteenth Arrondissement, where he exited from underground at the Place de Clichy. When he had visited Marielle five years earlier, she had been living with her mother in an apartment on Rue Caulaincourt. The building would be a ten-minute walk from the Metro station. Sean was in no rush. As he made his way along the street he allowed the memories to drift back to him one at a time. He spotted the Café de la Butte, where Marielle and he had spent time either enjoying croissants and café or glasses of wine.

Approaching 175 Rue Caulaincourt, Sean crossed the street so he would have a better view of the windows on the building's second floor. He remembered that Marielle and he had argued over the terms "first floor" and "second floor." She lived on the floor above ground level, and she insisted the proper name was the "first floor." That, she said, was what they called it in France. She didn't care what the Americans called it. Behind the curtains he could see a light in the apartment. He wondered if she might still be living there. He returned to the Metro by a different street. The next day he must make contact with the Kurds and begin moving the project forward.

9

A Walk by the Seine River

SEAN had nothing to do until suppertime, so he spent most of his third day in Paris reading in his room. He planned to return to the Kurdish restaurant in the evening to arrange a meeting with a cognizant Kurdish contact. By mid-afternoon, though, danger or no danger, he needed to get out of the small apartment. His legs and lungs wanted a change. A promenade along the Seine might quell his restlessness.

At the front door of the apartment building, Sean paused before stepping onto the sidewalk of Boulevard Traversière. He suspected his equivalent on the enemy's team was out there somewhere on the streets of Paris, so he also knew precautions were advisable. Satisfied that the few visible pedestrians appeared to be harmless residents of the neighborhood going about their business, he crossed the boulevard and proceeded toward the nearest Metro entrance.

He took the Metro to the Place de la Concorde, which was near the banks of the Seine River. At Quai d'Orsay Sean paused to watch the river. He found the everlasting flow of a river to be a consoling constant. He sought constants in the world, since he had few in his personal life. Turning right, he changed course for the Eiffel Tower. He found the cool, fall air invigorating. The chill in the air also gave him an excuse to wear a jacket without being conspicuous. Under the jacket, where he could reach it in an instant, he kept the Walther ppk at the ready. Sean preferred the Walther for his walks in Paris. Of course the French laws prohibited the carrying of a firearm, and he was aware of the danger. If the police caught him with it they would hustle him to an unaccommodating and uncomfortable jail. On the other hand, an adversary might inflict a worse penalty if he went unarmed, namely death. Sean concluded he needed the handgun.

All of those on Sean's side were aware that at least one of ISIS's men would be determined to find and terminate Sean. However, nobody knew anything about the person, his name, his height, language, nationality. Nobody had a physical description. The friendly informant had relayed only limited information about the person. Likewise, Sean's opposite within ISIS probably knew little of Sean, although in time he might have ways to locate and surprise him. Matthew had said that Sean's opponent was probably an Arab, but there was a slim chance he could also be a hired non-Arab operative.

Meandering along the quay, Sean thought about his situation and the project at hand. He believed walking always helped to clear a person's mind and to organize jumbled thoughts. He knew that the assignment was truly dangerous, perhaps even more than climbing up an Iraqi ravine with a squad of well-armed infantrymen. He reminded himself that taking assignments of his current type would not enhance his chances of living to middle age, let alone a ripe old age.

A mix of people was moving along the quay. One young couple, no doubt delighted with the pleasant fall day, was talking toward him. Sean expected an assassin to be experienced and of a serious demeanor. He would necessarily try to come close to Sean to do whatever he might have in mind. Sean moved to the side to allow the two strollers to pass by. Farther along, he spotted two men ahead on the sidewalk, conversing. Two men would always be a cause for concern; one could be an assailant and the second an accomplice. He changed his path to steer clear of those two. He did not wish to afford them a chance to assault him from a distance of a few feet. As the two men neared he saw they were deeply engaged in an argument. They were most likely French businessmen, although one cannot be certain. Sean again moved away, pretending to take a call on his phone, and the two passed without incident.

The need for constant vigilance was taking the pleasure out of Sean's outing. Besides, he realized that soon he must plan for his second visit to the Kurdish restaurant. Exiting the quay, he headed for the nearest Metro entrance and his apartment. Ahead, a lone man was moving along the sidewalk in his direction. Sean stepped into the street and crossed to the other side. Twice again he crossed streets to keep his distance from lone men on the streets. The sight of a telephone booth suggested that perhaps he should check in with the agency. In the eastern U.S. the time was mid-morning. He entered the booth and dialed the direct line to Matthew Barton. Barton answered immediately.

"How's it going, Sean?"

"Okay. No meeting yet although I believe it will happen soon. I'll be returning to the restaurant tonight. Oh, by the way, thanks for the package."

Ignoring Sean's comment about the package, Matthew said, "Glad you arrived safely. Our intelligence sources have nothing new to report. It's still a messy situation over there," he said. "The Kurds have difficulties making secure communications. Our man reminded us to watch for double agents. These are freelancers who owe allegiance to no one and they auction their information to the highest bidder. Be careful and slow to trust anyone. Just stay loose and keep in contact. And Sean, need I remind you to be careful. We don't want to lose you."

"Will do. I'll be in touch. Over and out."

10

A Treacherous Man

WHEN Jabir al-Ateri's father abandoned his mistress and his bastard son, life became difficult for the two. His mother struggled as best she could to provide food and shelter. She did wash, cleaned houses, begged on the streets of Bagdad. The day she concluded she could no longer take care of the child, she took him shopping and bought him new trousers, a shirt, and shoes. Holding him by the hand, they boarded a bus and traveled to a small village west of the city. They entered a restaurant, and she ordered a nourishing meal for each of them. With the bill paid, she left the boy and an empty purse at the table while she visited the washroom. From there she crept out the rear door and returned home, leaving behind both the ten-year-old and the purse. When the restaurant owner realized the woman's game, he drove the boy to an orphanage where the staff reluctantly accepted the child.

At the institution the staff developed a strong disdain for Jabir. He rarely followed instructions and frequently started fights with other boys. He became surly and stole food at every chance. Men at the orphanage would beat him and chain him to a bed for periods. They sat a slop jar within reach and fed him gruel once a day that was barely enough to keep him alive. The staff did their best to control the child. He was constantly unruly, and he never bent to abide by his guardians' rules. During one of the Muslim holidays a caretaker at the orphanage removed the chain from Jabir's leg so that he could clean the area, all the while hoping the boy would run away. Jabir seized the opportunity and ran out the back door of the institution. None of the staff pursued him.

Jabir gravitated to the Sehah neighborhood of Bagdad, one of the poorest areas of Iraq, if not the entire Middle East. In the streets he met up with other boys in similar predicaments. The boys were all accomplished thieves, and they taught Jabir how to survive. A few sympathetic merchants took pity on the boys and occasionally gave them money or food. In exchange the boys would sweep floors, clean washrooms, and run errands. The boys took care not to steal from the sympathetic merchants.

Life in the Sehah district was tough for Jabir. He became expert at fighting and stealing. The other boys learned he was quick and shrewd. Most boys avoided tangling with him because he had proved he could readily take care of himself, and he always had a knife in his pocket. He remained resentful and angry, yet was full of determination and the will to survive. At age fourteen he found shelter in a brothel. Jabir did odd jobs around the building, and in exchange for his help the owner allowed him to sleep on a mat in the basement of the building. Some days he also gave him meals.

Jabir found life at the brothel an improvement over his earlier days. Without prompting, he started trolling the streets of the city to find customers for the women. To assist his efforts he asked the owner for a pack of photos of the girls. He would flash the photos at candidates he saw on the sidewalks. His inventiveness and efforts noticeably increased traffic for the women, and soon the women began competing for Jabir's patronage. They started slipping him sandwiches and money along with other treats.

Through his work at the brothel, Jabir came to know the local police. The brothel owner let the police know that they were welcome at the establishment. Policemen regularly stopped by for free food, tea, and treats. Through his contacts with the boys on the streets, Jabir often passed along valuable information to the police. Several times he helped one of the policemen by suggesting and aiding in sting operations. As a result of Jabir's assistance, a policeman took a liking to him.

The growth of ISIS changed everything for Iraq and Jabir. At age twenty-seven Jabir learned of the Islamists and their agenda. Although he didn't give a hoot about Muslim religious ideology, he was attracted to the promise of a regular paycheck, food, and housing. He pretended to be a devout Muslim and joined the ISIS ranks.

At first, Jabir went through the rigorous training ISIS demanded of its soldiers. Because of the regimentation and exercise, he added weight and grew strong. However, the regular hours and the forced routine presented a new problem. Most of his life he had been accustomed to coming and going according to his whims. He was unaccustomed to taking orders, and he did not favor the prospect of facing an enemy that could shoot back.

When Jabir heard of the need for experienced policemen to deal with civilians, he did not hesitate to apply for a transfer. He claimed he had done police work in Bagdad and provided the name of a police officer that he said could provide references. He told the ISIS representatives he knew the reference would give him a good recommendation. What he did not mention was that the man had been killed in a confrontation. He thought he would let the ISIS people learn that on their own initiative. Given the turmoil in the region at that time, he believed nobody would learn of the man's demise.

To his delight, Jabir was selected for regular police duty in the towns overrun by the ISIS forces. In his new role, he was quick to prove his worth through his imaginative methods, and his capacity for obtaining information from captives. Shortly before his twenty-ninth birthday, a special request came in. A volunteer was sought to go to Paris to deal with an American who was in the business of bringing arms to the ISIS enemies. Jabir jumped at the opportunity. He was given a brief training in clandestine operations and provided with tools of the trade. A week later he took a flight to Paris and promptly made contact with the local ISIS operatives.

11

Memories

UPON returning to the apartment on Boulevard Traversière, Sean felt his eyelids growing heavy. He continued to contend with jet lag and a stomach that didn't know whether it wanted breakfast or supper. He lay on the bed and in seconds was asleep. When he awoke, the table clock read eight forty-five. It was time to attend to business. He changed his shirt, slipped into a jacket, and was moving to the front door when he remembered the Walther ppk automatic. Perhaps, he thought, he should bring it along, under his jacket. Nobody would notice it.

At nine in the evening Sean approached Restaurant Sirnak for the second time. From across the street he saw the patrons were the usual innocuous-appearing couples. He crossed the street and entered.

The waiter who had served Sean the previous evening, the man he knew as Azad Jibril, approached.

"Good evening, sir. Welcome back. One person again?"

"Yes, only me. How about that small table in the rear?"

"Yes, sir. Wherever you wish. Are you going to try the kofta tonight?"

"Yes, it sounds delicious."

Sean declined the waiter's suggestion for wine. Instead, he ordered a bottle of Perrier bottled mineral water.

Azad soon returned with Sean's order. Placing the meal in front of Sean, he leaned forward and whispered, "Sir, if convenient to you, one of our representatives would like to meet you here tomorrow at nine in the evening?"

Sean nodded as an acknowledgement and said, "Yes, thank you."

Following the lamb, which was as tasty as the waiter had promised, Sean had an apple tart and coffee for dessert. He had more than twenty-four hours until his scheduled meeting with the Kurdish representative. What to do with the time? Once on the sidewalk, he began another walk to breathe in the Parisian atmosphere. This time he headed for the Metro and shortly was on Rue Caulaincourt. Again he saw a light in the second-floor apartment where Marielle had lived years ago. Maybe, he thought, she still lived there. He considered going into the building and knocking on the apartment door. What would he say? He had not the slightest idea. What if a man answered the door? That, Sean reasoned, would embarrass and belittle him to the core. Besides, he had concluded he mustn't interfere in her current life. That would be wrong.

Moving beyond the apartment building, he noticed again the Café de la Butte. For old time's sake, he thought he might stop for a drink, much as he and Marielle had done years before. He took a seat at an outside table and picked up a newspaper someone had left behind. A German couple was seated nearby, enjoying a bottle of wine and paging through a guidebook of the city.

The waiter was occupied with customers inside the establishment, a group of six Spaniards who asked seemingly endless questions about the food and drinks. When the waiter approached Sean's table, he apologized.

"Sorry for the delay, sir. We are unusually busy tonight. Something to drink or to eat?"

"I'm in no hurry. Merely an Armagnac and a Perrier, please."

"Yes, sir. Right away." The waiter stood back, staring at Sean. "If I am not mistaken, you were here years ago. You were always with a pretty, young woman."

"You have a good memory."

"Thank you. I must admit, however, that I would not have remembered you if it were not for the young lady who accompanied you."

Sean considered asking if he had seen the woman recently, but he let the topic pass. He hadn't stopped at the café for the purpose of spying. He returned to his newspaper as the waiter went to the bar to pour the Armagnac. The German couple began arguing loudly over which sight they should see on their next outing. She wanted to visit the Versailles Castle, he the Eiffel Tower.

When Sean left the café, he walked toward the Metro. Passing the apartment building where Marielle had lived, he glanced up at the window of the apartment where Marielle had lived. The silhouette of a slender, spry woman crossed the curtains. Moments later the light went out.

12

Contact

SEAN returned to the Restaurant Sirnak at eight, one hour before the scheduled meeting with the Kurdish representative. He intended to have supper beforehand. It was Sean's fourth day in Paris. Sean noted the restaurant was half-full that evening. In typical French style, the patrons were talking quietly, almost in whispers, amongst themselves. The man who had waited on Sean the previous evening greeted him as he entered.

"Good evening, sir. I kept a table for you." Azad gestured toward a table for two that was near a window along the side of the room. "I trust this table will be satisfactory?"

"Fine, thank you."

A couple appeared at the door, and the waiter walked over to welcome them. Sean reviewed the menu and selected another Kurdish lamb dish. Having made his choice, he lowered the menu to the table. As he looked up he saw a man staring at him through the front window. When their eyes met the man moved to the front door and entered. Without waiting for a waiter, the stranger strode directly to Sean's table. In a heavy accent the man asked, "May I join you?"

Because Sean didn't expect to meet with the Kurdish contact for another hour, he concluded the Kurdish representative had arrived early. He rose and extended his hand.

"I'm Sean McDougal. Please have a seat."

"Latif Pirbal."

They shook hands.

The stranger eased into the chair across from Sean. He wore slacks, a dark-colored shirt, and a light jacket. Stocky and swarthy, the young man appeared to be fit and strong. Barely understandable, he asked Sean, "If all right with sir, we talk rifles for Kurds?"

Despite his reservations, Sean said, "Sure." He was puzzled and doubtful of the man's legitimacy. The man seemed like an unlikely representative of a government desirous of seeking major assistance form the Government of United States. The man was brusque and his wanting to discuss arms in a public restaurant seemed out of place.

Keeping his eyes fixed on Sean, the stranger took a piece of paper from his jacket and slid it across the table. The paper appeared to depict a map of some sort. With his left hand the visitor tapped on the paper in an effort to draw Sean's attention to it, all the while his right hand slipped into his jacket pocket. With a quick movement, the man turned his head to the left as though he had seen something of pressing interest outside the adjacent window.

That did it. The man's crude behavior, his poor English and demeanor all suggested the man to be a fraud. Sean turned his head only slightly, exposing the jugular vein on the left side of his neck. From the corner of his eye, he caught the glint of the man's knife as it traveled toward him. Sean jerked to the right as his right hand caught the man's wrist, deflecting the thrust downward. He acted too late to stop the forward momentum of the knife and the arm holding it.

Sean moaned, "Ah," as the knife went into his shoulder, a little below his collarbone . With both hands on the man's right hand, Sean stood and pushed the knife away from his body. The small table between them went flying. During his days in both Donora and the army, Sean had learned street fighting. The street had taught him what he needed to do under the present situation. Holding tightly to his attacker's right arm, Sean twisted the man's body so they were facing one another. He slammed his right knee up into the man's crotch, causing him to release his grip on the knife as he doubled over. Azad suddenly appeared brandishing a ten-inch butcher knife in his hand, no doubt with the intention of discouraging further aggression by the intruder. In France, using a knife on a man except for self-defense can earn a person time in jail. The man, appraising his situation, spun and hobbled to the front door before vanishing from sight.

Blood was rushing from the knife wound in Sean's shoulder. He paused to catch his breath and to take stock. Blood soaked the front of his shirt. Two patrons were on their cellphones, most likely calling the gendarmes. Above all, Sean did not wish to speak with the police. They would certainly take exception to his carrying a pistol. He had to get out of the restaurant and quickly. Without a word to anyone, he headed out the front door and turned to follow his assailant. He hoped to catch him near a dark alley and take lasting care of him with his Walther ppk. Rounding the corner, he spotted his attacker limp into a waiting car. He ran as best he could to catch up with the vehicle, hoping to come alongside so that he could open fire on the occupants. To his disappointment, the vehicle accelerated and was soon in the distance.

Sean started to feel light-headed from the loss of blood. He knew he had to get to a hospital and soon. First, though, he had to discard the pistol. He expected gendarmes to appear soon, and that would be too late. He spotted a dark alley and shuffled in. At the first garbage can he lifted the lid and jammed the gun below some trash that had the strong smell of rotten fish. He stumbled back to the sidewalk where he spotted a gendarme running toward the Restaurant Sirnak.

"Gendarme," he called out before slumping to the sidewalk.

When the gendarme approached, he said, "A man with a knife stabbed me. Please call an ambulance."

***

In the early morning hours, Sean opened his eyes at the hospital. His gaze wandered around the room and settled on a nurse sitting across the room. A gendarme sat in a chair several feet from her. When the nurse saw Sean move, she said, "Good morning, sir. How are you feeling?"

Sean hesitated before answering with slurred speech. "I guess I'm all right."

"Sir, you are a lucky man. The knife that went into your shoulder barely missed a major artery. Had the knife blade been a centimeter lower you may not be here today. We gave you a transfusion because you had lost a considerable amount of blood. Four bags, actually. The physician had to sew you up with fifteen stitches and then give you strong antibiotics."

Sean sat up in bed and asked, "When can I go?"

She said, "Not so quick, sir. Perhaps tomorrow, depending on your condition. We gave you some strong pain medicine so you may be groggy and unsteady on your feet for a day or two."

The gendarme, a man with a dour countenance, approached Sean's bedside. "Mr. McDougal, I withdrew the passport from your jacket. We would like to be sure you do not leave France before we investigate the altercation at the Restaurant Sirnak. In our opinion, the attack on you was both unfortunate and peculiar. We would like to learn more about the incident. When you can think and speak normally, we would like you to come to the police station in the Eleventh Arrondissement. We have some questions for you, and we want you to provide us with a formal statement. Also, we want you to look at a few photographs of some local miscreants. Perhaps you can assist us in identifying your assailant."

Struggling with the fog in his head, Sean tried remembering the project's schedule. Parts came back to him, only slowly. He recalled he was obliged to be in Oman soon. Nobody had discussed a contingency plan. He asked, "When may I have my passport?"

"Once we have gathered satisfactory information on the altercation, we shall return your passport. Until then we will be retaining the passport at the station."

***

On Sean's second day at the hospital, a nurse arranged for a taxi to take him to his apartment. The cabbie delivered him to the front of the building, and he went directly to the front door, pretending to play with his key. When he saw the taxi turn the corner, he went to the alley where he had deposited the Walther pistol in a garbage can. He realized he needed that pistol more than ever. To his disappointment, both the garbage can and the Walther were gone.

Back in his apartment, Sean sat in a lounge chair to reflect. The fog from the pain medicine was slowly dissipating. *How did that man know I would be at that particular restaurant? How did he know that I was an object of interest?* He needed to talk with Azad. The incident at the restaurant gave rise to too many unanswered questions. Nevertheless, returning that evening would be too risky. A visit to the restaurant and his next meeting with the Kurds must wait.

Sean dialed Hélène's number. She answered on the second ring.

"Hélène, this is Sean. Remember me?"

"Yes, of course, Sean. How could I forget you? Do you want me to come over to your apartment? I could be there in, let me see, two hours if that would be suitable."

"No, I don't need you to come here. I just want you to run an errand for me. You have my telephone number. Please write it on a piece of paper together with the name "Sean," and deliver it to a waiter by the name of Azad at the Restaurant Sirnak. Can you do that for me?"

"It's not the normal type of service I provide. Anyway, I'll be happy to do it for you."

"Good. I'll see you later then."

"Sure, Sean. I'll be your messenger. Of course, my hourly rate is still applicable."

"Understood."

When Hélène appeared at Sean's apartment an hour later, he paid her with a one-hundred euro note. She tucked the bill into a safe part of her dress before warmly embracing Sean. A part of Sean was becoming interested, but he told himself that was not something he really wanted. He allowed her to unwrap herself and step back. He said, "Hélène, you are a very attractive woman. I'll keep your telephone number handy."

***

Having completed his shift at the restaurant, Azad exited through the rear door of the restaurant to return to the apartment where he lived with his wife and three small girls. The couple had learned to enjoy life in France, and they never regretted leaving Kurdistan. Two blocks from the restaurant, he passed within a few feet of a two-passenger automobile that held a man in each of the seats. The men knew the route Azad took from the restaurant to his apartment, and they had been waiting for him. When Azad passed the waiting men, the driver started the engine and pulled onto the sidewalk behind Azad. Azad was fast on his feet, but he could not outrun an automobile.

13

Problems

THE pain in Sean's shoulder had barely subsided. Once back in his apartment, he popped two more of the pain pills the nurse had given him. Spotting his cellphone on a nightstand, it occurred to him he hadn't checked for messages in two days. He expected Azad to call him. The first message told him,

Mister McDougal, this is Rafiq Jaziri, owner of the Restaurant Sirnak. I am very sorry for the injuries you suffered at the restaurant. We hope you are recovering and will soon be well. I have several messages for you. First, I regret to inform you that our waiter, Azad Jibril, the man who came to your defense at the restaurant, was himself murdered. He was on his way home from the restaurant when men in a small automobile ran him down. His body was badly mangled. Several people saw the incident. However, the license plate had been covered with mud. So, there was really nothing to report to the authorities other than a description of the vehicle. We will miss Azad sorely. He was a fine and honest man. May he rest in peace. We feel confident Azad would have asked that we carry on. Your telephone number was on a piece of paper in his pocket. If it were not for that piece of paper I would not have known how to contact you.

As a result of the incident at the restaurant, we asked ourselves how that man who attacked you would have known you would be there. Because of our suspicions, we traced the telephone line at the restaurant and indeed found that the line had been compromised. An electronic apparatus on the roof of the building had been retransmitting our calls. We have chosen not to eliminate the tap as we might use it to our advantage at a future date. If you call the restaurant, please do not say anything of importance to our enemies.

My last message is this. We would like you to meet a representative of the Kurdish military at your convenience. In the meantime, I suggest you avoid visiting the restaurant. We have noticed unfamiliar men lurking in the neighborhood. We believe they are either plain-clothed gendarmes or persons inclined to do you harm. Please call me on my cellular telephone if you would like to arrange a meeting. God speed.

The call from the owner of the restaurant explained the attack on Sean. From the telephone tap, the Kurds' enemies learned an American man would be making contact with them, however they had no way of knowing his description. When the assassin approached Sean in the restaurant, he didn't know for sure that Sean was his target. He thought Sean might be the American contact, but he had no way of being certain.

It was Sean who inadvertently confirmed that he was in fact the American he was seeking. He realized he should have asked for a password before saying a word. Lesson learned!

Sean returned the call to Rafiq and advised him that he would be available for a meeting the following day. Rafiq Jaziri said their representative would meet him the following day at six in the evening at the gilded statues on the *Esplanade du Trocadéro* and near to the statue of *Les Oiseaux*.

Sean spent the morning in bed and had a light lunch at the apartment. Mid-afternoon he visited the "Troca" to familiarize himself with the place. He found the area to be expansive, with the *Palais de Chaillot* commanding one side. Numerous statues and fountains and the like were spread about. He failed to see any inconspicuous hiding spots.

The following day, Sean returned to the Troca before six and took up a position a good three hundred yards from the gilded statues. Peering through a pair of binoculars, he spotted a man approach the statue of *Les Oiseaux* at exactly six. The man placed his hand on its base and turned with his back resting against the base of the statue.

Sean put the binoculars away and approached the man. At a distance of ten feet he said, "You appear to be a Kurd. I thought I would like to go to Erbil one day."

The man turned to face Sean. "Oh, yes. I am Kurdish. Erbil is a pretty town but Kirkuk is more exciting. I suppose it depends on what a man is seeking."

Remaining apprehensive because of his previous experiences, Sean suggested they sit on a nearby bench. He had been tricked once by a man he thought to be a friendly Kurd. He would not turn his back to this man. Once seated, the Kurd was the first to speak.

"Mr. McDougal, I am sorry about your unfortunate incident at the restaurant. I trust you are recovering?"

"Yes, thank you. I'm feeling much better today."

"Good. I suppose you heard of our comrade Azad Jibril? Poor man. Cut down in a most cowardly manner. His murder was unnecessary. Azad was nothing more than a sympathetic Kurd who relayed messages. His role in our cause was minor. I believe the murder was a message from ISIS. They are saying: We can kill any of you at will and at any time we choose. Do not oppose us. Mr. McDougal, you may be aware we Kurds have been the object of oppression for centuries."

"I am very sorry about Azad. He seemed to be a decent man."

"The funeral will be tomorrow in a Parisian suburb. I suggest neither you nor I attend the service since our adversaries could be watching. We should remember Azad in our private ways."

Both men paused. The partisan continued.

"Sir, my name is Rojen Ghazi. The Kurdish authorities asked me to meet with you regarding the American shipment of arms to our side."

The two men shook hands. Sean said, "Sean McDougal."

Rojen continued. "Before we discuss specifics, Mr. McDougal, I must tell you that the Kurdish people greatly appreciate this most generous gift you propose. I will not bore you with talk about our plight. You no doubt are aware that the Kurds have been victims of both our Arabian and Turkish neighbors for centuries. We are unlike our neighbors and, I believe, in many ways much like you Americans. Unlike those who surround us, we believe wholeheartedly in democracy and women's rights. We do not suffer religious fanatics. All we ever sought was a land of our own where we would be free to govern ourselves. To make our own laws. To experience justice in our way of life. And now we have this new and terrible threat in the form of the despicable Islamic radicals. We are most desirous of dealing with these fanatics and putting to good use the arms you intend to deliver."

"Mr. Ghazi, I am not authorized to speak on behalf of my country," Sean said, "although I can certainly speak for myself. The American people have always championed human rights and decried injustice. If we can be of assistance to the Kurdish cause with this small arms shipment, we are happy to do so. We are especially desirous of assisting you in your fight with our common enemy. If it was not mentioned to you earlier, I will tell you that we expect no recompense for the arms shipment."

Rojen Ghazi bowed his head. "That is most generous of you and your countrymen. Our people are most grateful."

The men sat in companionable silence. Sean was obliged to tell Rojen what the man needed to know to meet the shipment and no more.

"The shipment is scheduled to arrive at an Iraqi port in two weeks. I will give you a more specific port and date of the ship's docking as the time approaches. You will need at least ten trucks to transport everything through Iraq to Kurdistan."

"Mr. McDougal, please be assured we will have the trucks at the port at the date and time you give us," Ghazi said. "In order to avoid attracting attention to the shipment, I suggest that the trucks meet the ship within several hours of its arrival. If the trucks are at the dock too long in advance of the ship's arrival, too many eyes might notice the unusual convoy. Those could be eyes of persons who may not have our interests at heart. It would be best if you keep us advised of the ship's progress. In advance of the ship's arrival we will position our convoy within some forty kilometers of the port. When the ship is near docking, call us and we will move the trucks to dockside. We will have ample hands to assist in loading the trucks. Our men will load the trucks promptly and we will move north while we pray. I shall be with the trucks. Do you plan to be with the ship upon her arrival?"

As Rojen was speaking, Sean noticed a middle-aged couple walking toward the bench where he and Mr. Ghazi sat. They appeared to be uninterested in Sean and Rojen. Nevertheless, one could not tell for certain what their intentions might be. True professionals were good at disguising their actual plans. Sean inclined his head toward the couple. "We should stop speaking."

When Sean moved his hand to grasp the Walter, he realized he no longer had the pistol. He cursed his bad luck. As the couple drew near, he recognized they were harmless Spanish tourists viewing the various statues. The pistol won't be needed after all. He answered Mr. Ghazi's question.

"Yes, I will be with the ship. As we approach the port I will call and give you an update."

Sean handed a thumb drive to Mr. Ghazi. "Here," he said. "If you put this encryption app on your mobile phone, we'll be able to communicate worry-free. I hope to see you at the Iraqi port."

When the men stood, Sean made a measure of the man standing before him. He told himself that here was a true patriot who was dedicated to a just cause. A sincere man who surely deserved respect as well as help in his cause. The men shook hands once more before parting.

14

Renewing Friendships

THE agency's schedule called for the arms shipment to arrive in Oman in approximately ten days, and they expected Sean to be there. Nobody had given thought to a plan B. Sean had given his statement to the gendarmes, yet they were still holding his passport. They gave no hint as to when they might return it to him. Without his passport, Sean would be unable to leave France and travel to Oman. He explained his dilemma to Matthew Barton who told him that his not meeting the British banana ship carrying the arms would be a big problem. The project schedule required Sean to be in Oman to coordinate transfer of the cargo to another ship, the *Sidra*, and then delivery to the Kurds. If one of the ships had to cast anchor to await Sean's arrival, the ship's owners would be sending demurrage charge. For the larger ship the charge might be around $8,000 a day. Matthew hinted he might send a replacement for Sean. The project had to advance.

With time on his hands, Sean visited sights in and around Paris. He often went running in one of the parks, and he strolled the streets. He rode the Metro and spent time listening to the foreign bands that played in the Metro stations. One day he went for a cruise on the Seine. Another day he took the tour of Versailles and the next day a bus to the Fontainebleau Castle. On his third trip to the Louvre he concluded he had seen enough antiquities and art for a time. Visiting sights alone was not all that enjoyable. Every night he went to a different restaurant. Three evenings he went to Rue Caulaincourt. Each of those evenings he stopped for a nightcap at the Café de la Butte, the café that Marielle and he had frequented years earlier.

The day before the arms shipment was due to arrive in Oman, a gendarme called and told Sean he could pick up his passport. Sean hurried to the police station and made a reservation on a flight to depart the following day for Oman. He called the skippers of the two ships scheduled to transport the arms and apologized for the delay. First he called the *Musa*, the large banana reefer ship that had been commissioned to bring the arms cargo to the Port of Salalah on the Arabian Gulf. Next, he called the skipper of the *Sidra*, a smaller ship that would carry the arms to a waterway in Iraq. Both times he apologized for the delay and said he would be arriving at Salalah the following day.

His last night in Paris, Sean stopped for one last drink at the café on Rue Caulaincourt. He sat at an outdoor table, and unfurled a newspaper he had bought down the street. People were passing by, enjoying the evening. Many of the pedestrians were commuting from their place of employment. A few people stopped at the café for an aperitif before supper. Three young and chatty nurses, dressed in blue uniforms, appeared on the sidewalk, no doubt returning home from a shift at the nearby hospital. A few steps behind the younger nurses, two older, more reserved nurses followed.

Sean's attention was drawn first to the young nurses. As his gaze shifted to the two women, he was shocked. Sean dropped his newspaper and stood. One of the women appeared to be Marielle. Both women noticed the man hurry to a standing position, and one of them stopped. She and Sean gazed at one another in silence. Lifting her hand over her mouth, she whispered, "Sean?"

Sean didn't move from his place at the table, and he didn't mutter a word. He was uncertain that he wanted this meeting to take place.

Marielle approached Sean, extending her hand. "Sean, what are you doing here?"

"Why, I was planning to have an Armagnac while I read my American newspaper."

As Marielle's companion continued on her way, she called over her shoulder, "See you tomorrow."

Both Marielle and Sean stood in silence, gazing at one another and wondering what to say next. In a low voice, Sean asked, "Won't you have a seat?"

"I would not be interfering, would I? What I intended was: are you alone? I still cannot believe my eyes. Did you come here to see me?"

"You would not be interfering, and yes, I'm alone. I've been alone for many years. And no, I did not come here to visit you. I came to Paris on business, and I stopped by your neighborhood as I had done in the past. In fact, I must leave Paris tomorrow."

Sean had a good view of his former girlfriend. In true Parisian fashion she had added no weight to her curvaceous figure. She wore no makeup and needed none. As he remembered, her hair was brown and luxuriant. Her movements feminine, her demeanor friendly, captivating. She took a seat across the table from Sean, leaning forward while searching his expressions.

"Sean, what a surprise finding you here. I thought I would never see you again."

Sean said, "I also thought I would never see you again, although I must say you are an unexpected delight to the eyes."

Marielle looked away. The waiter brought Sean's Armagnac and set it in front of him. Sean extended his upward-turned hand and asked, "Perhaps a glass of wine?"

She looked at the waiter and said, "Yes, a glass of the house white wine, please."

Sean told her, "You haven't changed. You are still as lovely as the last time I saw you on this very street."

She laughed. "And you too haven't changed. You're still full of bluster."

"It appears you are still in the nursing profession."

"Yes, I've been at it now for ten years. Because of my seniority I am no longer obliged to do the night shifts."

"How's your mother?"

Her expression turned sad. "Mother passed away last year, I am sorry to say. She lingered for a long time. I miss her dearly."

"I'm sorry."

A thousand thoughts raced through Sean's mind. He wondered if Marielle lived alone. Had she married? Did she have a beau? Asking outright would be tactless and might send the wrong message.

The waiter arrived with her wine. "I think you will like this," he said. "It's a Vouvray and very tasty! We have a whole cask of it in the cellar."

Sean could think of nothing appropriate to say. Marielle took a sip and nodded to the waiter. "Ah," she said, "this is delicious, which is unusual for a house wine."

She took another sip and, raising her eyebrows, said, "You said you will be departing tomorrow?"

"Yes, I will be traveling to the Middle East."

"Do you have time to stop by my condo? I would like to show it to you. I recently rearranged everything and bought a few new pieces. Besides, I'm a little hungry. I missed lunch today because we had so many patients. We can talk more at my place."

"Of course, I have time. I would very much enjoy seeing your place."

As they made their way along Rue Caulaincourt, Sean did not take Marielle's hand. He thought that might seem presumptuous. He did not know what to expect beyond the apartment door. Would she have a husband waiting for her?

Once inside the apartment, Marielle took Sean by the hand and led him from one room to the next. Sean saw no sign a man was living there. Standing in the living room, she said, "Why don't you watch the telly while I chase up something to eat. Are you hungry?"

"No, I'm fine. Don't bother. I'll see what's on TV."

As Marielle moved around the kitchen, Sean contented himself flicking around stations on the TV. His level of comprehension of the language was somewhere above intermediate, so he could understand only a part of what he heard. In a few minutes Marielle brought a dish with pieces of a baguette and slices of Camembert cheese for Sean. Back in the kitchen, she microwaved a frozen dinner. When it was ready, she brought it to the living room and sat beside Sean.

"So," she said, "tell me what you are doing with yourself these days. Should I assume you are no longer in the American army?"

Sean clicked off the TV and he set the dish on the coffee table. His interest in Marielle exceeded his appetite for food.

"I did six years in the army, and that was enough for me. I did my part. I now own a small gun store in rural Pennsylvania. I sell guns to hunters and farmers who mostly use the guns on the local wild game. I earn most of my income from the shop. I have a small project in the Middle East that will keep me busy for a few weeks. Upon completion of that contract I will be returning to America and the town where I have my gun shop. Enough about me. You might remember I don't like talking about myself. Tell me about yourself. Are you enjoying life these days?"

Marielle set her half-eaten supper on the coffee table as she turned to view her guest. She seemed pensive, a little sad.

"As you know I was with Médecins sans Frontières in the Middle East. I spent three years there. Those were worthwhile years. We assisted many of the unfortunate people who otherwise would have had no help. The sights and the people were heart-wrenching. In time, though, I was obliged to return to Paris due to my mother's deteriorating health. I haven't married. I could not under the circumstances. No sensible man would buy into that situation. Besides, the women of today do not feel the obligation to marry as did the women of generations ago. Mother left me the condominium and a little money. I live comfortably."

She studied Sean. Sean could tell she was thinking. He was delighted to see her again, but he told himself that perhaps he should be leaving. He finished the cheese and slowly stood. He said, "I must be going."

She was surprised and puzzled by his sudden announcement. Tilting her head, she sat back. She said, "If you must."

Sean said, "Thanks for the cheese."

Standing, she said, "Sean, you're a difficult one to understand. Your letters dribbled to nothing. I figured you found a new girlfriend. You know: Love them and leave them. Isn't that what soldiers do? You could have at least written to let me know what was going on in your life."

Sean spoke in apologetic tones. "You should know I'm not good with words and not much better at writing. Mostly, I could not see a future for us."

"I must tell you I am a little more than disappointed with your behavior. You were in Paris, yet you didn't have time to stop by to say hello."

Sean was flummoxed. He could not seem to find the right words to express his thoughts or feelings. He wondered: Should he make amends and perhaps renew a relationship with Marielle, knowing prospects for a future together were minimal? Or should he man up and leave? Stop pretending? Do the right thing!

He said to Marielle, "I really enjoyed seeing you again."

"I enjoyed seeing you too, Sean."

Marielle accompanied him to the lobby on the first floor. Standing beside him, she thrust a piece of paper into the pocket of Sean's jacket. "Here is my telephone number. Give me a call someday. I would like to hear from you, if only now and then."

She put her arms around his neck, pulled close to him, and gave him a long, firm kiss that Sean interpreted as a woman's invitation and a promise. With all kinds of thoughts running through his head, Sean backed away.

"I'll call although I'm not sure when. I'll be busy for a few weeks. *Au revoir*, Marielle."

He turned and opened the front door, gently closing it behind him. Leaving the building and Marielle behind him, he felt as though he was not doing the right thing.

15

The Bois de Boulogne

DISHEARTENED by the attack on their American contact at the Restaurant Sirnak, the Kurds held a conference to discuss the event and its implications. They were greatly disappointed that an American who had come to help them was viciously attacked in, of all places, a Kurdish establishment. They wondered how the assailant knew in advance the American would be in the restaurant. Was there an informer amongst the trusted Kurds? One of the men present at the meeting suggested that perhaps someone had placed a tap on the restaurant's telephone. He said he had surveillance experience, and that placing a tap on a telephone line could be done easily. Following the meeting, Rafiq Jaziri, owner of the Restaurant Sirnak, waited until all of the employees had gone for the day. With flashlight in hand he climbed to the roof of the building to trace the telephone line. To his surprise he found a tap and a transmitter that was sending calls to and from the restaurant to a remote location.

Except for the call to Sean, Rafiq kept the information to himself. Possibly, he thought, there might be a way to use that information to the Kurds' advantage. Indeed, he reasoned, action of some type was needed. Otherwise, the Kurds' enemies might very well succeed in terminating the American. If that were to happen, the Americans might give up on the idea of sending aid to the Kurds. At the very least, the Americans would regret that the Kurds had not done more to protect the American contact. Using his cellular telephone, Rafiq called a friend by the name of Tekan Hamza and arranged a meeting for that evening at Rafiq's home.

When Hamza came to his apartment, Rafiq told him about the tap on the restaurant's telephone line. "If you wish to help our cause," Rafiq told Hamza," this is what I ask you to do: Tomorrow, go to a telephone booth and call me at the restaurant. Do it in the morning. If someone else answers, say that you wish to speak with me. Once you have me on the phone, say your name is Najat. Speak as though you are a man with considerable authority within the Kurdish organization. I will act as though I am in a subordinate role. Tell me that you would like to meet the American tomorrow evening in the Bois de Boulogne, near the kiosk of the emperor. Suggest six in the evening and say you will be wearing a red scarf. Then ask if I can get in touch with the American. I'll say that I will contact him over the lunch hour."

***

Jabir regretted that his first attempt to terminate the American in the Kurdish restaurant had failed. He did not wish to be known as one who botched assignments as he had established a reputation that he valued. Because of his accomplishments he was shown great respect by the ISIS higher-ups, and he relished that status. During his younger years, he had been treated as though he were little more than human. So, the new respect was exhilarating. If he's to have another chance at the American, he will redouble his efforts. For weeks he waited in his apartment for another call to duty. His friends continued monitoring calls to and from the restaurant in hope that one day they would hear useful information.

One day a caller told Jabir one of the operatives intercepted a call at the restaurant and they learned the Kurds had scheduled another meeting with the American. The American would be wearing a red scarf at a meeting place in the Bois de Boulogne.

Jabir put on a disguise, gathered his tools of the trade, and went to the Bois four hours before the scheduled meeting. He wanted to be sure the Kurds were not setting a trap for him. Walking around the area, he found a suitable hiding place several hundred meters from the kiosk. With binoculars he would be able to see what was going on in the vicinity of the reported meeting spot. If all went as he hoped, he would use a hunting knife to do the job.

Two hours before the scheduled meeting, Jabir noticed four men wandering the area. With their dark skins, they appeared to be Kurds. In due time the men took up hiding places surrounding the kiosk. He easily spotted the amateurish trap. He stole away from the site and returned to his apartment to await a genuine opportunity at the American.

16

Wally and the Gun Shop

THE demands of operating McDougal's Firearms kept Wally busy in the weeks following Sean's departure overseas. Aside from the time he spent at the gun shop, he had his normal chores at his uncle's farm. He fed the horses at regular hours and mucked-out the stalls at least once a day. Wally also tried to ride one of the horses every day to keep them in condition. His uncle used the horses for fox hunting, and the exercise kept them strong enough for jumping hedgerows and fences. On many Sunday afternoons and holidays, Wally's uncle and aunt invited him to the main house for a dinner of lamb, a pork loin, or a beef roast. Wally did his best to show his appreciation by taking good care of the horses.

The first week, Wally maintained Sean's original shop hours, Tuesday to Saturday, noon to seven in the evening. The second week, though, he made some adjustments. He wrote the new hours on a piece of cardboard and taped it over Sean's original sign. The sign read: "OPEN 1 p.m. to 6 p.m." Wally sometimes made it to the shop by the advertised opening time. Yet, he was never known for his punctuality. Overall, Wally was doing a credible job of running the store. While he was not abiding by the advertised hours, the shop was open enough to Wally's way of thinking. And he sold a gun on occasion.

Many who lived in the town of Biglow considered Wally a strange individual. He did not have an automobile. His preferred modes of transportation were by bicycle or horse. He was not a good conversationalist, and he never cared to trade gossip. Yet he was nobody's fool, and in his endeavors he proved himself imaginative and intelligent. He knew computers, and during a period of employment years earlier had learned hacking techniques.

Wally pursued hacking for both the challenge and entertainment. He was generally careful to avoid malicious hacking, or at least what he considered malicious. He enjoyed using a skill set he had acquired over the years, and he tried to keep abreast of the latest and evolving techniques. A number of websites offered him opportunities to apply his skills. He tended to hack organizations of a preferred profile. He especially enjoyed annoying organizations that were against hunting and the "killing of wild animals." While Wally was not a hunter, he saw nothing wrong with those who pursued the sport. Since he had become friends with Sean and some of Sean's hunting customers, he came to view hunting as merely another recreational activity that Americans can enjoy in their vast land. He often posted anonymous and humorous messages on the websites of anti-hunting organizations. He considered the hacking as a gentle and harmless way of countering the maligned propaganda of the anti-hunters.

Wally particularly enjoyed targeting PETA, or "People for the Ethical Treatment of Animals," an organization that protested hunting. On occasion he would hack into the PETA website and enter a cooking recipe beside a photo of an animal. On a number of occasions, he posted recipes for a rabbit casserole beside PETA's photo of what many viewers might consider a cuddly rabbit. He had other recipes for wild game as duck, deer, quail, and pheasant. His antics infuriated the PETA people who had paid professionals to find and stop the embarrassing recipes on their website–all to no avail.

One morning Wally was in the mood for a little light entertainment. He had finished taking care of the horses, and he had several hours available with nothing in particular to do. He had a new venison recipe for PETA. He saddled the stallion, put his laptop in the saddlebag, and headed for the cabin in the woods. The horse was anxious to get going. It wanted to run. Wally started it at a slow pace along the roadside before letting the stallion break into a trot. Nearing the path to the cabin, Wally spotted an auto parked to the side of the road. Not a good sign! No one had ever parked near the cabin in the past. He pulled back on the reins and brought the horse to a walk while he considered the parked auto. Seeing Wally stop, a man in a blue uniform opened the car door and stood by the roadside, waiting for Wally to come closer. Wally didn't care to converse with anyone in a blue uniform. He started the horse into a run, jumped the guardrail at the roadside, and took off through the woods, leaving the man behind. Posting the venison recipe could wait. He would not be visiting the shack for a few days.

17

Sean in Oman

WITH the returned passport in his jacket pocket, Sean flew from Paris to the city of Salalah in Oman. Because the plane landed late in the day and he was tired from traveling, he went directly to the Fanbar Hotel where he had made a reservation. He thought he should call the *Musa* and the *Sidra* to allay any anxieties his contacts aboard the ships might have developed because of his delayed arrival. Besides, he wanted to be certain the *Musa* was still nearby and prepared to come to port. He hoped the skipper hadn't pulled anchor and sailed away.

A Lieutenant Carson answered the call. "Oh, there you are," he said to Sean. "We were wondering where you were."

Sean asked, "How's it going?"

"The food is terrible. The English cooks work hard to maintain their bad reputation. It's boiled this, boiled that. Their oatmeal and pudding are great, though. Other than the food, no complaints. The mates are good company. Passage through Suez was slow. Too many ships in front of us were crawling along at a snail's pace. As far as your being late, it's no skin off my nose. I couldn't care less. I'm on the clock, if you know what I mean. The skipper was getting anxious, I can tell you, and I'm sure he will be relieved to learn you finally showed. Yesterday he mumbled something about an invoice for the unanticipated idle time at anchor. I didn't say anything since I'm not in the circle. That's something that is between you and him."

"Please tell the skipper to bring the *Musa* to dockside at his convenience," Sean said.

"Will do. Chances are we won't make it till mid-afternoon tomorrow. We'll need to clear with the port authority, get a berth, and find a tug. You know the drill."

Sean dialed the skipper of the *Sidra.* In response to Aziz el-Amin's "hello," Sean said, "Mr. el-Amin, this is Sean McDougal. I arrived in Salalah this evening. A few minutes ago I talked with personnel aboard the ship with the cargo, and they told me they expect to come to dockside mid-afternoon tomorrow.

"Mr. McDougal, I'm pleased to hear from you. We have been waiting at anchor, and I was becoming concerned."

"I'm sorry for the delay. As you are no doubt aware, in this business one often encounters delays. They are unavoidable."

Sean gazed at the ceiling, unsure as to how his deceit might be received.

The skipper responded, "In any event, sir, let us continue with our business."

"I just called the ship with the cargo, and they are standing by. I shall keep you advised of their progress so that you may prepare to come in."

"That will be fine. We shall await your further instructions. May I ask where you are staying? If convenient to you, I thought I would come ashore to meet you and have a chat."

Sean assumed the man was concerned about payments. He was also aware that in the Middle East, men prefer to discuss business face-to-face. He responded, "I'm at the Fanar Hotel. Yes, I would like to meet with you. Please come ashore and we will have a conversation."

"Give me time to catch a shuttle. That may take as much as two hours. What if we meet on the veranda at the hotel?"

"I'll wait for you there."

For a time Sean read the *London Times* in his room. He tried watching TV until he became bored with the programs. When he went to the veranda, a waiter told him a gentleman was waiting for him at a table. As Sean approached, the man rose and extended his hand.

"Aziz el-Amin."

The man was a slender individual, dressed in western style trousers and shirt. His clothing seemed to hang on him. Sean guessed that, as most seamen, he was not in good physical condition. Aboard ship he probably had little opportunity for physical activity. His skin had an olive cast, and Sean guessed he was probably younger than he appeared. He spoke with a gravelly voice.

Sean said, "Sean McDougal. Pleased to make your acquaintance."

When a waiter came to the table, Sean ordered tea for the two of them. He turned to el-Amin and remarked, "Beautiful day today. Not too hot and not a cloud in sight."

El-Amin smiled. "Yes, I understand that Westerners favor a sunny day and one such day might be called a beautiful day. However, here in the Middle East we have a different opinion. We tend to call a rainy day a beautiful day. When it rains, the clouds shade us from the relentless sun, and the water that the clouds bring is needed to sustain life in this arid climate."

In response, Sean answered, "If I lived here, I might have the same point of view."

The two men exchanged small talk. Eventually, Mr. el-Amin said, "Mr. McDougal, I was told your shipment consists of medical and office equipment. Please believe me when I tell you the owner of the

Sidra is delighted to have your business, and we sincerely hope that you will have more shipments for us in the future. I must say, however, that I find the shipment unusual. Goods of the type you describe almost always come to Iraq aboard large ships that dock at Umm Qasr, which is more suited to ships with a high draft."

Sean was aware that he must be careful with his words. Although the captain's question suggested he doubted what Sean had told him, Sean intended to stick with his original story.

"My customer asked for the shipment to be delivered to the Port of al-Zubair. I'm unaware of their reasons. Perhaps it would mean less trucking on their part. Or maybe they had a bad experience at Umm Qasr and stopped bringing their business there. I didn't ask."

"Fair enough. It's not that important. Nevertheless, perhaps in time we shall learn their reasons."

Sean steered the conversation to the weather and international affairs. The waiter appeared with a pot of tea, cream, sugar, pastry, and cups for two. Sean, acting as host, poured tea into both cups. Aziz el-Amin took a sip from his cup and replaced it to the saucer, regarding Sean.

"Mr. McDougal, if you do not object, I would like to discuss payment for transportation of your merchandise."

He didn't wait for a response from Sean. "We understand you are not an established, large firm with a proven credit history. In fact, we could find very little in the way of financial data on your past business activities or your creditworthiness. For this reason I prefer to confirm your intentions. According to our agreement, you will pay us half in advance and the balance upon delivery of the shipment. May I assume you still intend to abide by those terms?"

Sean nodded firmly. "Of course. I will pay you half the contracted amount as soon as the shipment has been loaded aboard your ship and the other half when the goods have been transported and off-loaded at the destination. I trust those arrangements meet with your approval?"

"Yes, what you suggest is entirely satisfactory. I hope you do not mind my asking how you propose to pay–by bank check, wire or by other means?"

"If you will give me your bank account number at dockside, I will transfer the funds to your account."

"Excellent. One more question. Could you tell me the weights of the components of the cargo? I will need to balance the cargo in the ship's holds."

Sean reached into a trouser pocket. "I'm glad you asked. Here is a summary of the packages and the respective weights and sizes. I anticipated your question. According to my request, the crates should be numbered."

Sean handed the list to the skipper. The man glanced at it, and put it in a shirt pocket.

He said, "I must get back to the ship. I begin to feel ill at ease on land. Allow me to pay for the tea."

"The tea is on me. You had better run along before you get land sick."

The man smiled slightly. "Thank you, Mr. McDougal. I'll repay you with tea aboard ship. We shall await your call."

Sean said, "I shall see you later."

The skipper took his leave, walking toward the dock where he planned to take a shuttle back to the *Sidra.* As Sean watched Aziz el-Amin disappear around the corner of the hotel, he started to have an uneasy feeling about the man. Perhaps the eye contact was not what Sean thought it should have been. As Sean had learned during his earlier days, things in the Middle East often were not what they appeared. Anyone slow to understand this trait would pay a penalty for the shortcoming. Since the U.S. government usually went with the lowest bidder regardless of all other considerations, he wondered if they had conducted a thorough vetting of el-Amin's outfit. And what dangers lurk ahead?

18

At Dockside

EARLY afternoon, Lieutenant Carson called Sean at his hotel room and reported, "The tug's now available so we are pulling anchor and moving in. The port authority told us we will be at Dock Number Three. If all goes according to schedule, we will be unloaded by fifteen-hundred hour and be on our way back to Suez. I'm sure the dock workers will be surprised to see something other than bananas coming out of a banana reefer."

Sean responded, "I'll go to Dock Three and watch for you. The *Sidra* is anchored a short distance away, and the skipper told me they will be prepared to come in on short notice after you depart."

Sean checked out of the hotel, and, with a small bag in hand, headed to the dock where he expected the *Musa* to arrive. He wanted to confirm the dock was clear and that a crane operator would be available.

Upon arriving at the dock he waited where he could see out to sea and watch for the *Musa* to appear.

An hour later Sean saw the *Musa* appear behind a tug. As the ship drew near the dock, the tug maneuvered the large ship toward the dock. Sean called the *Sidra* and notified the skipper the cargo would be unloaded shortly.

The *Musa* was a fair-sized ship that was primarily intended for hauling large quantities of bananas on the high seas. Painted the color of ripe bananas, the ship had two large holds forward and two aft. She was neat, tidy, and clean. The *Musa* touched the dock and men tied her up. Three men came ashore from the ship and approached Sean. Lieutenant Carson, dressed in civvies, introduced himself. In turn, he introduced the skipper of the *Musa* and the second mate. All three men were brusque and businesslike. None showed either cordiality or an interest in exchanging small talk. They seemed miffed by the delay caused by Sean's late arrival. Clearly, they wanted to unload and be on their way–the sooner the better.

Crewmen aboard the ship opened both a fore hatch and an aft hatch in preparation for unloading. The port's crane operator swung a boom out over the ship, preparing to lift the cargo to the dock. Sean stood by to watch. The cargo consisted entirely of sturdy wooden crates. Sean wanted to be certain no crate was dropped or lowered too swiftly. He also recorded the number on each crate as it was positioned dockside. In less than an hour, the cargo was unloaded. Men aboard the *Musa* secured the hatches, the ship's engine came to life, and side thrusters pushed the ship away from the dock. Lieutenant Carson appeared on the bridge and gave one grand wave at Sean. Not waiting for a response, he disappeared into the bridge. Sean sat on one of the wooden boxes as he watched the *Musa* move out to sea.

While the *Musa* was sailing away, Sean spotted the *Sidra* approaching. She was much smaller than the *Musa*. As she came closer, he saw she had only two holds, one forward and one aft. Because of her smaller size, the *Sidra* was able to come in and dock more quickly than the *Musa*. In comparison to the *Musa*, the *Sidra* was a shabby-looking affair. Much of the paint on the ship's hull had been bled over with rust that had oozed down from higher unpainted spots. The bridge was made of wood and some of the panels displayed rotted sections. While the crew tied her up, Aziz el-Amin came ashore and approached Sean.

"Mr. McDougal, is your entire shipment here?"

The skipper took a few minutes to circle the pile of boxes. When he returned to Sean, Sean said, "I checked the shipment against my list, and it's all here."

Scratching the back of his neck, el-Amin said, "The shipment seems smaller than what I expected. Considering the thickness of the boards on those crates, I would say those boxes are relatively heavy."

The skipper's expression suggested he would be receptive to more information on the cargo. He probably doubted the boxes contained the medical and office equipment he had been told comprised the cargo. Sean had no rebuttal that would sound genuine, so he said nothing.

"Unlike many of the shipments we handle," the skipper continued, "I expect the crane operator should have no difficulty transferring the load to our ship. The straps and cables all seem to be substantial and in the proper places."

Crew members aboard the *Sidra* opened hatches, and el-Amin signaled the crane operator to commence loading. El-Amin went aboard to supervise the loading. When the entire cargo had been on-loaded, the hatches were secured in preparation for departure. Sean came aboard, carrying his small bag. The skipper walked over to Sean and stood nearby, much as a schoolboy waiting for his allowance. Sean withdrew his sat phone and said, "If you will tell me your bank and the account number, I'll pay you now."

El-Amin reached into a trouser pocket and handed Sean a piece of paper that contained the account number and routing. Sean punched the numbers into his phone and transferred fifteen thousand dollars to the account. El-Amin stepped away a few steps, cell phone in hand, to confirm receipt of the funds.

Sean asked, "May I have a signed receipt?"

El-Amin obliged Sean's request. The second mate started the engine, and a crewman went ashore to remove the lines holding the ship to the pier posts. The ship moved out to sea and turned northward. Sean and el-Amin stood side-by-side at the bow as the *Sidra's* speed increased. The sky was perfectly blue without a cloud in sight. A mild breeze stirred up three-foot waves and white caps. Sean's sense of dread would not go away.

19

Visitors

DURING the first hour out of Salalah, Sean and the skipper stayed on the foredeck. The air streaming by confirmed the ship was underway and making progress toward its destination. The seagulls stopped following the ship, abandoning hope for a free meal, and flew westward where they knew they would find land. In time, the skipper turned to Sean.

"Mr. McDougal, may I repay you a tea? I believe our cook has baked some of his famous scones. We'll be eating supper later this evening."

"Thank you, Mr. El-Amin. I was up early and have developed a good appetite. Tea would be fine."

"Shall we adjourn to the galley then? We're lucky to have a good cook. He's an Indian chap and he takes his cooking seriously."

In the galley, two crewmen were already seated and eating snacks. Aziz El-Amin didn't introduce them to Sean. The cook, seeing the skipper and Sean enter, abandoned the carrots he was preparing and came over to the table where they were sitting.

"Good day, gentlemen. Would you like a tray of cold cuts or perhaps pastry?"

Sean said, "I've heard you are well known for your scones."

"Thank you, sir. I can bring you scones if you wish. I baked them only this morning."

Sean said he would have two scones and tea. The skipper ordered the same. As the cook turned to complete the order, Sean excused himself, saying he needed to go topside to make a call.

El-Amin seemed concerned over Sean's pending departure. "Why don't you continue with our tea?' he said, frowning. "We have a long trip ahead of us, and you'll have plenty time on your hands later."

Standing, Sean responded, "I need to advise my business associate of our progress. He may wish to know our approximate landing time."

Sean took the stairs to the aft deck. Stepping outside, he noticed the rear hatch cover was up. Curious, he thought. He walked over and looked down into the hold. A man with a crowbar was tearing boards off one of the boxes, a box Sean knew contained rifles. He shouted at the man, "Hey, what are you doing down there?"

Surprised, the man looked up. He said something in Arabic as he pointed to the box with the removed boards. El-Amin came up beside Sean, and together the two peered down into the hold. El-Amin shouted at the man in a tone that suggested he was berating him. The man answered meekly and climbed out of the hold. He secured the hatch and disappeared below deck. El-Amin turned to Sean.

"I am sorry for this intrusion. I believe the man was looking for something to steal, although he said he was fixing loose boards. In any event I believe he did not find anything of value. He is new with us. Please believe me when I tell you I have difficulty finding dependable men. I will get rid of this one as soon as we return to our home port. In the meantime I cannot afford to be too tough on him. These men know a dozen ways of getting revenge on a skipper."

Sean didn't know what to make of the incident. The intruder obviously had learned the crates contained weapons. He wondered: Would the man keep that information to himself? Or was he sent there by the skipper on an information-gathering mission while the skipper kept Sean occupied in the galley? As they were standing near the closed hatch, Aziz el-Amin suggested, "Mr. McDougal, shall we return to the galley? I believe the cook will have our tea by now."

Remembering he had not completed the call he had started earlier, Sean replied, "You go ahead. I'll be down in a few minutes."

"As you wish. I'll wait for you in the galley."

"By the way, what was the man's name?"

"We know him as Kamil Najem."

The skipper returned to the galley, leaving Sean to his thoughts. When he looked back, away from the stern, he noticed the second mate watching him from the bridge. On second thought, Sean had developed an appetite. He returned to the galley and took a seat across from Aziz el-Amin. The cook delivered the scones, cups and a pot of tea. Both men ate and drank in silence. Aziz el-Amin conveyed an attitude of regret while Sean tried to figure out what it all meant.

One of the crew approached El-Amin and mumbled something about a pump problem. The skipper stood, excused himself and disappeared down the hall. Sean climbed the stairs to the aft deck. He withdrew his phone and sent an encrypted message to Rojen Ghazi. *We are at sea on our way to Iraq. I estimate we are two days from port. Our docking may be delayed depending on port traffic. Will advise....Sean*

Rojen replied immediately. *We shall mobilize and plan to meet you at the time and place you designate. Please keep us informed of your progress. God be with you.*

The remainder of the evening Sean spent his time reading, either on the aft deck or in his cabin. At dusk he went to the galley and the cook made him a platter of baked chicken, mashed potatoes and carrots. That night he had no problem sleeping. The rhythm of the ship's engines and the gentle rocking as the ship moved along made for a good night's sleep. On the second day at sea he rose late and ate alone in the galley. He saw little of the crew, including Aziz el-Amin. The crew had their chores, and Sean stayed out of their way. Midday he went up to the fore deck to enjoy the scene and the sea air. On occasion he saw ships in the distance. Most were cargo ships of various sizes and most were sailing either north or south. Enjoying the sights and smells of the sea, Sean happened to glance off the port side, where he spotted two small dots on the horizon. As the dots grew larger it became apparent that the objects were two small ships traveling at a high speed and on a course that would intercept the *Sidra.* As they drew near, Sean saw the ships were slender and built for speed.

At a distance of a kilometer, one of the boats held back while the other proceeded toward the *Sidra.* The purr of the boat's engines suggested power that, if needed, could propel the ship along at a good clip. In the near boat, one man sat at the wheel while two men stood at midship facing the *Sidra.* Concerned, Sean hurried to the bridge. The wheelman and el-Amin were peering down at the small boat. Sean joined them.

One of the visitors in the boat stood and waved a rocket-propelled grenade over his head. He didn't aim it at the *Sidra.* It seemed his sole intention was to show personnel aboard the *Sidra* that he had the weapon. He set the weapon down and reached for a sign with a telephone number.

Aziz el-Amin dialed a number on the ship's telephone and started speaking with someone. Returning the ship's telephone to its cradle, Aziz El-

Amin spoke to the helmsman, who promptly turned the ship's wheel. The ship began to turn on an arc.

"What's going on?" Sean demanded.

El-Amin shrugged. "These men are pirates. The man down there demands that we follow him. If we do not comply, he said he will sink our ship. I believe he has the means to carry out his threat. An RPG delivered to the right spot on our hull would bring us to the bottom in minutes. We have no alternative and are obliged to do as he says. Most likely he intends to take us south to a port in Yemen or to the Yemeni territorial waters. Outlaw factions operate there without restraint or interference."

Sean assumed someone aboard the *Sidra* had learned the true nature of the cargo, and that person, perhaps the skipper, had placed a call to make a deal with the men in the fast boats. He knew any one of many groups in the Middle East would pay handsomely for either an arms cargo or for information that led to capture of the cargo.

Two additional crewmen came to the bridge, perhaps because they had sensed the ship's change of course. As Sean looked around, he noticed that none of them seemed concerned or worried by the developing situation. Clearly, he was amongst dangerous men. His days, or hours, might be numbered.

20

Going South

SEAN'S GPS told him that the *Sidra* was indeed headed on a southerly course. Ahead, the pirate ship continued leading the ship to an uncertain and possibly dreadful future. Far off to the port side, the second ship continued traveling on a parallel course. No doubt men aboard the far ship were watching developments. The scenario suggested the pirates were following the modern-day playbook. The commander and his lieutenants watch and supervise the operation from a distance while their minions, usually poor young men, do the dangerous work in a second ship near the target.

Sean understood that Aziz el-Amin would not wish to lose his ship, and that might explain his willingness to cooperate. Beyond that, though, Sean wondered if the skipper might be complicit. Was the skipper anticipating a handsome finder's fee if, in fact, he had alerted the pirates to the shipment? Whatever was going on, Sean realized he was about to lose the cargo to a nefarious group of ill-doers. The munitions aboard the *Sidra* might be headed to America's enemies rather than to her allies. And, what would become of him once they had taken final possession of the stolen goods? Would it be a bullet to the head or a swim far out to sea?

Sean considered the pirates' action strange given that none of them boarded the *Sidra.* They seemed confident the *Sidra's* skipper would cooperate. Whatever was happening, Sean was not going to go down without a struggle. When he was certain nobody was watching, he went to the aft deck and hid his sat phone in a lifeboat. Not having access to his cell phone would be a major problem. He needed to speak with el-Amin and returned to the bridge.

The second mate was manning the wheel while nearby Aziz el-Amin peered through binoculars at the pirate ship off the port side. Hearing Sean enter, both turned toward him. El-Amin lowered the binoculars and said, "We have become the victims of an unfortunate situation. Apparently you will be losing your shipment to some desperate people."

Sean was quick to respond. "Mr. Aziz el-Amin, let me ask you a few questions if you don't mind?"

"Certainly."

"Why haven't any of the pirates come aboard? One would think they would like to be near you, to talk with you, and to give you directions."

"It is their way of showing us respect. They want us to likewise show them respect and go along with whatever they want. The implication is that if we do what they want, they will harm no one and we shall be allowed to return with our ship undamaged. Nevertheless, I expect that as we near their destination, one of them will want to come aboard to give us specific orders."

Keeping his distance, Sean said, "Another question. Why don't you call the Coast Guard in Oman? Would they not wish to offer help and perhaps pursue these outlaws?"

"Mr. McDougal, I can think of no one I may call. First of all, we are in international waters and not the territorial waters of Oman. I am not a citizen of Oman. I am Iraqi, and the ship is not of Omani registry. So the government of Oman has no incentive to risk losing a ship, a plane, or personnel in a fight with these people. Besides, the pirates have most likely made payments to certain authorities in Oman to ensure that they ignore what might happen in nearby international waters. It's how things work in this part of the world. Perhaps you get my point."

Flabbergasted, Sean concluded he had nothing of significance to add. He said, "Disgusting."

Returning to his cabin, Sean considered his options. Above all, he did not want to lose the arms shipment to these crooks. That would be a terrible outcome. Doing a few mental calculations, he estimated they would be traveling the remainder of the day, that night, and at least one more day and one more night. While he had no weapons at hand, he knew of an ample supply of weapons only a few yards away. Reviewing the list of munitions, he realized the heavy sniper rifles and the matching ammunition were in the rear hold. One of the boxes also contained 9 mm Beretta handguns. He hadn't used either weapon in years, but he knew he could still employ them with competency. When the crew was eating at the regular suppertime he wandered the ship looking for a crowbar and flashlight. When he found what he needed, he brought the items to his cabin.

Sean had a late supper and returned to his cabin to read. At one in the morning he quietly made his way to the rear hold and opened the hatch. He flipped the lights on, and with the crowbar and flashlight dangling from his belt climbed down the ladder. He worked quickly, as he didn't want someone closing the hatch over him and locking him in the hold for the rest of the voyage. He found the crate with the big sniper rifles and used the crowbar to pry away several of the boards. The crate contained a number of M82 Barret .50 caliber sniper rifles. He retrieved one and set it near the ladder.

The ammunition for the big gun was in watertight canisters in three different crates. He removed several boards from one of the crates to find forty canisters of the cartridges. One container was marked ".50 cal blue tips." Those were the incendiary bullets–not exactly what he wanted. Another was marked "black tips," or armor-piercing. Those would do if he could not find the ones he wanted. With a little more searching, he found the canister with the red-tipped bullets. Those, which were a combination of armor-piercing, incendiary, and tracer. Perfect for the situation at hand! The bullets were over five inches in length and more resembled an antiaircraft round than the type of bullet used in a shoulder-fired weapon.

Sean withdrew eleven of the red-tipped bullets and stored them in the pockets of his jacket. Because the bullets were heavy and bulky he felt he could not easily carry more. He still needed a revolver. His list showed the Berettas and matching ammo to be in Box Number Seventeen. He moved several boxes around until he found the one he wanted. He removed more boards and grabbed a revolver and several clips of ammo. Lifting the twenty-six-pound rifle, he slipped his head through the sling. The handgun went into his belt and under his shirt. He climbed out of the hold and closed the hatch, all the while taking care to be as quiet as possible. The moon was casting enough light so he could make his way along the deck. He entered his cabin, certain nobody had seen him. At dawn he would launch his attack.

Lying in bed, Sean kept his hand on the Beretta. In case someone broke through his cabin door, he would have a surprise for the unwelcomed visitor. He tried to sleep because he anticipated an exhausting day ahead. Nevertheless, sleep didn't find him. The adrenalin in his bloodstream and the many thoughts racing around in his head worked to keep him well awake. An hour before sunrise he sat up. The time for action had arrived. Carrying the heavy rifle, he eased past the bridge and lay prone on the bow with the rifle pointing forward. He knew the man at the ship's wheel would see him and would certainly would alert the skipper. No matter! Sean expected to finish his work before men aboard the *Sidra* got organized and tried to stop him.

Sean figured he needed less than a minute to complete his attack. The light was at exactly the level he wanted. The scope on his rifle was a light-gathering optic so when he looked through it everything in sight appeared brighter. The lens produced the same effect as a bright light illuminating the pirates' boat and the men in it. Yet the prevailing low light level would not allow the men in the pirate ship to see him as he lay on the deck.

Sean cycled one of the red-tipped cartridges into the rifle's chamber. The scene reminded him of times in the past. Truly in his element, he felt a moment of elation. Peering at the pirate ship through the telescopic sight, he could see one man at the wheel. The other two were probably still asleep in the small cabin. The three men had no way of knowing their end was near.

Sean had several possible choices to evaluate. He could aim for the man steering the pirate ship. However, the *Sidra* was swaying, and he would have difficulty holding the crosshairs on the small target. Sean might very well miss him on his first shot. If the bullet missed its target, the man most certainly would give the ship full throttle and take off at a high speed. A fast-moving ship would be a difficult target, and Sean could easily miss with a second or third shot. The pirates might escape, only to return at night to do their dirty work.

The other option, which Sean favored, was to aim for the ship's engine–a much larger target. The red-tipped bullets had the capability to penetrate one inch of hardened steel. Depending on the point of impact a single bullet could easily destroy the engine and disable the boat. The pirate boat would become dead in the water and an almost stationary target. With the ship steady in the water, he could take his time giving the pirates the punishment they had earned.

Sean put the crosshairs on a spot where he estimated the ship's engine was located. He squeezed the trigger, and the rifle recoiled against his shoulder. The tracer showed the strike was low and below the ship's water line. At the sound of the shot, the man at the boat's wheel spun around. He didn't know what had happened or the source of the sound. Sean adjusted his scope to raise the strike of the bullet. He cycled another round into the chamber and repositioned the crosshairs. He took a deep breath, left half out of his lungs and slowly squeezed the trigger again.

Upon the bullet's impact, smoke shot up from the engine compartment. Debris flew high in the air, and the ship stopped, dead in the water. Sean spotted the gooseneck where fuel would be entered to fill the tank. The gooseneck indicated the probable location of the fuel tank. His third round struck the fuel tank, and the rear section of the ship burst into flames. The incendiary part of the bullet performed perfectly.

The man who had been steering the pirate ship stood up with a RGP on his shoulder. As he aimed at the *Sidra*, he was looking directly at the bow, which offered a small target, and his boat was rocking violently. He fired nevertheless. The rocket flew wide of the starboard side of the *Sidra*. Sean's fourth shot blew a hole through the man's midsection. The other two men on the ship grabbed life jackets and jumped overboard. Either they feared bullets from Sean's rifle or the temperature from the fire was not to their liking. To ensure that the ship would sink to the bottom, Sean put two more bullets in the ship's hull a little below the waterline.

21

Under Attack

SEAN had taken less than a few minutes to make the six shots on the pirate boat leading the *Sidra.* He expected the second pirate boat, the one carrying the overseers of the operation, would realize the plight of the first pirate boat and perhaps try to take revenge on the *Sidra.* While they would lose their stolen goods, they might consider the loss a cost of doing business. Their retaliation would send a message to future targets: Go along with us or live to regret the consequences; we mean business.

Sean hurried to the bridge, where the lone helmsman was manning the boat's wheel. When Sean entered with the fearsome-looking rifle, the man raised his hands. Sean motioned for him to lower his hands and said, "Keep the bow facing the second boat. Otherwise they will sink us. You have that?"

The man said a few words in Arabic and shrugged his shoulders. He didn't understand what it was that Sean wanted.

With his hands, Sean indicated that the helmsman should turn the ship to face the oncoming pirate ship.

Realizing Sean's intent, he answered "Yes" and proceeded to turn the ship toward the pirates.

Sean knew that if the pirates intended to sink the *Sidra*, they would want a broadside shot. The RPG rockets are designed to impact a target perpendicularly to a surface. The rockets functioned properly only in that orientation. An RPG shot from a position facing the bow or stern would most likely cause no damage. Even if it glanced the ship's hull and exploded, the missile would cause only superficial damage.

Sean returned to the position he had used for the first series of shots and lay on the deck. Because of the deck's height above the waterline and the low light level, he still held an advantage over his adversary. Chances were they would not be able to see Sean whatsoever. Even when the daylight improved, they would be able to see no more than a small part of him. Yet he would have no difficulty seeing them. To port, Sean saw the second pirate boat increase speed and turn a course toward the *Sidra.* They ignored their men in the water near the first pirate boat.

Sean started to think that perhaps he should have brought more of the .50 cal cartridges. As directed, the helmsman turned the *Sidra* to face the oncoming pirate boat. At 1,000 yards the pirates changed to a circular course, intending to race into position for a broadside shot at their target. The helmsman increased the ship's speed so he could more quickly realign the *Sidra* to face the pirate boat. Because the Sidra was only two hundred and fifty feet in length, the helmsman had no trouble quickly altering her course to face the pirates. Twice the pirates tried to maneuver into position for a broadside shot, but each time the *Sidra* successfully turned to face the small boat.

Soon the pirates realized their only hope for a broadside shot at the *Sidra* would be to come within several hundred yards or less. If they remained too far out, the *Sidra* would always have time to turn so they would not have a broadside shot. At the same time, they were reluctant to come too close. They understood that someone aboard their target ship had the capability to sink the first pirate boat, and they did not wish to suffer the same fate. The driver of the boat gunned the engine and headed for a point slightly ahead of the *Sidra*. They would sink the *Sidra* as she turned to avoid them.

At five hundred yards, Sean let fly his first shot. The second boat posed a difficult shot because it was moving fast and diagonally from upper right to lower left. The tracer bullet showed Sean that the shot hit the water behind the boat. He reloaded and aimed further ahead of the fast-moving boat. In a short period of time, the pirate's boat was at four-hundred yards and closing fast. The second shot blew a three-inch hole in the near hull and passed through to the far hull. Unfortunately, the point of impact was too far forward and too high above the waterline to do any damage. The strike would not hinder the boat's progress. Sean had three more cartridges. He reloaded and fired again. The shot struck mid-ship, causing flames to erupt and the engine to sputter.

Although damaged, the pirate boat maintained speed. Still a dangerous threat, it turned to get away from the *Sidra.* Perhaps the pirates intended to move away for the time being so they could devise another strategy. There might be reinforcements they could call in. Sean realized his adversaries could be a continuing and dangerous threat if they escaped. If the boat remained operable, they might very well shadow the *Sidra* and sneak in close at night. At close range they would have an easy broadside shot that would guarantee sinking the *Sidra.* For the safety of the *Sidra* and his mission the surviving pirate boat must be destroyed.

When the pirates turned to flee they gave Sean an unintended gift. As they motored away they were no longer a difficult shot going from left-to-right, right-to-left, or at an angle. They had become the next best target to a stationary shot. All Sean had to do was get the lead correct. Sean's first shot went high and hit the water ahead of the pirates. Too much lead! He inserted another round, the last one on his person, into the chamber. He adjusted for less lead, and squeezed the trigger. The bullet struck the engine and the boat erupted into flames. It stopped moving and the two men aboard jumped overboard.

Standing at the bow of the *Sidra*, Sean waved to the men in the water and shouted, "Have a nice day." Carrying his rifle, he strode to the bridge. The skipper, two other crew members, and the Indian cook were waiting there. Aziz el-Amin, wearing pajamas, said "Good shooting, Mr. McDougal. We will pray for them."

Sean said, "You do that."

Sean did a quick calculation. If Aziz el-Amin was in with the pirates, he had just lost whatever commission they had promised him. On the other hand, perhaps his cause was not lost. If he brought the ship to Khor al-Zubair in accordance with the original contract, he could still collect the other half of the contracted fee. Yet, there was another possibility. Aziz could kill Sean and sell the cargo to the highest bidder. That might be the most profitable of all options, although Aziz would need to find a reliable buyer. He would also need to worry about repercussions from unknown sources. In any event, Sean told himself he must proceed with the utmost care.

"Shall we continue our journey north?" he asked the skipper. "It seems we had a distraction and a brief delay."

Aziz turned to the helmsman and gave him orders. The helmsman redirected the ship onto a northerly course. Facing the cook, Sean said, "I worked up an appetite. How about two eggs, steak, and toast?"

"Yes sir. I'll start right away," the cook responded. "How do you like your steak?"

"Medium rare, and tea, please. I'll be down in a few minutes."

Sean was not in the mood for small talk. Especially, he did not care for conversation with the skipper. He made his way to the stern and retrieved his cellular phone from the lifeboat where he had hidden it earlier. He sent coded messages to both the Agency and Rojen Ghazi to advise them that he would be delayed by a few days. Next, he went to the galley and sat at a table. When the cook brought Sean a cup of tea, he asked. "Milk or sugar, sir?"

"No, thank you. Plain will be fine. I like your tea. Is it from India?"

"Yes, the tea is from the Assam Province, much as myself. I am pleased you like it. I'll have your breakfast in a few minutes, sir."

Sean smiled his gratitude. He started to believe the Indian cook was an honest man and perhaps the only member of the crew he could trust.

That evening Sean ate supper alone in the galley and later went to his cabin. The day's activities and the engagement with the pirates had tired him. The tension, the adrenalin rush, the fear for his life reminded him of his combat experiences in Iraq. Before lying down, he checked the Beretta to confirm there was a round in the chamber. He would sleep with his hand gripping the Beretta. His eyes became heavy, and his thoughts drifted to the time his army buddy, Mason, took a bullet. He often thought of Mason and the tragic day he had led his squad into a trap near the Iraqi town of Usit. He sometimes blamed himself for not having been more cautious, for not being apprehensive of the high ground above the road into the town. His thoughts wandered to Mason's parents and the day Sean visited them at their home near Barlow, Pennsylvania.

In advance of his visit to the Kellers, Sean had called the couple to ask if they were agreeable to his stopping. Mr. Keller told him they would like to meet him and please do so. They agreed on a Wednesday afternoon. On the day of the visit, Sean found the Keller's house without difficulty. The small, white frame house sat amongst aged oak trees on a large lot. Mr. Keller greeted him at the front door. Mrs. Keller joined them in the living room. She forced a smile at meeting Sean while trying to conceal her overwhelming grief. They talked quietly in the living room for a time. When the conversation slowed, Mr. Keller suggested that if Sean was interested they could visit Mason's grave. He said the grave was a short distance away and behind the Lutheran church they attended periodically.

Sean concurred with the suggestion and Mr. Keller drove.

At the cemetery, Mr. Keller led the way as they walked to the headstone that acknowledged the remains below were those of the Kellers' son, Mason. While the three stood in silence with bowed heads, Mrs. Keller reached over and took Sean's hand. Not a word was spoken until the three returned to the Keller house.

In the Kellers' living room, Mr. Keller offered Sean a beer. Mrs. Keller, with watery eyes, told Sean that Mason was their only son and they missed him dearly. "Mason had so much promise," she said. "He hoped to go to college when he got out of the army. It's so sad." She asked Sean if he had known Mason well and if he was with Mason at the end. Sean obliged with several tales of his times together with Mason. He told the story about the occasion he and Mason both came down with bad cases of poison ivy during boot camp. "We were in the dispensary for three weeks, recovering," Sean said. "Later Mason and I had to repeat the entire boot camp." Mrs. Keller seemed consoled by the tales of her son's army experiences. She said Mason hadn't told her about the episode with the poison ivy. No doubt, she said, he didn't wish to worry his mother. With regard to Mason's last moments, Sean didn't tell all that he knew. He acknowledged he was with Mason that fatal day, while omitting the parts about Mason's screams before he passed.

The Kellers asked Sean to stay for supper, but he begged-off, saying he appreciated the offer. Beside his car, Mrs. Keller gave Sean a hug and held him tightly for a time. She thanked him for the visit and said he should stop by again. They would like to see him again, and perhaps the next time he could stay for supper. Struggling to hold back tears, she waved as Sean backed onto the main road and drove away. Farther down the road, he passed and took notice of the old Esso gas station that he eventually bought for his business venture.

At first, Sean had thought the gun store was a great idea. After his military service abroad, he longed for a quiet scene, one away from the ruthlessness and turmoil he had experienced. He thought he needed a place where he could take time to renew. With time, though, he started to have doubts about his original choice. Barlow and its people were so different from everything he had come to know. So parochial.

Sean's eyes were growing heavy. He thought of Marielle … how pretty she was… the strange and lonely life he had been living. He resolved to give more thought to his predicament …to Marielle…another day….

22

Sailing North Again

THE *Sidra* was once again cruising north, on a course for Iraq. Although it had been at sea for four days it hadn't moved any farther north from its starting point. The *Sidra* and Salalah were still at the same latitude. The ship continued on her journey toward Khor al-Zubair where, if all went as hoped, Sean would supervise unload of the cargo for the waiting Kurds.

Several times el-Amin approached Sean with a conciliatory demeanor. Regardless, Sean showed no interest in conversation. He did not wish to give the skipper a chance to come close so he could slip a knife blade between Sean's ribs. The episode with the pirates had heightened Sean's distrust of the man and his intentions. Yet, Sean needed him to take the ship to the Iraqi port. Better to keep a distance and the relationship professional. The crew sensed the chill between their skipper and Sean. As a result, no crew member wanted to be seen conversing cordially with Sean. Their behavior was a show of respect for the ship's master. The cook was an exception. He didn't seem to care one way or the other. He tried to be friendly to all who visited his galley.

The cook, Mandar, was by nature an outward and gregarious individual. His English was on a par with Sean's, and in some regards better. As he explained to Sean, he came from a village in India where English was the first language. The two would sometimes sit in the galley between meals, compare notes, and exchange observations. Mandar told Sean that the small pay he received as the ship's cook he sent to his family in India. There, he had a house, a wife, and six children. Once a year he made a trip home to see them. Otherwise he was away from home and his family. He said he once considered emigrating to America, Canada, or the Middle East. However, these days, he explained, emigration was little more than a remote thought. His love of India and its ways delayed him from making a move. He hoped one day he would return permanently to his homeland.

Traffic on the Arabian Sea was busy. Ships could be seen traveling north and south any time of the day or night. The ships were either loaded with fresh cargo or returning to port for another load. By far the largest and most numerous of the ships were the oil tankers.

Now and then Sean would go to the stern to watch the traffic. On occasion a southbound ship would pass within yards of the *Sidra*, the helmsmen on both ships not wishing to change course to any large degree. Approximately one hundred nautical miles northeast of Salalah, Sean spotted a boat far off on the horizon. It was traveling at a moderate speed and its bow was headed to intercept the *Sidra*, much as the recent pirate boats had done.

Alarmed at the sight of the approaching ship, Sean scurried to his cabin to retrieve the heavy-duty sniper rifle and a handful of cartridges. He laid on the deck to follow the ship through the scope on the rifle. If they were more pirates, he would deal with them early on. As he peered through the rifle's telescopic sight, following the ship's progress, he gradually realized those on board were uninterested in the *Sidra.* The ship, a fair-sized pleasure yacht, crossed the *Sidra's* path heading toward the Omani coast. Sean guessed the vessel was most likely carrying the son of an oil-rich Arab and his friends out for a cruise. A woman in a red bikini waved at the *Sidra* as the yacht sped by. Relieved, Sean returned with the rifle to his cabin.

Two days ahead of their anticipated arrival at the Shatt al-Arab Waterway, Sean sent an encrypted message to Rojen:

Mr. Ghazi. *I estimate we will arrive at the mouth of the Shatt al-Arab Waterway the morning of the day after tomorrow. I've been told that travel up the waterway is often at a snail's pace. We might dock the morning of the tenth. If we cannot make dockside that day, we will delay so as to dock on the morning of the eleventh.*

Ghazi replied: *Mr. McDougal, we have the trucks and men mobilized and standing by. We are most anxious to see you and the cargo arrive safely. Please call me again when you are near the entrance to the waterway. When we hear from you, we will move to a point near the port. From there we will move to the port when the cargo is about to be unloaded or shortly after it has been unloaded. We hope to promptly load the trucks and move out before too many eyes take notice of the shipment.*

Sean also sent a message to the agency and advised them of his progress.

Sean's thoughts continued to wander back to Paris and Marielle. How wonderful it was seeing her again. What a charming, lovely, and sincere young lady. Feeling a need to talk with her again, he dialed her number. On the tenth ring he pushed "off." Perhaps she was on duty at the hospital.

In the galley, Sean found Mandar peeling potatoes and singing in English. When he saw Sean enter, he asked, "Tea, sir?"

Sean responded, "Tea would be fine. Why don't you have one with me?"

"Perhaps I will. I need a break. I've been on my feet for hours. I'll bring the tea over in a few minutes. Please have a seat. If you are so inclined, you will find some American and French magazines in the corner. The mates page through them on occasion, although they can't read the text. Mostly they like the girlie pictures."

Sean sat near one of the portholes. He wanted to be able to see out to port side. Paging through the assortment of magazines he saw nothing of interest. Most were over five years old. Others were missing pages. In due time Mandar brought a tray with a pot of tea, two cups, warm milk, sugar, and a selection of his freshly-baked cookies. Gesturing toward the tray, the cook offered, "Help yourself."

Sean responded, "Thank you. I will." Indian style, Sean poured the warm milk into one of the cups and followed the milk with tea.

Mandar did likewise and followed with several shakes of pepper to his cup.

Waiting for the tea to cool, Sean tasted a cookie and asked Mandar, "Tell me if you are so inclined. Has the *Sidra* been hijacked by pirates in the past?"

"Mr. McDougal, you are asking a dangerous question. You could get me fired or thrown overboard. Even if I knew of any pirates from past adventures on the *Sidra*, I could not tell you. I expect you know that."

Mandar's answer was revealing. If the ship had not been involved in a hijacking to the man's knowledge, Sean assumed he would have emphatically so stated. His answer allowed Mandar to deny later, if asked, that he had said anything about a hijacking, yet his coded answer suggested that perhaps the ship had been involved in pirate encounters in the past. Sean helped himself to the tea along with two more of Mandar's cookies. When the teapot had been drained, he thanked Mandar and returned to his cabin. The cook had indirectly confirmed Sean's doubts about el-Amin and his ways. In the coming days, Sean realized he must be extra vigilant. Having the handgun in his belt would offer a degree of protection.

On Sean's second attempt, Marielle answered the call. Her "Allo" raised Sean's spirits.

"Greetings from a ship in the Persian Gulf," he said.

"Sean, how are you? Safe and well, I hope."

She sounded distant, which Sean thought to be appropriate, considering his noncommittal behavior the last time he'd spoken with her.

"I'm fine, Marielle. I've been thinking of you and our last meeting. You're right. I was equally stupid and asinine at the same time. I'm not good with people the way you are. I called to say I'm sorry, that I keep thinking of you and that I miss you."

There was a long silence during which neither spoke. At last, and in a more relaxed tone, she said, "Don't fret over it. I was delighted to see you again after all those years."

There was another pause before Marielle asked, "Do you think you might be stopping by Paris again within the next five years?"

"That is why I called. When my assignment is finished here, I'll be traveling through Paris. I was thinking of spending some time…what I meant to say was maybe a few weeks in Paris."

More cheerful, she said, "Why don't you? I would like to see you again. Tell me your favorite French dish, and I will make it on your first day back. We will have a small celebration in honor of our returning adventure-seeker."

Her response delighted Sean who felt like a little boy who had just found a shiny new bicycle under the Christmas tree. Why was he risking life and limb amongst people of dubious intent when he could be enjoying life back in Paris with Marielle? Of course, down deep he knew the answer. The call of adventure had drawn him into a spider's web of intrigue and danger. He had made the choice and he had agreed to supervise the arms shipment. He was going to try his best to see the project through to a successful end.

Sean's pulse had increased dramatically at the sound of Marielle's voice and the thought of spending worthwhile time with her. Afraid of becoming tangled up in a stream of words, in typical Sean McDougal fashion, he ended the conversation by telling her, "I'll call."

23

Docking at Khor al-Zubair

STANDING on the bow of the *Sidra*, Sean gazed into the distance toward the mouth of the Shatt al-Arab Waterway. As the *Sidra* drew near, he could see traveling lights aboard numerous ships that had anchored and were waiting their turn to enter the waterway. The *Sidra* continued forward, although at a slower speed, and when the ship had almost come to a halt the skipper dropped anchor.

The following morning the line of ships began entered the waterway, each keeping a distance of at least a thousand yards behind the preceding ship. The *Sidra* followed in turn, moving at ten knots.

Sean called Rojen Ghazi in the open. When Ghazi answered, Sean said, "This is Sazan, the baker. We've encountered a few delays during our travel. Anyhow, we expect to meet your delivery truck first thing tomorrow morning. Would that be satisfactory?"

Ghazi said, "Yes, Sazan, that will be fine. See you then."

Late in the day the *Sidra* pulled into a dock at Khor al-Zubair. Men aboard ship opened the hatches, and a port worker climbed up to the crane cabin. Aziz el-Amin approached Sean. "Mr. McDougal, the hatches are open and we are prepared to commence unloading your cargo."

Sean nodded. "The sooner the better."

Aziz responded, "I am truly sorry our voyage took so long. I assume you are likewise disappointed because of the extra time and the dangers we encountered. As you are well aware, I came close to losing my ship as well as my men."

Sean knew where Aziz was going with the discussion, although he chose to remain silent for the moment. In the meantime, he noticed the crane operator was not proceeding with the unloading. He was sitting in the crane's cabin, watching Aziz and Sean.

"As you might understand, Mr. McDougal," Aziz continued, "this trip has taken my ship and crew on a much longer and more costly trip than we had bargained for. I had added expenses in the form of wages, fuel and food. I had bargained for a charter of only three days. Yet your shipment kept me engaged for many more days. In short, Mr. McDougal, I am obliged to ask for a surcharge of thirty thousand dollars."

Sean looked the man in the eyes. "Mr. El-Amin, I know that you almost lost the *Sidra* as well as the crew, yourself, and me. Tell me, please: Who saved the ship and all of the men? Need I spell it out for you? I could tell you that my fee for my efforts amounts to more than the surcharge you are requesting."

Sean considered objecting further and more vigorously. He knew that according to the terms of the contract, he was not responsible for *force majeure*, unforeseen expenses, or delays. The terms of the contract excused him from any surcharge. He hesitated to say more. Any argument with the skipper would only result in further delays, and complications. He needed the cargo on the dock and he needed it there promptly. The Kurds would be arriving soon, and he must have the shipment available for them to load it on the trucks and depart without delay. Arguing with Aziz could take hours, if not days. It would be better to let Aziz have his way for the moment. Besides, Sean thought he might have recourse. He said, "I'm sorry about your added expenses, and I can understand your position. If I were you I would expect similar consideration. Perhaps your request for additional payments is warranted. I'll pay the added fee if you start unloading immediately."

Aziz motioned to the crane operator that he should proceed. He said, "Mr. McDougal, I have been advised that we must move the *Sidra* away from dockside as soon as we have unloaded the cargo. A man from the port authority told me they wish to have the dock space available first thing in the morning. Because I do not wish to travel the waterway in the dark, we will move only a short distance before we drop anchor for the night. If you have no objection, perhaps we could settle our accounts without further delay?"

Sean withdrew his cellular phone. "Fair enough." He moved away a few feet and punched numbers on his telephone. He waited a few seconds before pushing the "off" button. "There's your payment including the surcharge," he said.

Aziz said, "Give me one minute please, while I check my account." He turned, pushed some numbers on his phone. Placing his phone in his pocket, he said, "Thank you, Mr. McDougal. It's been a pleasure doing business with you."

Sean said nothing as he continued to check the crates emerging from the bowels of Sidra.

Having completed the transfer of the cargo to the dock, the crane operator descended from the cabin of the crane and headed for the port's canteen. Crewmen aboard the *Sidra* confirmed the holds had been emptied and they secured the hatches. Aziz, who had remained on the dock during the unloading, came over to Sean. He rubbed his chin before speaking. "Mr. McDougal if I were you I would not allow the cargo to rest on the dock for very long. And I suggest, too, that you have someone guard it while it rests here."

The man was trolling for information. Sean was not going to give him anything of value. "No problem," He answered.

"I'll say goodbye then. We'll be departing as soon as the crew returns from the port store with their smokes and snacks."

El-Amin turned and walked toward the ship. Sean realized the man knew the true nature of the shipment and could sell that information for a sizeable commission. Yet again, he realized he was in a precarious situation. He hoped Rojen and his men would arrive soon.

Sean sat on one of the cargo's wooden boxes so he could watch the *Sidra* depart. A crewman from the ship came down the gangplank, removed the lines from the dock posts and returned up the gangplank. The ship's engines started, the crewman retrieved the gangplank, and the *Sidra* eased away from the wharf. Sean felt an association with the *Sidra*. Possibly he had saved her and the crew from a watery grave. As the ship was disappearing into the darkening distance, Sean faced out to the ocean. The boxes behind him, he reasoned, might protect him from any sniper who would be outside the port's fence. He anticipated a long night. The gates on the road to the dock would be locked until early morning. As the evening air cooled, he withdrew a jacket from his duffel bag and slipped into it. He likewise withdrew the Beretta automatic he had placed into the duffel bag before leaving the *Sidra.* While it was a little large, he was able to squeeze it into a pocket of his jacket.

Prompted by the skipper's demand for more money, he sent an encoded email to Wally.

Hope all is well. I'll be home in a few weeks, although not sure exactly when. I'm going to stop over in Paris for a little R *and* R. *Do me a favor if you don't mind. I was just cheated out of thirty-thousand dollars by a dishonest swindling SOB. Do you think you could retrieve the funds? The transfer was from my account, which is Account Number Scarlet 26797743 with National Suisse in Bern, Switzerland. The swindler's account is 777239611 with the Royal National Bank of the Bahamas. If you can do it, don't transfer the funds back into my account in Bern. That would be a telltale giveaway. Instead, transfer the funds to an account I have with Banque Germain & Cie SA in Geneva. The account there is 827-926553-843. See what you can do. While you are at it, a little more than thirty would help even the score. ….. YKW.*

24

Jabir

JABIR al-Ateri returned to the small apartment that had been made available to him in the Eleventh Arrondissement. An anonymous person had mailed the keys and the address to him prior to his arrival in Paris. He didn't know who owned the place and was not inclined to inquire. Over the years he had learned in was best to avoid asking more questions than were absolutely necessary.

He smiled as he entered the apartment, thinking of the minor adventure in the Bois. *Such amateurs. Those stupid Kurds apparently have little practical experience in subterfuge.* On the other hand, he knew that even persistent amateurs might succeed if they tried enough times. The experience of the trap told him there were people bent on either capturing or killing him. He resolved to watch his back.

Jabir had been given no additional instructions since he was sent in pursuit of the American in the

Kurdish restaurant. While he awaited a call and new orders, he had time to enjoy the sights of Paris. He thought he would go for a walk on the Champs-Élysées, France's main street. He took the Metro, exiting at the Place de la Concorde. He found the Champs to be a beautiful and exciting part of the city. He hadn't seen anything like it in Iraq. He enjoyed watching the crowds of tourists and looking in the windows of the shops. Now and then he heard Arabic spoken by those on the streets. He especially enjoyed observing the Western women, who had no interest in wearing head scarves and who carried themselves with casual confidence. They seemed so different from the women of the Middle East, who were mostly covered, demurring, almost cowed. He admired the women's long hair and, too, the lovely necks. The merchandise in the display windows all seemed of excellent quality although extremely expensive.

At the upper end of the Champs he had a good view of the Arc de Triomphe, one of the most famous sights in the city. Noticing people moving back and forth at the top of the structure, he thought the view from up there would be worth the climb. Mounting the stairs was a more arduous task than he had anticipated. By the time he reached the top, his legs were burning. Once at the summit, he moved to several spots to survey the city. So beautiful!

Descending the stairwell, he saw two young men below him who were coming up the stairs. When they drew near, he heard them speaking Arabic. He thought he might enjoy a chat with someone from the Middle East. A pause would also give him a chance to rest his legs. He commented in Arabic, "It's more of a climb than you might think."

Smiling, the two men stopped to engage him. "You are from the Middle East?" one asked.

He said, "Yes, and you?"

"We are both French. Neither of us has ever been out of the country. Our parents were Algerian, so they were free to come here."

"You like living in France?"

"Yes, we are Frenchmen. Where would we go?"

"What country are you from?"

"I'm from Iraq."

"Do you enjoy life in Iraq?"

Jabir reflected on their strange question. He never thought about enjoying life. Survival had always been his sole aim. Jabir didn't answer the two young men as he continued down the stairs. Over his shoulder he said, "You will like the view from the top."

One of the young men looked at his companion and shrugged his shoulders before the pair continued their climb.

When Jabir returned to the apartment, he noticed the blinking light on the answering machine. The caller said that the following day Jabir was to go to the Charles de Gaulle airport, where a flight reservation had been made in his name. The ticket will be at the Emirates Airline check-in desk. He was to fly to Kuwait City, where a reservation had also been made for him at the al Jahra Hotel. The message reported that Jabir's "American friend" was on a ship in the Arabian Sea with the anticipated shipment of arms. They believed the ship might land at an Iraqi or Kuwaiti port. The Port of Umm Qasr was said to be the more likely landing spot. In Kuwait, the messenger said, Jabir would be well positioned to travel to any of the likely ports on short notice. He would be given additional instructions following his arrival.

Jabir had a light snack in his apartment, and when his legs felt rested he considered another walk. The sight of the feminine necks and the long hair stirred the testosterone in his blood. Before he departed Paris, he wanted something to remember Paris by. He checked his finances and took a Metro to Place Pigalle. On the first side street he passed several of the ladies of a more haggard appearance. Most of them had positioned themselves up against building, waiting for approaches. He was hoping for a more youthful *fille de joie*. In the second block he sighted one who caught his eye. However, the price she quoted was beyond his budget. He returned to the first block where he had started and began negotiations with one of the more experienced ladies. She said her name was Michelle. Actually, Jabir didn't care what her name might be. She said she wanted full payment in advance. Jabir said he would pay half in advance and the rest afterward. Reluctantly, she agreed, saying she had been cheated on occasion. Jabir cheated her again when he realized she was a freelancer and had no pimp to enforce the terms of an agreement.

As directed, Jabir packed his few belongings and the following day took a bus to the airport north of Paris. In Kuwait he checked in at the designated hotel and waited again for further instructions. The days went by without any messages. In a way, he didn't mind the wait. He was enjoying the fancy meals and the fine accommodations, all of which were charged to an anonymous account. In time, though, he started to believe that his handler had forgotten him. Or, perhaps his services were no longer required for this special assignment. Possibly another assassin had been chosen.

The call came when Jabir had only recently returned to his room from the hotel's restaurant where he had downed a seven-course meal. The caller said that the American, together with the arms shipment, were to arrive in two days at the Port of Khor al-Zubair. A driver would be sent the following day to the hotel where Jabir was staying. He and the driver were to go to Khor al-Zubair and shadow the shipment to its destination.

Because of some discomfort he had been experiencing, Jabir went to the lobby and asked the concierge if he knew of a pharmacy in the neighborhood. He said he had a sore throat. Actually, he needed something to kill the small crabs that had infested his crotch. He truly had a memento of his visit to Paris and Place Pigalli.

25

Trucking to Erbil

THE sound of seagulls cackling awakened Sean. The rising sun to the east was casting a faint light over the ocean, and he realized the port would soon be coming to life. He sat up and stretched. In time the hum of ship's motors confirmed the port was starting its daily activity. A ship moved toward land to dock where the smaller *Sidra* had been tied up the previous day.

As Sean watched the ship approach the dock, he heard vehicles approaching. Standing, he looked over the pile of crates to see what was happening. A line of army trucks stopped on the access road, where a port attendant walked over to speak with the driver of the first truck. The two men spoke briefly before the attendant opened the gate to allow the convoy to enter the dock area. As they entered and moved toward the cargo, Sean counted ten trucks. The trucks stopped beside the stacks of wooden boxes. An officer exited the first truck and shouted commands in the direction of the trucks. Instantly, over a hundred soldiers descended from the trucks and assembled in formation on the wharf. A lone sergeant stood in front of the men. They all stood rigidly at attention. A small group carried rifles at port arms while the larger group had no rifles. Sean didn't know what to make of it. Were these people friends or otherwise? The officer disappeared behind the third truck. When he reappeared, Rojen Ghazi, wearing an army uniform and the insignia of colonel, walked at the officer's right side.

The officer held back as Rojen came over to Sean. The two shook hands.

"Good to see you again."

"I'm delighted to see you too."

"I am sorry to learn of your difficulties at sea."

"All part of the job! We should be satisfied with the outcome. It could have been otherwise."

"Yes, indeed. With your approval we will start loading the trucks so we may be on our way."

"Sure, go ahead."

Rojen gave the officer a hand signal, and the man responded with a short command to the sergeant standing in front of the assembled soldiers. The sergeant saluted, turned to the men, and shouted several orders. The soldiers who were holding rifles ran to perimeter positions while the unarmed men started toting crates to the trucks. Once the boxes were loaded, the soldiers boarded the trucks while the officer stood near the first truck waiting for further instructions.

"Mr. McDougal, I suggest you ride with me in the third truck," Rojen said. "The officer in command of the men will be in the second truck. The first truck is almost always the first that suffers a road bomb or snipers' bullets, so the third truck is a little safer. We continually have the trucks change positions so as to alternate risk to the first truck."

"Whatever you suggest. Perhaps you and I should stay together."

Rojen signaled the officer before he and Sean climbed into the bed of the third truck, joining the eight soldiers already seated on the benches in the truck's cargo area. Four soldiers sat on one side, across from another four on the opposite side. Two large crates had been positioned between them on the bed of the truck. Sean noticed the Kurds had installed steel plates behind the benches. One of the soldiers, a corporal, nodded to Sean as he and Rojen took their seats. The greeting was intended as an acknowledgement on behalf of all the men in the truck. The convoy slowly moved away from the dock.

"We will be going to our post in Erbil, where we shall unload the arms," Rojen said. "I expect we shall arrive at our garrison in the early morning hours. In case you are hungry, I will tell you that we are all hungry. None of us have eaten since lunch yesterday.

We prefer to be in the open desert before we stop to eat. We'll stop in an hour or two."

Sean did not wish to appear as approving or disapproving of any of Rojen's plans. Despite the emptiness in his stomach, he responded, "No problem. I'm not that hungry."

Outside the gate to the port, two men in an Iraqi army vehicle awaited the return of the Kurdish trucks. Their vehicle sported an Iraqi flag and an antennae that extended high in the air. When the trucks had passed through the gate, the Kurdish officer walked from the second truck to the waiting Iraqis and spoke with them briefly. The Iraqi vehicle pulled away and entered the main road. The ten Kurdish trucks followed, one behind the other, and the convoy headed north to its destination.

As the trucks rolled along the road out of Salalah, Rojen asked Sean, "Have you been to Kurdistan before?"

"I've only seen parts of southern Iraq."

"We are proud of our homeland. You will see Kurdistan is unlike these lower and desolate regions of Iraq. We have trees and green hillsides, farms. I believe Kurdistan is a beautiful part of the world."

Sean nodded, "I'm looking forward to seeing it."

Traveling along the roads from Khor al-Zubair the trucks stayed in a tight formation. The purpose of the tight grouping was to minimize the chances of a truck making a wrong turn and becoming separated from the assembly. With each truck close behind the truck in front of it, the trucks' wheels kicked up billowing clouds of desert dust. The grit entered the men's nostrils, ears, and eyes.

The Kurds didn't hesitate to put their shemagh scarfs to use, covering their mouths and noses. Sean searched his duffel bag for a garment he could use to filter the sand. The most suitable cloth he could find was a T-shirt, which he tied behind his head. It covered his nose and mouth, providing some relief. Two soldiers in the truck exchanged glances that acknowledged the newcomer's susceptibility to a common element of life in the Middle East.

Several miles away from the port and its surrounding villages, the trucks spread out to allow several hundred yards between the vehicles. While the tactic was intended to minimize damage from a broadside attack, it also reduced the nuisance from the dust. Both the soldiers and Sean removed their makeshift face masks. As the trucks lumbered along, the wooden benches and the trucks' stiff springs amplified the irregularities in the road. Sean considered siting on his duffel bag so as to soften the shocks. Reconsidering, he decided the move might make him appear soft in the eyes of the soldiers, who were being stoic about the torturous ride.

Due to the rough ride and the high temperatures, most of the soldiers dozed off. Some leaned sideways on a comrade's shoulder. Others slept with their heads tilted forward. Sean had had next to no sleep the previous night, so the ride through the desert likewise cast its spell on him. He was sleeping when he sensed the trucks slowing. He immediately snapped awake, wondered if a truck had stopped for a mechanical problem or for a more serious reason. The trucks all drew close to one another again, and gradually they pulled to the side of the road. When the convoy came to a halt, the soldiers exited the trucks and clustered in a group near the center of the convoy. A mullah came to the front of the gathering and started reading aloud passages from the Koran. In unison, the men answered. The prayers continued for twenty minutes before the men returned to their trucks. The drivers started their engines and returned the trucks to the road.

The convoy stopped again later in the morning for an early lunch. The drivers pulled to the side of the road at a stretch of the desert that had no hills or obstructions nearby that might hide a waiting enemy. Cooks carried several stoves from the last truck to a spot off the road and began to prepare meals for the men. At the mess sergeant's announcement, the men lined up for slices of mutton, lentils, rice, and bottled water. The soldiers displayed a relaxed and seemingly carefree disposition, much as they might at a friendly soccer game. Rojen, the officer in command of the operation, and Sean were the last in line for eats. The cooks served themselves, and took five minutes to eat before hauling the stoves back to the last truck. Resuming the trip north, the drivers again allowed a separation of several hundred yards between vehicles.

Toward dusk, the convoy pulled off a side road so the cooks could prepare supper. Guards were sent to the perimeter, prayers were said and the evening meal was served. While Sean was eating, his phone rang.

"Sean, this is Matthew," said the caller. "Just wanted to let you know there's been an automobile trailing your convoy. We've been keeping an eye on it. They keep back a distance, so that might explains why your people might not have noticed them."

"Thanks for the intel. Ill mention it to Rojen although I don't think we can't do anything about it"

When he signed of, Sean told Rojen, "We have a tail."

Rojen responded, "The car might be Iraqi police. Regardless, we Kurds have no jurisdiction or right to stop a vehicle on the roads of Iraq. As long as they cause us no harm, we must leave them alone–whoever it might be."

26

A Brief Firefight

THE convoy continued northward along dusty, rutted roads. They were making steady progress toward their destination when, near the town of Al Hadithah, a thunderous explosion rattled Sean's truck and raised the front of the first truck into the air. The explosive device instantly killed the driver and the man beside him. Whoever detonated the roadside bomb had allowed the Iraqi vehicle to pass. At the sound of the explosion, the Iraqi vehicle raced ahead and disappeared down the road. Bullets began striking the sides of the trucks, although with little effect. The steel plates the Kurds had inserted performed as intended. It seemed those who launched the attack underestimated the Kurdish resolve. The soldiers in the trucks didn't risk exposing themselves by returning fire from the trucks. They had other plans.

The response of the Kurds suggested to Sean that they had expected an attack and they were well prepared for it. As soon as the driver of the second truck saw the explosion beneath the truck in front of him, he sped past the wreckage. The third and fourth trucks followed, and the three trucks rushed down the road in what appeared to be their efforts to escape the ambush. The fifth truck pulled up next to the damaged first truck so that the men aboard could check on their comrades. When they realized the men in the cab were dead they allowed the bodies to remain in-place for the time being.

The men in the cargo area of the first truck were shaken by the explosion although no one was badly injured. With some help, the men changed to the truck that had stopped next to their vehicle. When all the men had transferred, that truck also sped down the road and away from the attackers' bullets. The remainder of the trucks turned and went back the way they had come. If the ISIS attackers thought the Kurds were fleeing the scene, they would have been mistaken. Sean recognized the maneuver. The Kurds were not fleeing. They were going to pursue their attackers with a pincer movement.

The four trucks that had advanced forward on the road stopped a short distance from the spot where the attack had occurred. Some forty men jumped from the trucks and assembled beside the road. Sean did likewise and stood beside the road, uncertain of what to do next. He noticed Rojen remained in the truck. He seemed shell-shocked, silent, dazed. On the other hand, the commanding officer seemed in his element as he calmly issued orders and organized the men into squads. Except for the officer, every man had a rifle slung over his shoulder. They appeared anxious to take the initiative.

Looking back toward the trucks, Sean saw Rojen had stretched out flat on the bed of a truck. Perhaps he thought he would be better protected there from rifle fire. Sean immediately recognized that Rojen had no combat experience, and in fact he might have had a lingering fear of combat. Sean guessed that Rojen probably was awarded the rank of colonel because of family influence and political connections. Such practices were common in the Middle East. As the groups were about to move out, Sean had an idea. He wanted to assist.

Although Sean preferred to avoid interrupting the officer who was busy addressing the soldiers, he realized he must. His message was too important. When Sean approached, the officer turned to meet him. Sean said, "I see your men have only rifles. Do you intend to use mortars? I believe mortars would be very helpful in the current situation."

"Sir, I wish we had mortars, however, I am sorry to say we have none. If our enemy has positioned themselves behind obstructions, we shall have a real problem. We will soon find out."

"I know some of the boxes in the trucks hold mortars," Sean said. "If you will allow me, I would need two men to help me. We will unpack one of the boxes and put one of the mortars to good use."

The officer shook his head. "None of our men are familiar with mortars. We would not know how to use them."

Sean said, "I know how to use a mortar, and I will come with you."

The officer said, "Certainly we could use your assistance." He selected three men from the third squad and instructed them to go with Sean to retrieve a mortar from one of the trucks. He ordered two of his sergeants to take the first two squads and advance toward the enemy. He told them their immediate objective was to prevent the enemy from escaping. He said to delay attacking until he issues orders to do so. The third squad would wait for the mortar and then follow the first two squads. A fourth squad would stay to protect the trucks and their cargo.

Upon checking his list, Sean noted one of the boxes contained 60 mm mortars. Two other boxes had the mortar rounds. However, he didn't know which truck held those boxes. He indicated the three Kurds should follow him to the trucks. He searched the first two trucks without finding the box with the mortars. He hoped the mortars were not with the four trucks that had turned southward. His last hope was in the third truck, where he luckily located a crate with mortars. The men helped him tear the heavy boards away from the box. Inside were three sets of mortars. He retrieved one mortar tube, a bipod, and a base plate. In another box he found the mortar rounds.

With hand signals, Sean indicated two of the men should carry the ammunition for the mortar. Between them, they could carry forty rounds. The third man was to carry the heavy base for the weapon, and Sean would carry the tube and a bipod. Together with his three assistants, Sean hurried to join the third squad. The sergeant in charge of the squad led them toward the area where the fight was about to commence. The officer remained with the squad defending the trucks in order to coordinate operations.

The first report from the Kurds positioned to the south of the enemy was disappointing. The sergeant in charge said the enemy had positioned their men behind mounds that they obviously had built up. He reported that attacking the enemy's position would result in too many casualties. The area surrounding the enemy position was largely open terrain that offered little protection. He said the enemy had selected their position with care. The officer told him to stay put for the time being while other plans were being developed.

The squads to the north of the enemy's position reported the same problem as the southern group. The enemy had positioned themselves behind earthen mounds they had constructed at the site. The surrounding landscape was mostly flat and offered few hills or obstructions that would allow the Kurds to approach without being exposed to murderous rifle fire. A sergeant suggested to the commanding officer that the Kurds retreat because they were up against am unfavorable situation.

Seeing the Kurds halt their advance, Sean immediately realized the problem. He borrowed a radio from the sergeant of the third squad and spoke with the officer. He said the enemy had not anticipated the Kurds would have mortars in the trucks. He said he would begin launching mortars with the officer's permission. He said the mortar rounds might roust the enemy from behind their earthen mounds. The officer told Sean to proceed.

At a distance of five-hundred yards from the entrenched enemy, Sean set up shop. With hand signs he explained to his three assistants what their respective roles would be. He would aim the mortar tube, and one of his assistants would drop the rounds into the tube at Sean's signal. The ammo bearers would hand rounds to the man who was to drop the rounds into the mortar tube.

Sean's first round fell well beyond the enemy's stronghold. He adjusted the elevation and alignment of the tube, signaled for another round to be fired, and sat back. The second round fell just outside the small circle of mounds. The third mortar fell amidst the troops within the circle of mounds. Immediately men near the burst of the mortar shell were shouting to one another. Sean had the range. The fourth round resulted in screams and more shouts, yet nobody within the mounds came out. Sean knew that soon his targets would realize they were on the wrong side of the mounds. The next round fell again within the mounds, and immediately some thirty ISIS men rushed from within the circle of the mounds to lay on the sand outside the mounds. Seeing their opportunity, the Kurds advanced from both the north and the south. They had the enemy exposed and in a cross-fire.

To keep the enemy off guard and frightened, Sean changed the target area every few rounds. Soon the enemy became disorganized. Randomly falling mortars will induce fear in the bravest of men. Individual soldiers began running from their entrenchment. The Kurdish snipers started picking off targets, one at a time. Sean had just dropped a round inside the circle of mounds when a bullet whizzed past his head. One of the enemy riflemen had seen Sean firing the mortar and was intent on taking him out. Looking into the distance, he saw no one. The sniper, wherever he was positioned, was well concealed. If Sean were to remain in the same position, he certainly would take a bullet. Whoever was shooting at him would continue until he succeeded.

Sean grabbed the mortar tube and indicated the men with him should follow. He found a gully to his right and set up shop at the bottom of the gully. There, he and his men would be safe from enemy bullets. He stationed one of his men nearby and indicated the man should let him know where the mortar rounds were falling. He resumed firing mortar rounds in and near the mounds. In time the enemy stopped responding to the Kurds' rifle fire. The men who had been there were either dead or they had run off into the desert. The ISIS fighters had expected their initial attack to decimate the Kurds as they sat in their trucks. In case the attack didn't go as expected, they had an alternate plan in the form of a well constructed defensive position. Nevertheless, the Kurds were well prepared for the event and in the end had out-smarted and out-gunned their attackers.

When the Kurds returned to the trucks they brought with them a number of rifles they had taken from the grasps of their dead enemies. Two Kurdish soldiers were carrying a comrade who had a leg wound. A medic tended the wounded man, gave him antibiotics, pain pills, and helped him to a bed of blankets in back of one of the trucks. The commanding officer dispatched one group of men to go with a truck to retrieve the bodies of the two men killed by the roadside bomb. He sent another truck to salvage the boxes of arms from the demolished truck. They abandoned the truck that had been demolished by the road bomb.

The bodies of the men killed by the road bomb were wrapped in white sheets and brought to the area where the men and the officer waited to the north of the encounter. All the men gathered around while the group's mullah read prayers. An assembly of men carried the bodies to one of the trucks for transport back to Erbil and burial amongst the remains of relatives. The five trucks that had sped south before the firefight rejoined the northern group. When they regrouped, the trucks continued their trip to Erbil. Sean's phone rang.

"This is Matthew again. We've been watching you by satellite, and we saw your contingent was ambushed. Are you all right?"

"Okay here."

"I should perhaps tell you we also watched the pirate episode. You might like to know we had dispatched a Navy destroyer as a precaution. Under no circumstance were we going to allow those arms to fall into the wrong hands. The destroyer was on a course that would have brought it to an interception with the pirates. Before they arrived, we saw you took control of the situation. Congratulations for a job well done!"

"Will make a note. Over and out."

As the convoy moved north toward Kurdistan, Sean noticed that, exactly as Rojen had promised, the countryside improved. The stretches of flat, barren sand and rocks of southern Iraq changed to rolling hills covered with greenery, more similar to the environs he knew in Pennsylvania.. Farms and orchards occupied the valleys. Rojen sat silently on the bench in the cargo area of the truck, peering at the floor near his feet. He hadn't said a word since the explosion that upended the lead truck.

27

Hacking for Fun and Money

WALLY rode his bicycle in the rain to the gun shop and secured it with a chain and padlock to a tree behind the building. He had arrived forty minutes later than the shop's advertised opening time. Entering through the back door, he hung his wet rain jacket in the small corner office and proceeded to a position behind the counter. He plugged his laptop into an outlet and prepared for an afternoon of fun and relaxation. If someone showed up shopping for a gun, of course he would do his best to accommodate that person too.

Naturally reticent and distant by nature, Wally realized he was not nearly a salesman of Sean's caliber. He did not exude warmth and friendliness. Nevertheless, he tried his best because he wanted to sell guns while Sean was gone. He tried to be congenial and polite to all prospective customers entering the store. It occurred to him that he should smile more. Most salesmen, he realized, smile a lot. Some days, when he first came to the shop, he would go to the small washroom in the back and practice smiling. He figured that exercising his smile muscles might assist him in showing a more natural, friendly face. Once he tried the wide, show-the-teeth smile. He quickly gave up on that since the curl of his upper lip gave his smile the appearance of a sneer. Eventually he settled on a gentle smile that more resembled a grin.

Despite Wally's resolve to accommodate customers, some people tried the limits of his patience. Just the day before, a man came to the shop and insisted on buying a handgun on the spot. Wally told him that he would be delighted to sell him a handgun. First, though, he had to complete some forms, and then there was the mandatory waiting period. The man had asked Wally to fudge the papers, forget the state regulation and let him take a six-shooter home that day. The man told Wally he was willing to pay a little extra to make it happen. He wanted a handgun, and he wanted it that day. Wally responded that he couldn't do that. The state prohibited instant handgun sales and doing what the man requested could get the shop in all kinds of trouble. The state might pull the shop's license. The man became belligerent and insisted that where there a will there's a way. He said he would be back again with cash, and that Wally should do the paperwork in the meantime. To avoid the man, Wally had closed the shop early the previous day and went home.

While standing behind the counter and tinkering with his laptop, Wally heard a car pull into the parking lot. When he looked up he recognized the car. It belonged to the man from the previous day who had been in a big hurry to acquire a handgun. Wally resolved he was not going to deal with the gruff character. He scurried to the front door, where he turned the "Open" sign to "Closed." He locked the door, turned the lights off, and stood with his back against the front wall where the man would not be able to see him if he peered in the front window. Waiting in the darkened showroom, Wally heard the man try the door. Next the man started swearing and kicking the door.

With the sound of squealing tires and flying gravel, the car tore out of the parking lot and sped down the road toward the town of Barlow. Wally put the cash in the safe, slid his laptop into his backpack and went out the rear door. If somebody wanted to shop for a gun, he or she could return another day. Besides, he reasoned, few people would be shopping for a gun on a rainy day. He unlocked his bicycle and headed for the cabin in the woods. *To hell with selling guns to crazy people.* He wanted to continue working on Sean's recent request from Iraq. Plus, he would find time for a little relaxation, enjoyment, and what to Wally's way of thinking was harmless mischief.

The cabin that Wally used had probably been built by deer hunters many years in the past, when the region had more woods and fewer farms, and the prospect of sixty pounds of venison for the cost of a rifle bullet was an attraction to many men who lived in the region. The cabin stood in the midst of a patch of woods not far from the east road out of Barlow. Despite its age, the building remained in relatively good condition. The siding was weather beaten and aged although it continued to repel rain. The single room inside held a tier of bunks against one wall. A pot-bellied stove stood a few feet from the back wall. Over the years various people had found use for the cabin. Some used it as a love nest. Wally had put a new roof on it once. He also had the cable company extend a line to the cabin.

At the only door to the cabin, Wally punched in the code to the digital padlock and entered. He preferred a digital padlock to a key-operated padlock. If caught, he could say he didn't buy and install the lock. No, he did not have a key on his person for the padlock. He could say that by trial and error he figured out the code. Entering, he heard the usual mice running above the ceiling. They liked the dry area beneath the roof because their numerous predators couldn't get to them up there. Wally and the mice shared the same philosophy: Don't bother me and I won't bother you.

Once he'd connected his laptop to the cable, Wally resumed his attempts to hack into the Royal National Bank of the Bahamas. On previous days he had spent hour after hour attempting to breach the bank's firewall. He knew from past experience these projects took time, patience, and his type of skill. However, he couldn't get past the firewall that day so he gave up for the time being. Hacking into banks was too much like work. He needed some fun to counteract his unpleasant experience at McDougal's Firearms earlier in the day. He decided against giving PETA trouble. He knew of similar, equally deserving organizations.

For his afternoon entertainment, Wally selected the website of Hunt Saboteurs Association, a group that advocated the mischievous interference with hunters in their legitimate pursuit of foxes. Wally had become sympathetic to fox hunters because it was the only sport his uncle enjoyed, and the uncle had been generous to Wally. His uncle explained that when the animals were too numerous they became a rabies threat to humans. They also developed mange that caused the poor animals to lose their hair and slowly freeze to death over the winter. So, thinning the wild population was the right and humane action.

To Wally's way of thinking, people who enjoyed giving mischief in turn deserved mischief done to them. Hacking into the Hunt Saboteurs website was easy. Once beyond the firewall, Wally posted a story of a local twelve-year-old girl who had been bitten by a rabid fox along with the statement in bold letters that declared, *She was saved from death only by a series of very painful inoculations.* Beside the story he added the words, in red letters: *More fox hunting might have prevented the infection to this poor, unfortunate little girl who came close to losing her life in a painful and horrible way.*

Having completed his share of mischief for the day, Wally returned to the challenge at the Royal National Bank of the Bahamas. If he could, he wanted to help Sean with his finances. While tinkering he suddenly remembered a similar challenge from his earlier days as a paid hacker with a government bureau. To breach the firewall: invade the BIOS of the bank's server, modify the register in the CPU, enter with a Trojan download patch. Why hadn't he thought of it earlier?

He had often given thought to the possibility of lawmen inquiring into his hacking. Wally maintained the opinion that he was not seriously harming anyone although he understood that some persons might disagree with him. For that reason, he had prepared defense strategies. Near the stove he had modified a floorboard that could be removed in seconds. Beneath, he had installed a shelf where he could hide the laptop if the need should arise.

Wally had just completed the small project for Sean when he heard knocks on the door. He quickly disconnected the laptop and delivered it to the shelf under the floor. With paperback in hand, he opened the door. Two burly men wearing dour expressions and blue uniforms stood outside. Mustering a friendly voice, Wally asked, "May I help you gentlemen?"

The older of the two, standing forward of the second deputy, spoke for the pair.

"We are sheriff's deputies and we have a warrant to enter this building and conduct a search. What is your name?"

"My name is Wally Woodrow."

"Do you live here?"

"Nobody lives here."

"Then what are you doing here?"

"I come here to escape the drudgery of everyday life, people with silly ideas, and the world's ugly people. I find this to be a quiet and wonderful place to think, read, or meditate. A kind of retreat if you will. I don't know who else visits the place. I saw a man here months ago. He didn't give me his name. In fact he didn't say anything. From his attitude, I would say he didn't like me showing up here. When I arrived the gentleman packed his things and left without saying a word to me. You could say he was not the friendly type. I think that would be a fair statement. To answer your specific question, I was reading a paperback book. This one."

Wally held the book up for the men to see.

"What you had to say, Mister Woodrow, is interesting. Anyway, we'll have a look around."

"Do you mind my asking what it is you are looking around for?"

"No, I don't mind. It seems some individuals are upset with hacking that has been traced to this building and the cable service. I trust you are familiar with the laws against cyber stealing and the willful destruction of other people's websites."

"I understand. Yes, I can believe hacking could aggravate a person. If I had a website, I certainly would not appreciate someone hacking into it and doing destructive things to it. I hope you find the rascal. Come in and have your look around. I'm going to leave. I won't be able to read with you guys nosing around. You might want to lock the door when you leave."

"Before you leave, sir, I would like to see your driver's license? I need to confirm your name and address."

"I don't have a driver's license."

"Why don't you have a driver's license? Was it taken away because of a DUI?"

"I don't have a driver's license because I don't need to drive. I don't have a car." Wally gestured to his bicycle.

"Whatever. If we drive you to your home will someone there be able to confirm that you are who you say you are?

"I prefer that you wouldn't do that. I live with my aunt and uncle. If they see me with a policeman they will automatically come to the conclusion I did something illegal. They may kick me out of my apartment because they don't like law breakers. That would be unfair to me, don't you think? I didn't commit any crime and I don't deserve a bad reputation."

"I don't have any other choice."

"What if we go to Boyer's Grocery Store in town? I regularly buy my groceries there. They know me and can confirm my name and address."

"Okay, we can do that. We'll finish our job here and later take you to Boyer's. You can wait outside if you like."

Wally sat on a tree stump while he pretended to read his paperback. Eventually the deputies completed their search, and joined Wally outside the cabin. The younger man, who had climbed to the space above the ceiling, had cobwebs on his shirt and thick, brown mouse dirt smeared on his trousers. The senior deputy drove the three to Boyer's Grocery Store, where Mr. Boyer confirmed Wally's name and address. Afterward, the deputies drove Wally back to a point on the road near the shack.

The sheriff slowed the car to a stop near the cabin, and Wally tried to open the car door. He wanted to get away from these two men ASAP, but the door was locked from within. Slowly the policeman turned to Wally.

"Mr. Woodrow, a word to the wise. The next time we come here we might catch you at your hacking game. You should understand that if we do, you might be obligated to spend time in the pokey. If I were you, I wouldn't be using this place to do your mischief. I hope you appreciate the good advice I'm giving you?"

"Sure, Deputy, I certainly appreciate your invaluable and well-intended advice."

The deputy pushed a button on his door that unlocked the passenger's door. Wally stepped out. Before he closed the door, the deputy said, "Goodbye, Wally. Don't take it personal if I tell you I hope I don't ever see you again."

"The feeling is mutual, Captain."

Wally climbed through the woods to the cabin, unlocked his bicycle, and steered for home. The laptop, safe below a floorboard, would remain there until his next visit.

28

Arriving in Erbil

HAVING regrouped after the ambush near Al Hadithah, the Kurds' convoy continued their travel toward Erbil. The Iraqi vehicle that had raced away from the scene of the attack on the convoy resumed its position at the head of the group. The assembly stopped only for a change of drivers and prayers.

When Sean again mentioned the automobile that was shadowing the convoy, Rojen seemed unconcerned. He reminded Sean that the Kurdish militia operating the convoy had nothing to do with the Iraqi Army. His soldiers were all Kurdish volunteers. While the Iraqi Army included numerous Kurds, that was a different situation. The Kurdish convoy was traveling through the Arabian section of Iraq with the approval of the Iraqi Army, and that was the reason for the Iraqi escort. The Iraqi authorities would not view with favor any Kurdish interference with the travel of a vehicle on an Iraqi road. It was agreed that no effort would be taken to halt, let alone attack, the automobile. The occupants would be allowed to continue with whatever travel plans they might have in mind.

The convoy arrived at Erbil in the middle of the night, and the trucks went directly to the army garrison. Once the trucks were parked, the commanding officer called the men to a formation, where he complimented them for their resilience and bravery. He told the men to return for a formation at fourteen hundred hour. In the meantime, he said, they were on their own. An ambulance was called to transport the wounded man to a nearby hospital.

Rojen offered Sean several options in the way of accommodations. He said Sean could stay in the officers' quarters at the garrison or at a hotel. The choice was his. He added that the officers' quarters were safe and adequate although not nearly as posh as a hotel. If Sean were to choose a hotel, he would send two plainclothes guards with him. Rojen would take care of all expenses. He suggested the Altin Hotel was a good possibility and mentioned that the hotel gave him and the military special rates.

Sean asked, "How's the food at the hotel?"

"You will like the food at the hotel, and there are other restaurants in the neighborhood. However, I suggest you minimize travel away from the hotel."

"I'll go with the hotel."

"I'm sure you will like it there. Your guards will stay with you and drive you anywhere you wish. The names of the guards are Osman Anter and Karim Qadir. They are well trained and experienced as body guards."

"Do you think that is necessary?"

"I believe in precautions. Kurdistan has a variety of factions, and everyone living in Kurdistan is not necessarily sympathetic to the Kurdish cause. To be sure, spies are mixed in with the population. In any event, you are free to go anywhere according to your choosing."

Sean said, "I'll try to be careful."

"Please do. About tomorrow–please come over to see me at the garrison when you are rested. I would like to discuss the agenda for the coming weeks."

"How about early afternoon?"

"I'll be here," Rojen said. "When you arrive we can go to the officers' club for tea and tarts."

"Sounds good. I'll save room at lunch."

As Sean began to turn, Rojen added, "By the way, if there is anything you might want while you are here, please do not hesitate to speak up. You are our guest, and we will try to make your visit here as pleasant as possible. If you like, we can arrange companionship for you."

"Thank you for the offer. I live alone back home, so I'm accustomed to rooms without people. See you tomorrow."

***

As the convoy approached the outskirts of Erbil, Jabir told his driver, Salim, to move within sight of the trucks. He needed to ascertain exactly where the arms were being delivered. He didn't care if the soldiers spotted him. To his dismay, he saw the trucks approach the Kurdish garrison, the gates open and the trucks disappear within the safety and protection of the armed compound. A sturdy fence surrounded the installation and armed guards patrolled the perimeter. Jabir saw no means whereby the arms could be salvaged. The ambush had provided no gain. The soldiers lost in the firefight were for naught. He would report the disappointing news to his handler.

Although Jibir could see nothing more to be done about the arms shipment, his mission had not come to an end. He had yet to settle the vexing problem with the American. His people wanted to be sure that the American would not be available to facilitate any future arms shipments to the Kurds. An act of violence to the Americans' representative would send an important message to their enemy.

Salim pulled to the side of the road at a spot where he and Jabir could continue to watch the entrance to the garrison. Jabir told the driver to sleep while he took the watch. They were exhausted from the demands of the trip from Khor al-Zubair and in need of rest time. At the same time, they did not wish to miss an important vehicle entering or exiting the garrison.

Later, when he saw a sedan exit the garrison, Jabir shook Salim's shoulder and told him to follow the vehicle. At the Altin Hotel, Jabir saw three men leave the auto and enter the hotel. In the darkness, he could not distinguish any of the three. Nevertheless, he suspected the group consisted of the American and men who might be bodyguards. He expected the Kurds would treat the American to first-class accommodations.

Once Jabir knew where the American was staying, he decided he could find a hotel for himself and his driver. Salim drove around in search of an inexpensive hotel. Several blocks from the Altin, they found suitable, inexpensive lodgings. The night clerk, reading a paperback behind the check-in counter, looked up when he heard footsteps. Jabir was leading, and Salim followed, carrying two bags. The clerk put the book down and greeted the newcomers, "Good morning, gentlemen. Are you looking for rooms?"

Jabir said, "Yes, we need a single room with two beds."

The clerk immediately pegged the speaker as an Iraqi from Bagdad, and he also thought the man might be a policeman. He carried himself with the air of righteousness and arrogance. The man with him was obviously in some subservient role. He carried the bags and remained quiet while the other man spoke for the two of them.

"Yes, sir we have a room available."

The clerk, a through-and-through Kurd, hated the Arabs from Baghdad. He remembered the day the Iraqi authorities of Bagdad delivered the nerve gas attacks on Kurdish civilians in northern Iraq. The gas caught and killed his parents and one sibling. Every day, he remembered them in his prayers. Every day, his hatred of the Iraqis lingered, unabated. Regardless of his personal feelings, the clerk felt obliged to be cordial to all visitors. He asked Jabir to sign-in and said, "The room is up the stairs, third door on the right."

Jabir said, "I'll take it. By the way, do you have room service? My friend and I are hungry."

The clerk handed Jabir keys to the room and told him, "Sir, the kitchen is currently closed."

Jabir appeared disappointed as he turned away, thinking.

The clerk added, "The cook will be in shortly. If you like, I could have him send a breakfast to your room once he has opened the kitchen."

Jabir said, "Make it eggs, potatoes and lamb."

"Yes, sir I will do that."

Jabir and Salim disappeared up the stairs. The clerk waited five minutes before going to his room in the basement of the building. In his medicine cabinet he retrieved six laxative pills of the type he used on occasion. When the cook came to the hotel, the clerk told him about the "devils" from Bagdad. They discussed the visitors' request and jointly agreed that eggs, mutton, and mashed potatoes flavored with ground-up laxatives would be appropriate for the Baghdadi guests. A painful poison would have been preferred. However, a fatality might have brought police, complications, and a loss of paying customers. Both the clerk and the cook had families to consider. A good cleaning-out of their guests' systems would do for the day.

Later in the morning a waiter delivered breakfasts to the recently arrived guests. The two ate with relish. Neither guest was seen that day nor the next. Two days after their arrival in Erbil, the clerk saw the pair walking through the lobby as they exited the hotel. He guessed they had in mind a restaurant other than the one off the lobby at the hotel.

29

Rest Time

SEAN slept until noon. Dressing, he realized how hungry he had become. When he opened the door to the hall, the two guards were standing a few feet away. The more senior of the two, Karim, greeted Sean.

"Good morning, sir. May we assume you will be having breakfast?"

"Yes, indeed. Have you both eaten?"

"No, sir. We were waiting for you."

On the way to the lobby Karim walked beside Sean while Osman walked behind the two. Karim explained that while he spoke English with some proficiency, Osman knew only a few words of the language. One at a time, they entered the hotel's restaurant. According to a prior understanding, they pretended they did not know one another. Each would sit at a different table. Later Osman drove the group to the garrison. While Sean went into the building to find Rojen, Osman and Karim waited near their vehicle.

Sean found Rojen's office, a sparse room similar to the offices of many higher level officers regardless of their country. The colonel's desk appeared to be mahogany with a glossy sheen. Except for a few papers on one corner, the top of the desk was bare. Two flags, one of Kurdistan and one of Iraq, had been posted behind the desk. Rojen rose to greet his visitor. "Good afternoon, Sean. I hope you enjoyed your rest. We were all tired from the trip and the engagement. Thank God we made it to Erbil with the arms. I regret we lost two men in the effort. Later today I must visit their families."

He held up a piece of paper. "We checked the arms inventory, and found it agrees exactly with the delivered goods. The Kurdish people are most appreciative. We intend to put every item in the shipment to a worthwhile cause and soon."

"You are welcome," Sean said. "We wish you success in your struggle, and are pleased to be of assistance in this small way. Again, I ask that you make no public statements acknowledging this gift from America. The arms all are stamped 'Made in USA;' so I suggest we allow people to come to their own conclusion. The official American position is that the Kurds paid for the shipment, and I, as a private arms dealer, took care of the arrangements. The Turks may suspect otherwise. Let them draw their own conclusions. We don't care what the ISIS people think. For obvious reasons we ask that none of the arms be turned against the Turks. The Turks are more or less considered friends of the United States, and we don't want to worsen an already fragile relationship."

"I understand. We intend to abide by your stated conditions."

"I should perhaps add that we expect to make more arms shipments in the near future."

"That is indeed great news. I will pass that information along to the Kurdish authorities. I guarantee they will be delighted. Now, sir, if you don't mind, I would like to talk about your stay with us and the agenda we have in mind."

"Sure. Anything you wish to discuss."

"First, I must tell you that much of the weaponry you delivered is new to us. If you are agreeable, we would like to have you train our junior officers on their use and maintenance. Our fighters are intimately familiar with similar shoulder-fired rifles, so those weapons pose no problem. The large caliber sniper rifles are different because they are new to us. We are most anxious to use them, I might add. We have heard about their lethal results on the battlefield. Our men would like to be trained in their use. We should know more about their capabilities and their limitations. In addition, we would like to hear you talk about the light mortars and the hand grenades. I am sure we will also have additional questions about other items you provided. In short, we would like you stay with us for about four weeks. Do you think you could accommodate us to that extent?"

"Thank you for the invitation, and yes, I will do as you ask. However, I don't believe four weeks would be required. I'm sure I could go over all the material adequately in two weeks' time. I've included training manuals in some of the boxes, and you will find they contain all the answers you might need. If you would still have questions or concerns, contact me and I will get you a resolution. If needed, I can also arrange to send over a weapons specialist to stay with you for an extended time. The arms manufacturers all have personnel available for this kind of service. Generally they charge only a small fee for their time because they hope for repeat orders."

"Two weeks it is then. We will set up a program around a stay of that length. I suggest we start with the sniper rifles. Our men will be occupied three or four days unpacking, cleaning, and storing the arms. Friday is our day of rest. Shall we plan to begin training Monday morning?"

Sean said, "Monday will be fine."

Rojen nodded as an acknowledgement. "Now that we have the training schedule finalized, may I invite you to the officers' club for dessert? We can continue our discussion there."

"That's right. You promised me dessert. Let's see if your cook is as good as you suggest."

The officers' club was empty since lunch had been served earlier and the tables had been cleaned. A waiter hurried over to greet the pair and indicated they may sit anywhere they wished. Rojen told the waiter they were only having dessert, perhaps tarts, and tea. The waiter told them, "I suggest the cherry tart. Cherries are in season and our cook made up a batch this morning."

While they waited for their orders, Rojen mentioned the ambush the convoy had experienced on the road to Erbil. "We anticipated that certain individuals would learn of the arms shipment and those individuals would be sorely tempted to sell that information to the highest bidder. The information alone could command a small fortune. So, we knew there was a good chance our adversaries would try to intercept us as we traveled to Erbil. We had trained for the ambush, which we expected to happen. That is also why we brought along one hundred armed soldiers which were far more than what was needed to load or transport the arms."

"I'm inclined to agree with your analysis," said Sean. "I believe the skipper of the *Sidra* was the informer. He probably sold the information first to the pirates, who then pretended to hijack the *Sidra.* They paid him a pile of money for that episode–or promised to pay. When that charade went sour, he saw an opportunity to sell the information a second time. The second sale would explain the automobile that followed us from Khor al-Zubair. Someone in that vehicle was continually reporting our route and progress."

The waiter brought a tray with tea and two tarts. He poured the tea, and discretely withdrew."

"Before traveling to meet with you in Khor al-Zubair," Rojen said. "We had practiced several maneuvers we thought might be suitable in the event our trucks came under attack. When the attack actually happened, we were well prepared. From the initial volley of rifle fire we estimated the attacking forces to be of a size we could countermand. Had their forces been, say, twice as large, we would have escaped as best we could. We knew from the start we could overcome them. Unfortunately we could do nothing to prevent the damage from the road bomb."

After they had finished their tea, Sean and Rojen returned to Rojen's office where they continued their discussion. When the conversation slowed, Ghazi clearly thought that their meeting was about to come to an end and stood. Suggesting he might wish to discuss another topic, Sean remained seated.

"Colonel, if you have the time, I would like to discuss another subject with you."

As he resettled behind his desk, Rojen said, "Of course."

"As perhaps you know, I was with the American Army during our mission in Iraq. We were up against a variety of factions. Those who were against us were also sometimes fighting one another. Treachery and betrayal were everyday occurrences. One day the squad I was in became a victim of betrayal. We were tricked into approaching a small village by the name of Usit. You've probably never heard of it. It's near Tikrit. We had information that there was a band of Taliban fighters near the town. As we approached our enemy, we were ambushed. Enemy riflemen killed two men in my squad on that excursion. I was wounded and lucky to have survived. Today, I believe there are men in that town who are aligned with ISIS. If you are game, I would like to revisit Usit with some of your men."

Rojen hesitated before speaking. "Let me ask you. Do you still consider the people who attacked you to be a current enemy?"

Sean said, "I didn't come here to find and fight them. Still, they are an enemy of my country. You may call them Taliban, ISIS, Islamicist or whatever. Regardless of the term, they are bent on fighting and killing Americans. Why do you ask?"

"Mr. McDougal, revenge can be a dangerous frame of mind. For the sake of revenge, a person may be inclined to forgo those precautions he might otherwise take. If it's solely revenge you have in mind, and only revenge, I suggest you forget Usit. If revenge is your criteria, you might be inclined to take reckless measures, and you might lose some unfortunate soldiers in the process. If an operation is to be taken, it should be undertaken because there is an expectation of a successful mission and one that will assist us in our eventual goal. It should not be undertaken for the purposes of revenge. That would be unprofessional."

"You are quite right," Sean responded. "While I cannot deny I would like to see some of those from Usit suffer the consequences of an attack, I deny the purpose would be for revenge. No, I see the opportunity for a successful mission, and only for this reasons did I made the suggestion. Of course, I can understand your reluctance. Please do not volunteer men if you have reservations."

"If you feel confident that the proposed mission has a good chance of success with the potential for losses at a minimum, I will support it. I am sure we have men who would be delighted to join you on a skirmish with our enemy. Tell me the details so that we may find the right men for the mission. I know just the officer to lead them. He speaks English and he has a strong hatred for the followers of the Taliban or ISIS. We could go any day you might prefer. How about the day after tomorrow. If you are agreeable, we will meet at six in the morning. Come to my office at that time, and I will introduce you to the lieutenant who will go with you."

"I will be here at six hundred hour the day after tomorrow. I predict you will be pleased with the outcome."

30

A Run in the Park

HIS meeting with the Kurdish colonel concluded, Sean joined guards Karim and Osman near the sedan that had been made available for Sean's use.

On the drive back to the hotel, Sean commented to Karim, "I would not mind going for a run. I've been stuck in cramped quarters in ships and trucks for days. I would like to find a place where I can stretch my legs and breathe in fresh air. Do you or Osman enjoy running?"

"Sorry, sir. Osman and I lift weights and skip rope to stay fit, but neither of us is a runner. If you wish to run along a back road, we could follow you in the sedan."

"Do you think you could find a place where I could run and where there are few people?"

"Certainly, sir. We will find a suitable place for you."

Osman drove back to the hotel, where Sean changed into shorts, a tee shirt, and running shoes. When he rejoined the guards, Karim told Sean he knew of a park on the outskirts of Erbil. The city maintained the park and it was known for its greenery. The trees were mostly conifers and most of the bushes were evergreens so most of the park was green year round.

"Great. Let's give it a try."

Osman drove to the park, which was a few miles from downtown Erbil. In the parking lot, Sean stretched for a few minutes near the automobile where Osman and Karim waited. Before turning to take off down a gravely path, Sean said to the guards, "I'll be about an hour."

Sean started down a path that wound through a thicket of bushes. He found the park a delightful location for a relaxing run. The city had placed picnic tables here and there for its citizens to enjoy time outdoors. The paths had been covered with gravel of a type that was ideal for running or walking. A few fields were interspersed between the trees and bushes. To Sean, the park was a lovely and inviting place.

***

Jabir al-Ateri and his driver, Salim, saw the American and his guards take off in their automobile, and they had followed at a distance. When Osman pulled into the park, Salim continued along the road and pulled to the side out of sight from the parking lot.

Thinking he might finally have an opportunity awaiting him, Jabir cycled a round into the chamber of his 9 mm automatic. He might wish to fire as soon as he withdrew the gun. He walked behind a row of houses that bordered the park and entered the park several blocks from the main road. Nobody was around. He would not need to worry about witnesses.

Jabir thought a runner would prefer to try different courses rather than repeat runs along the same paths. Scouting the area, he found a path that he speculated his target might use on his run. He found a bench beside the path and near a turn in one of the paths. If Sean rounded the bend and saw Jabir, he might be too close to turn and escape the ambush. Jabir took a piece of paper from his pocket and pretended to be reading. When he heard the sound of running feet, his pulse increased. His prospect for success was near.

Running at a brisk pace, Sean rounded the turn in the path and then saw a man sitting on a bench nearby. Jabir moved his right hand into a pocket of his jacket where he had the automatic. Sean noticed the suspicious motion, did a quick turn-about, and retreated back around the bend. Jabir had erred in judging Sean's alertness. He ran to the corner, thinking he may still have a chance for a shot. He was too late as Sean had already traveled a good distance. He raised his pistol and was about to fire when he reconsidered. Because of the distance, he knew his shot might miss.

And, the sound of a pistol shot might attract police, an inquiry, and a search. An investigation by the police could result in a search and jail time. True too: If he missed the shot would alert the American that he was the object of a hunt. When he pulled the trigger, he wanted to be sure of a kill. Jabir cursed his continuing bad luck. Still, he thought perhaps he could intercept Sean before he returned to the safety of the parking lot where the two guards waited.

Jabir realized he had come upon an exceptional opportunity, and he hated to let it slip away. The American was finally away from his guards and unarmed. Jabir may not find such good luck again. If he could beat the American to the parking lot, he might have another chance at him. He could see no path that led directly to the parking lot, so he took off running through the brush. After a few feet, he fell and scratched his face. He continued running, but soon was panting for air. He had to slow his pace. In the meantime Sean had found a path that would take him directly to the sedan and his armed guards.

Nearing the parking lot, Jabir's awkward motion in the brush gave him away. The American noticed the motion. Quickly, Sean dashed off the trail to the right and through the brush in order to arrive at the parking lot along a different route. Not being a runner himself, Jabir knew he would be unable to catch up to his target. He cursed and stamped his foot to the ground.

When Jabir called his handler in the evening, he reported he'd almost had success. "I was right behind the American in the park," he said. "I pulled your gun from my pocket and pulled the trigger. To my great disappointment, the gun didn't fire. I pulled the trigger twice, again nothing happened. For my next assignment, perhaps you will be able to provide me with a handgun that actually shoots. Tomorrow I'll take it to the suburbs and test it. Too bad, I almost had him."

The handler was disappointed with Jabir's report and doubted most of what was reported. He told Jabir that time was running out. Jabir explained that he had a difficult situation due to the two guards who were constantly near the American and protecting him. He added he would continue to be alert for another opportunity. With luck he would soon have good news to report. The handler told Jabir that he must continue his efforts and that he should "try harder." He said the American probably would not remain in Erbil much longer.

***

Disappointed with Jabir's report, his handler called Bashir Masri, a man with whom he had a business association and who in the past had demonstrated a capacity for solving difficult problems. He related the difficulties related by Jabir in his pursuit of the American. The next morning, Bashir again visited Marwazi Alwan, a man within the organization who had both considerable influence as well as access to resources. As was his practice, Marwazi Alwan kept Bashir waiting. He used the imposed delays to demonstrate his right to do so. Bashir sat in the outer room with Alwan's personal guard, Nawaz Hadid. Later, when Marwazi's guard led Bashir into Marwazi's office, the ISIS official was curt with Bashir. He was in a poor mood as the situation in the field had not been going well for their fighters. Bashir briefly explained the problem in Erbil. Marwazi told him to take his personal guard, Nawaz, who he said would certainly solve the problem. The guard, he said, had experience with similar problems in the past. Before Marwazi dismissed his visitor, he said to him, "Bashir, of course we appreciate your support of our common cause. Please understand, however, I am a busy man with significant problems. If you need assistance with a situation that is of great importance, please come to see me. Do not hesitate. I shall do my utmost to be of assistance to you. Otherwise, try to solve your minor problems by whatever means you have at your disposal."

Bashir said nothing in response, bowed, and backed away before exiting the room. Inside he simmered. His problems and best efforts had been classified as being of minor importance. In an outer room, Bashir related to Nawaz what Marwazi had told him. He asked the guard to come to Bashir's house in two days. At that time, he would provide him with an automobile and connect him with their people in Erbil. Without another word, he turned and let himself out of the mansion.

31

Returning to Usit

SEAN came to the garrison early in the day, where he found Rojen waiting for him with an assembly of fourteen soldiers. The Kurds had prepared two vehicles for the mission. To avoid appearing out of place, Sean had dressed in a Kurdish military uniform that Rojen's secretary had given him. The two stripes on his sleeve suggested he was a corporal of the Kurdish forces. In truth he would be guiding the excursion. Rojen introduced Sean to the lieutenant who would be in command of the soldiers. The officer bowed slightly.

"At your command, sir."

Sean said, "Let's do it."

The officer called out a command to the enlisted men, who then climbed aboard the vehicles. We'll ride in the front vehicle," he said to Sean. "The drive to Usit will take about three hours."

On the way to their destination, Sean became pensive. The trip brought back memories from the previous time he had traveled to the village. Then he was wearing an American army uniform with US Army corporal stripes that the company commander had given him only days before. He'd been proud of the distinction, and that along with the promotion to corporal, he was made squad leader of eight men in an infantry company. At the time, the American forces were playing a mortal game of hide-and-seek with the Taliban.

Sean well remembered the day the platoon's officer called him to the headquarters tent to discuss the assignment. He told Sean that MI had referred a paid informer to the company. The man, together with a translator, was in a nearby tent. The lieutenant said Sean was to meet with the informer and evaluate what he had to say. That day the lieutenant would be going on an urgent assignment east of camp with the remainder of the platoon. Based on the discussion with the informer, Sean was to take appropriate action if warranted. The lieutenant left the tent and a short time later returned with the translator and the informer.

The informant, who the translator introduced as Shakir Rahal, was a young man, small in stature and slightly stooped. He seemed nervous as he spoke. Through the translator, he told Sean that he had learned of a Taliban camp about an hour's drive from the American camp. In fact, he said, he had seen the camp from a distance. He said the camp consisted of about twenty Taliban soldiers, mostly recent recruits who were inspired although poorly trained and poorly equipped. Almost in a whisper, he said he hated the Taliban for their atrocities. He would be happy to lead the Americans there if they wished to attack the camp. Convinced of the validity of Rahal's report, Sean gathered his squad in preparation for an assault on the enemy camp. They used three vehicles, and Rahal rode in the first vehicle with Sean.

At Rahal's suggestion, Sean parked the vehicles two miles from the target. With his hands, Rahal indicated to Sean the route to the camp. Rahal and one soldier stayed with the vehicles while Sean and his squad headed for the reported Taliban encampment. Near the village where the enemy was supposedly encamped, bullets and grenades started raining down from the cliffs above. One of Sean's men, his close friend Mason Keller, was killed and a second man wounded. Sean took a piece of shrapnel in his leg. Sean was forced to retreat with the squad in the hope of fighting a better battle another day. When they returned to their vehicles, they found the soldier who had remained with the vehicles dead of a bullet to the head. Shakir Rahal had disappeared. The tragic events of the day were seared into Sean's memory. Likewise the name Shakir Rahal. Every day he thought of his dead comrades, their foibles and idiosyncrasies. He believed his gullibility caused the death of those two men. A thousand times he told himself he should have been more careful and less trusting.

The small village of Usit sat at the end of a ravine approximately a mile off a main road, and it consisted of some twenty houses. Hills bordered the village on two sides. A single-lane dirt road led to the small hamlet. As the two Kurdish vehicles drew close to the dirt road that meandered to Usit, the drivers pulled the vehicles to the side of the road. Sean, the officer, and four men gathered their gear and dismounted. According to the Kurdish practice, the officer carried no weapon. Sean and the four soldiers each carried a rifle.

Sean mounted an American flag on the first vehicle. He went to the front right tire on the first vehicle and allowed a slow stream of air to escape. The drivers then moved the vehicles down the road and parked beside the road so the flat tire and the American flag could be easily seen by anyone traveling along the road to Usit. Together, the flat tire and the American flag comprised the bait.

A sergeant would oversee operations along the road. Sean and the accompanying group walked off into the brush and climbed the hill that ran parallel to the main road. Travelers on the main road would not be able to see their movements due to the thick brush and the occasional tree. The group continued up the hillside until they came across a trail that meandered along the summit. Silently they followed the trail to the south. Sean's map indicated the path would bring them to the overlook above the dirt road to the village. Once at their destination they would be well positioned to shoot down on their adversaries. According to their prior understanding, the two Kurdish groups were to avoid communications until the assault was initiated. Although Sean thought nobody would detect radio transmissions, he didn't want to take the risk.

Halfway to the summit overlook, the group rounded a turn in the trail and came to a section of the path where the trees and brush had been cleared from the west side of the trail. A small meadow lay below the trail and a number of sheep were grazing on the lush grass. From the path the men could see over the meadow to the village of Usit in the distance. The view caught Sean's attention and at first he failed to see a shepherd who was some fifty yards away, watching over the sheep. About the time Sean noticed the young man, the shepherd turned and saw Sean. Immediately the youngster took off running toward the village, his dog following him. The lieutenant, realizing the problem, shouted at one of his men, "Pashew, go catch that youngster."

The soldier, carrying his rifle in one hand, took off chasing the boy. As the soldier was gaining on the young man, the sheep dog took notice of the man chasing his master. Growling, the dog went for the soldier's leg. Although it missed a leg, it had a solid grip on his soldier's trouser. The soldier lost his balance and fell, his rifle butt slamming into a rock. Continuing to growl, the dog held tightly to the mouthful of clothing.

While the dog kept the soldier occupied, the shepherd was making his escape. The soldier tried to shake loose from the dog's grip although without success. Apparently he didn't want to kill the dog. The officer saw the problem and told a second soldier to go after the youngster. The second soldier caught up to the shepherd in the distance and grabbed him by his shirt. The boy knew better than to struggle. With one hand on his captive's collar, the soldier led the young shepherd back to the group. "Bring the youngster along with us," said the lieutenant. "First stuff a rag in his mouth so he won't be able to shout. We will tie him to a tree farther along the trail." He repeated to Sean in English what he had told the soldier. The dog trotted over to be near his master's side, its tail wagging contentedly.

The group proceeded along the trail to the vantage point above the dirt road and waited for the prey to appear. Sean and his group saw no locals until mid-afternoon, when a woman drove down the road from Usit. Perhaps she was going shopping in nearby Takrit. She showed no outward interest in the two vehicles. Later a man in a car drove up the road to Usit. He might have been returning from employment in Takrit. The next car up the road held two men.

Late afternoon, Sean spotted the first signs of the quarry. A group of six men appeared on the dirt road near the houses in Usit. Each was dressed in black and carried a Kalashnikov rifle. The men displayed neither urgency nor anxiety as they moved toward the main road where the two army vehicles were parked. Sean expected the men would proceed along the dirt road to a field near the army vehicles. There, the terrain was elevated slightly above the vehicles, and they would have clear shots at the vehicles. On their way to that location, the Taliban fighters would pass beneath Sean and his group of Kurdish soldiers. The Kurds would have easy targets, much as Sean and his squad of American soldiers had been easy targets for the Taliban five years earlier.

Sean watched the Taliban fighters as they advanced along the dirt road. He thought they were marching directly into his trap. However, when they were well out from the overlook, two men split away from the group. One went right and one went left toward Sean and his men on the hill. Their commander was sending scouts to guard the group's flanks. The four Taliban on the road held back while the scouts climbed to the higher ground. Sean had not anticipated the Taliban would send scouts to their flanks. It occurred to him that these men had at least a modicum of training in battlefield tactics and therefore could present problems. The day's conflict was not going to be the easy turkey shoot he had anticipated.

32

Retribution

As Sean and the Kurdish fighters with him watched the Taliban scout approach, Sean asked the Kurdish officer, "What do you think?"

The officer responded, "I suggest we stay where we are. If we change positions, they might see our movement. We should wait and see what they do. Whatever happens, we have the high ground and the upper hand."

The four enemy fighters were still far away on the road. They were waiting for the scouts to check out the flanks. If the Taliban were truly wary of possible enemies in the hills near the American vehicles, they most certainly would have waited farther back along the road. Their behavior suggested only a modest caution on their part.

As the left scout began to climb toward the crest of the hill where Sean and the Kurdish group were waiting, he had his rifle slung over his shoulder. His behavior suggested he did not actually expect to encounter an enemy on the hill. He was merely following orders. Once at the crest of the ridge, he followed the trail toward the overlook. When he spotted the shepherd tied to a tree, he paused. Strange, he thought. The Kurdish soldier who had been assigned to watch the shepherd, well hidden in the nearby brush, watched the Taliban scout approach the shepherd. His rifle followed the man's movements. The scout walked to the shepherd and removed the rag from his mouth. The shepherd's dog was barking continuously at the recent visitor.

"What is this all about? What happened to you?" asked the Taliban scout.

The shepherd started crying and said to him, "Please remove the rope. I must go home. My father will be worried. He will beat me."

"If you will tell me who did this to you, I will untie you."

"A group of men?"

"What kind of men? How many?"

"Maybe five. They were in uniforms. Soldiers, I guess."

The scout set his rifle against a tree and removed the ropes that bound the shepherd to a tree. As soon as he was free, the youth took off running toward Usit, his dog following. The scout withdrew his cellphone and related the shepherd's information to his comrades on the road below.

Upon receiving the message from the scout atop the adjacent hill, the four men on the road unslung their rifles from their shoulders and cycled rounds into their rifles' chambers. Sean knew these were brave men who were not afraid of engaging enemy forces. In fact, they might welcome a firefight. Their type considered bravery in the face of the enemy a special badge of honor. The group held a brief discussion amongst themselves before they moved toward the hill where they knew the scout was located. They had a mission.

The Kurdish soldier who had been assigned to watch the shepherd was watching the Taliban soldier from behind a clump of brush. Sean, watching from a distance, understood the man's dilemma. If he fired at the scout, the sound of the shot would alert the other Taliban fighters and spoil the trap that had been set for them. Yet he could not allow this enemy to wander over the summit of the hill where Sean and the other Kurds were waiting. Before the man moved to retrieve his rifle the Kurd stepped from behind the concealing brush, and with his rifle pointed at the scout, indicated that the man should raise his hands. The man complied. A Kurd near Sean had seen what happened and he walked over to tie the man's hands. behind his back. He then retrieved the Taliban's cell phone and stomped on it.

As the four Taliban started up the hill toward the point where Sean, the Kurdish officer, and three soldiers were waiting, Sean told the officer, "You go with two men a short distance out the ridge. I will remain here with one man. The four Taliban will stay together as a group. We shall catch them in crossfire from our high positions. Allow them to come close before firing so that we shall have easy targets."

The officer selected two men and together they moved out through the brush, staying at the same elevation. Sean and the soldier with him were well hidden and protected behind the trunk of a fallen tree. They waited quietly and patiently for the enemy to approach. When the four Taliban were halfway to the crest, they tried to call the scout for an update. When the scout failed to answer, they slowed, although continuing to climb cautiously toward the crest. Showing good soldiering, they spread out in a single file with a gap of some twenty-five yards between them.

Sean and the soldier with him watched the approaching enemy from behind their secure position. The Taliban soldiers continued moving cautiously uphill, peering right and left into the brush. When the lead man was near the spot where Sean and the two Kurds were hiding, Sean could not believe his good luck. He could see the nearest man had a beard–a beard the man didn't have the last time Sean had seen him. He still had the same stooped shoulders. It was Shakir Rahal, the man who was the cause of the ambush that had killed two of the men in Sean's squad.

Sean wanted Rahal to see him before he died. He stood and shouted, "Allahu Akbar, Shakir, you son of a bitch." Shocked at the sight of a man suddenly appearing close by and shouting his name, Shakir froze. When he saw Sean lift his rifle to shoot, Shakir fired his Kalashnikov from the hip. The round flew by Sean's ear. Before Shakir could respond with a second round, Sean had his rifle up and fired. Shakir's next shot went up toward the clouds as he fell backward with a bullet through his heart.

From their positions behind the deadfall, Sean and his companion opened fire on the remaining Taliban fighters. The nearest Taliban fell immediately. The other two who were farther down the hill, ran into the brush to the west. To their misfortune, they ran into the Kurdish lieutenant and two of his men. The Kurds hated the Taliban and especially the Iraqi Taliban. The two Kurdish shooters believed the enemy deserved no mercy and they showed none. A volley of shots completed the day's mission.

Sean's group collected the guns, ammunition, and wallets from the dead Taliban fighters. Sean placed small American and Kurdish flags in the pockets of each dead man. Sean remembered the one enemy combatant they didn't get and said to the lieutenant, "We didn't get the second scout. He could possibly open fire on our men at the vehicles. We should warn them and tell them to move up the road to the point where we left the road to climb the hill. Our group will follow the trail we took coming in along the crest of the hill, and meet the vehicles at the road."

The Kurdish lieutenant called the men at the vehicles and advised them of the possibility of a Taliban shooter on the adjacent hillside. He directed them to immediately inflate the flat tire and remove the American flag. He said they should move to the point two miles up the road where they had earlier deposited Sean, the men and him.

The victors moved out along the crest of the hill before descending to the waiting vehicles. The soldier who had stayed with the shepherd brought his captive along. The lieutenant explained to Sean they would keep the captive for a possible trade for a captive Kurdish soldier. Once all were aboard the vehicles, the drivers headed for the garrison at Erbil. On the trip, Sean went through the confiscated wallets. One of the wallets confirmed that Sean had killed Shakir Rahal. Sean spread the cash amongst the Kurds and threw the empty wallets out the window. He believed justice had been served.

33

Training

WHEN Sean was not at the garrison, he stayed mostly within the confines of the Altin Hotel, reading, watching TV or sleeping. Remembering the experience at the park, he believed someone very well might be out to do him harm. Excursions away from the hotel would only be offering more opportunities to his pursuers. The two guards were always lingering nearby, and that was a consolation. On the occasions they visited a restaurant away from the hotel, Sean took care to be especially wary.

In compliance with Rojen's request for training on the recently received American weapons, Sean returned to the Kurdish garrison for the beginning of two weeks of classes. Rojen had designated fifteen of his junior officers to attend the classes. Once those men knew the weapons, they would be able to teach a larger number of soldiers. Since only a few of the men knew English, a translator repeated Sean's words in Kurdish.

On the first day of classes, Sean started with the .50 cal sniper rifle. The Kurdish soldiers had explained that much of the combat with ISIS had been in towns and around buildings of masonry construction. The ISIS fighters would hide in these buildings and periodically peer out to shoot at the Kurdish soldiers. The bullets of the small caliber, shoulder-fired rifles used by the Kurds could not penetrate those walls. Accordingly, the fearsome .50 cal rifles would be a game-changer. The bullets from the new sniper rifles could easily penetrate masonry walls of a substantial thickness and bring death to those hiding behind those walls. The Kurds looked forward to learning the capabilities of the new rifles, the bullets that go with the rifles and, especially, they wanted to put the new armaments into service in the field.

In his classes, Sean emphasized the importance of firearm maintenance. He brought three of the big rifles to the classrooms, and he regularly disassembled and reassembled one of the guns. As part of the instructions, he had each of the men in the class repeat the procedure. Reports of the gun's use in the field stirred the Kurds interest, and they were looking forward to witnessing live demonstrations in the coming days.

On the second day of classes, Sean reviewed American practices as applicable to sniper teams. He explained the reasons for the two-man teams, which typically consisted of a shooter and a spotter. Despite Sean's insistence, the Kurds failed to see the need for a spotter. Sean assured them they would eventually see the merits of the arrangement. The soldiers agreed they would follow the American practice and keep an open mind. Sean also went over the telescopic sight that is affixed to the rifle, the markings in the scope, and how the crosshairs are repositioned to correct the strike of the bullet. For long shots, the spotter would calculate the needed adjustments for drop and wind and advise the shooter how to reposition the crosshairs.

Sean's daily routine started with breakfast at the hotel's restaurant while Karim and Osman, each at separate tables, ate nearby. From the restaurant, they would travel to the garrison, where Sean would continue the training classes. While Sean was busy with classes, Osman and Karim typically went to the barracks to catch up on sleep or relaxation. At midday Sean would have lunch with the soldiers attending his classes. In the evenings he, Karim, and Osman would return to the hotel, and in an hour or so all three would go for supper.

Sean resolved he would not be running anymore while in Kurdistan. He continued to think of the man in the park who had reached into his pocket when Sean came near him. Was the man reaching for a pistol, or was he merely searching for a handkerchief? Although

Sean didn't have a clear view of the man's face, he thought he might have seen him before.

For the program on the third day, Sean scheduled a visit to a rifle and mortar range. He wanted to have live demonstrations with both the .50 cal rifles and mortars. The group included five junior officers, ten noncommissioned officers, a translator and several recent recruits who would be manning the targets. Sean went in the sedan along with the two body guards and one senior officer. The truck with the trainees followed Sean's sedan and was driven by one of the NCO's.

The range was located fifteen miles east of Erbil at a relatively flat section of bare land. Markers indicated the distances to the targets out to five-hundred meters. A mound of earth ten feet in height extended behind the rifle targets to absorb bullets. Five masonry walls of a substantial thickness had been recently constructed at the two-hundred meter distance for use with the large sniper rifles. Upon arrival at the range, Sean directed the soldiers to carry the three sniper rifles to benches at the firing line. One-by-one he had each of the trainees fire a single bullet at a one-hundred meter target. Next, Sean divided the group into teams of twos. The three rifles were moved to the ground along the firing line so that the teams would be firing from the prone positions. Sean began to discuss team operation of the rifles when he noticed in the distance a military vehicle speeding to the range. He told the group to stand-by while he walked over, along with the translator to meet the vehicle. When the vehicle stopped, Rojen stepped out and hurried to Sean. He looked serious.

"This morning we received urgent transmissions from our general in command of operations to the south. The ISIS fighters have concentrated on a section of the battlefield and have succeeded in inflicted severe casualties on our brave fighters. The battle line has been pushed north and east toward Kurdistan. We must quickly form a battlegroup from our garrison and move to aid our men to the south. I am sorry to interrupt your classes, but the new and grave situation deserves our immediate response. You must finish training here immediately so that our cadre can return to the garrison."

Rojen walked over to those gathered around the rifles and spoke to them. When Rojen finished speaking, those present gathered everything they had brought to the range and returned to the truck. Rojen asked Sean and Karim to ride back to the garrison with him. In a matter of minutes, the truck and the two sedans headed for the garrison.

On the way, Rojen told Sean, "I don't know what to tell you. We were hoping you would have time to instruct our cadre personnel on the use of the American weapons. Unfortunately, we now have no time for that. If ISIS continue as they have the last few days, they will have a clear path to Erbil. Then we would have a terrible problem. They would terrorize our populace. Once they enter into the city, it would become twice as difficult to extract them. And the price in blood would be great. At all cost, we must stop them before they advance to our capitol."

Sean remained quiet. He was at a loss for words. Rojen continued.

"Sean, perhaps it would be best if you return to America. You would be safe there and out of harm's way. If all goes well, you could return another day."

Sean said nothing. Rojen, looking dismayed, stared out the window as the vehicle made its way to the garrison. Part way to their destination, Rojen said, "You may have noticed: The soldiers we have at this garrison are mostly recruits, soldiers who only recently joined our ranks. Except for the training cadre, few have any battlefield experience."

Sean looked puzzled. "Do you think it is wise to send your inexperienced soldiers against the battle-hardened ISIS soldiers. As you know, ISIS trains their soldiers well. Their programs are long and tough. Your fresh, inexperienced soldiers will have a hard time of it up against the fanatics. Are there no other Kurdish forces you could send until the soldiers here have more training and practice with the new weapons?"

Rojen had been exceptionally polite and accommodating to Sean, but he started to show exasperation with Sean's council.

"Perhaps you don't fully appreciate our dilemma. If we send our inexperienced men and women into combat against ISIS, the mortality rate will be high. On the other hand, if the ISIS forces make it to Erbil, they might all die anyway."

Sean was at a loss for words as the driver continued toward the garrison. When the gates opened at the garrison to admit the vehicles, Sean said, "Could you get me a Kurdish uniform again? If you will allow, I'll come with your forces to fight ISIS."

Rojen showed surprise at Sean's request.

"You needn't, but you are most welcome to join us. Your battlefield experience would be of great help to us. You could also help us with the American weapons since we have not yet had the full benefit of your training and demonstrations. I'll get you a uniform and insignia that will identify you as an officer in the Kurdish forces. I'll send Sergeant Karim Oadir with you to serve as translator and personal body guard."

34

Call to Arms

THE radio stations throughout Kurdistan announced the disheartening news received from the battlefield. The ISIS forces overran the town of Mosul, the Kurdish line had broken and the enemy was posed to move eastward with Erbil as their objective. The civilian population in Erbil was panic stricken by the news. Everyone in the region knew of ISIS's reputation for brutality, rape and murder. Many of the residents were packing possessions into vehicles and leaving the city. Some were traveling to towns far to the east to stay with relatives.

The military garrison in Erbil became a beehive of activity. Soldiers and military vehicles were in constant movement. It was announced that at fourteen-hundred hour Colonel Rojen would address the soldiers at the parade grounds.

Sean was given a set of combat fatigues and a duffel bag with extra boots, underwear, socks, a blanket, a sleeping mat, soap and shaving gear. As a side arm, he would have one of the Beretta automatics he had brought to the Kurds. Sean met up with Karim and together they went to the mess hall at Company A, where Rojen told him they would be assigned. Rojen said the commanding officer of Company A spoke English and Sean should have no difficulty conversing with him. A lavish meal with ample cuts of lamb had been prepared for the soldiers who would be traveling to the front.

Each of the companies designated for the southern mission marched, one at a time, to the parade grounds. Each unit consisted of approximately one-hundred soldiers. Two of the units were all women. Although most were young and inexperienced soldiers, they all marched smartly. Their steps were in unison and the lines were straight as they moved. They projected a professional image. As each unit entered the parade ground, it first marched to the far side of the field, did two left turns and then moved smartly to a position in front of the speaker's platform. Sean and Karim were in the Company A group. When the last unit was in place, all the soldiers were called to attention and a band beside the platform played what many considered a national anthem. When the music stopped, Colonel Rojen slowly climbed stairs to the platform. Loud speakers to the right and left of the platform amplified his voice. Rojen seemed well prepared as he spoke without notes.

"Soldiers of Kurdistan, I believe you have all heard the sad news from the front. The savage and ruthless ISIS forces have overrun the town if Mosul and are moving toward our sacred homeland. They claim to be doing Allah's will, but they are not. They are a despicable band of uncivilized fanatics who rape, pillage and murder at will. If they make it to Erbil, we all know thc rcsults will be catastrophic to our population, to our loved ones and especially our women.

"Many of you are new to soldiering. Your officers had hoped to train you for a longer period of time in the business of fighting so that you would become truly expert. Unfortunately, the situation to the west has unfolded before we at the Erbil garrison were entirely prepared for it. I know that each of you will willingly go to the front to defend Kurdistan from this plague. I also know that if you had your choice, you would rather die fighting our enemy far from Erbil rather than knelling before an ISIS devil in Kurdistan.

"Thanks to generous friends of the Kurdish people, we now have at our disposal the latest military weapons for use by our light infantry. If your unit has not been issued the recently-received rifles and mortars, you will receive them before we move out today.

"Go with fervor and know that the people of your homeland wish you well. God speed."

Rojen nodded to his right and immediately the band started playing a military march. A major who had been standing between the speaker's stand and the assembled troops, turned to face the assembly and gave a brief command. One after the other, the units marched away from the parade ground. Sean and Karim went with Company A to their barracks. Before they were dismissed outside the barracks, the unit's commander announced the riflemen were to collect their new rifles and be in one of the trucks within an hour. The mortar teams were to likewise pick-up their weapons and ammunition before going to the trucks. Five trucks were parked near the Company A buildings, fueled and ready to transport the warriors to their upcoming conflict. Each truck towed an enclosed trailer that would carry the duffle bags, extra ammunition, canned meals, water, cans of gasoline and first aid kits.

Since Sean was assigned to Company A, he felt he should introduce himself to the company commander. Rojen had been occupied with a thousand considerations and didn't have time to go with Sean to meet the company commander. The Company A headquarters was in a small building next to the barracks. Sean opened the front door and entered. Inside, a clerk sitting behind a desk asked, "Sir, what is your business, please?"

Sean said, "Colonel Ghazi told me that Sergeant Qadir and I are assigned to this company. I thought we should introduce ourselves to the company commanding officer."

The clerk said, "Sir, I will ask Captain Mirzo if he is available."

The clerk opened the door behind his desk and disappeared into the small office. Shortly he reappeared and closed the door to the office. "The captain will see you now. Remove your hat, knock on the door and enter when the captain says to do so. Approach the captain's desk, salute, state your name and the purpose of your visit."

Sean thought *Just like the American army.*

After Sean had knocked, entered and approached the desk where the captain sat, the captain continued writing on a notepad. Sean held his salute and said, "Lieutenant McDougal reporting for duty. Colonel Ghazi sent me to join your unit."

Captain Mirzo wrote a few more lines, set his pen on the desk and saluted. "Colonel Ghazi called to tell me you were coming. I suppose the colonel sent you to my unit because I speak a little English. No matter. I am uncertain as to what, exactly, I am to do with you. I already have three lieutenants in my unit. One for each of the three platoons. You might only get in the way. The colonel said you were in the American army. Is that correct?"

Sean knew he should answer without elaborating. That, no doubt, is what the captain would expect.

"Yes, sir."

"What was your rank in the American army?"

"Corporal, sir."

"From the lower classes, then. I'm surprised the colonel made you a lieutenant. That's not what we normally do in Kurdistan. No matter, though. It's only for a brief period, so no harm done. Anyway, we'll be boarding the trucks shortly so be sure to find a seat on one of them."

Sean thought that in recognition of the free equipment that he had recently delivered to the Kurds, he could expect a somewhat more polite recognition.

Sean answered, "Yes, sir. Sir, may I speak?"

"Yes, what is it?"

"Sergeant Qadir of the Kurdish forces is traveling with me. I thought you should know."

"Very good. I'll introduce you to the other officers along the way. Dismissed."

Sean saluted and march-stepped to the door.

35

Moving to Mosul

SEAN and Kamir went to find a seat in one of the trucks assigned to Company A. The first two they came to were fully packed with soldiers and gear. The third truck was likewise full, but they decided to climb aboard regardless. When they pulled themselves up to the bed of the truck, a lieutenant sitting near the end of one of the benches recognized Sean from the classes he had started. He nodded to Sean as an acknowledgement. The men slid over to make room for the two newcomers. The lieutenant in the truck also recognized Karim and told him, "Please tell Lieutenant McDougal that I enjoyed his classes. All the men did."

Karim related the message to Sean, who, in turn nodded to acknowledge the compliment. At exactly seventeen-hundred hour, sirens throughout the city started wailing. The citizens of the city were saying

"God speed, Kurdish fighters." Almost in unison, the truck drivers started their engines. The gates to the garrison swung open and fifty-five trucks slowly passed through on their way to the front. Most of the vehicles belonged to the army and were of a sand color. Behind the military vehicles, another ten trucks of various sizes, colors and conditions followed. These were commercial vehicles trucks that had been commandeered to haul food, tents, medical beds and other supplies to the rear echelons at the combat zone. Four ambulances followed the commercial vehicles.

The major in command of the operation rode in an armored vehicle at the head of the assembly. The trucks carrying the soldiers of Company A followed immediately behind the major and his armored vehicle. The convoy took a road out of Erbil that led directly west to Mosul. Several police cars from the city followed the trucks and, after several miles, stopped. They would halt all traffic going west behind the convoy. They intended to prevent spies from reporting the progress of the convoy. Five miles from Erbil, and well out of sight from the city, the convoy took a road heading north. It was thought that if ISIS were to place road bombs along the way, they would obvious do so on the direct route between Erbil and Mosul. After traveling some distance north, the convoy again turned west again. They would approach the outskirts of Mosul from the north.

Sean noticed every soldier in the truck with him and Karim were holding one of the new American rifles that he had brought to the Kurds. Most of the men didn't know gun safety rules as indicated by the muzzles that pointed randomly at their comrades. A young man next Karim, holding a rifle between his legs, smiled and asked him, "Sergeant, have you fought ISIS before?"

Karim said, "Yes, for a year I helped fight them in Syria. Some of their units are very good, but not all of them are equally capable. Sometimes they press recruits into action without much training. Some units have little gear beyond their rifles and a few mortars. A few fighters use large caliber automatic weapons mounted in the back of pick-up trucks."

The young man said, "I hear they are terrible people, but that they are good fighters."

Karim said, "The ISIS fighters are fanatics and most of them fight bravely. A lot of them are anxious to be a martyr and go straight to heaven."

Everyone in the truck was listening intently to what Karim had to say. Karim asked the young man, "I see you have one of the new American rifles. I guess you haven't had a chance to shoot it?"

"No, sir. I've never fired a gun of any kind. I think they were going to teach us how to fire weapons at the garrison after our boot camp training. Anyway, I think I could learn quickly. Shooting a gun doesn't look complicated. You know. A person just puts the safety off, aims and pulls the trigger."

Karim told Sean what the young man had told him. Sean said nothing although he found the man's comments revealing. Everyone in the truck grew quiet, thinking about what Karim had said about the enemy they were about to engage. The face of the young man who had talked with Karim showed concern and a little fear.

An hour out of Erbil, the convoy turned south onto a side road that led southward. Sean's GPS indicated they were only several miles from Mosul. The city would be southwest of their position. The trucks continued along the dirt road until they were directly east of the city. The terrain there was relatively flat and open. The trucks all came to a halt and military police emerged from trucks that were already at the site. They directed the trucks to park at various spots along a line that stretched north and south for three miles and which was two miles from Mosul. In all, there would be seven fighting units along the line, including one that was all women. The commanding officers of the seven companies gathered their junior officers and issued orders. For the present, the Kurds will be forming a defensive line to counter potential movement of ISIS to the east. Should the ISIS fighters come out to do battle, the Kurds wanted to be prepared.

Company A was given a section that extended nine hundred yards north-to-south and faced Mosul. Along that length, the fifteen squads of Company A would each establish defensive zones. Each squad would build a circular shaped compound. Sand bags were to be filled and stacked to protect the soldiers against small arms fire as well as shrapnel from mortar rounds. Captain Mirzo dismounted from one of the trucks and waited for the three platoon leaders to approach. When the platoon commanders were near, the captain pointed to sections along the defensive line while giving orders to the men. Shortly the lieutenants hurried to the trucks to organize their men.

Within an hour there were some seven-hundred soldiers along the defensive line filling bags with sand and stacking them in a circle. The circles were about twenty-feet in diameter, just enough to accommodate a squad of twelve soldiers. A smaller circle of sand bags were positioned a short distance to the east of the main line for Captain Mirzo, his aids and a radio operator. Sean and Karim went with the commander officer of the third platoon, the lieutenant who nodded to Sean when he had entered the truck for transport to Mosul.

Three hours after their arrival east of Mosul, most of the squads had constructed circles of sand bags to a height of several feet. The bags would be enough to protect the Kurds in a prone or sitting position. The men were tired from the work and the heat. Late afternoon, most soldiers stopped filling bags with sand to rest and wait for supper. The women of the service company had erected three tents behind the defensive line and were preparing supper in each tent. In shifts, the soldiers wandered back to the mess tents to eat. As the sun was setting over Mosul the soldiers were mostly within the circles of sand bags they had piled around themselves. A few spread their mats on the ground and went to sleep. Others sat on sand bags and chatted. A few were smoking. Everyone wondered what surprises, if any, ISIS might have for them during the coming night.

36

The First Night

SEAN believed he knew a little battlefield psychology. He'd been exposed to it numerous times in Iraq. His experience told him ISIS was not about to let their new adversaries enjoy a good night's sleep. No, ISIS would help their cause by applying a little psychological warfare. The maximum effect would be to cause a disturbance during the small morning hours. With these considerations in mind, Sean spread out his mat and went to sleep early. He kept night goggles and a .50 cal sniper rifle by his side. Before their departure from the garrison, Sean had placed the sniper rifle in one of the trailers. It was the only large caliber sniper rifle that the Kurds had brought with them, and Sean had it at his side.

At 1:00 a.m. Sean awakened. He speculated there would be ISIS action of some type in the coming hours. He sat up and rubbed his eyes. He moved to the front of the small compound and sat behind the wall of sand bags. Everyone within the circle was sleeping. He put the night goggles on and surveyed the field between his position and the outskirts of Mosul. There was no sign of movement. He continued watching. Another hour went by. Sean nodded, and then he fell asleep with his head tilted forward. When he heard a loud explosion to the rear and to his right, he came awake with a startle. He was angry with himsclf. Had he stayed awake, he might have spotted the source of the explosion. He thought the explosion might have been a mortar round. If it was, there would be more and soon. There was a clear sky and a partial moon. With the night vision goggles, the plain in front of the Kurdish line was lit like a stage with overhead lighting. He scanned from left to right but failed to spot anyone. A second explosion occurred, more near one of the circles of sand bags.

The soldiers within the circle near Sean were turning over on their mats, uncertain as to what to do. Others sat up, listening for the next explosion. Nobody wanted to stand up because the upper half of their bodies would be exposed to shrapnel if one of the rounds landed nearby. Sean scanned the field a second time, going more slowly. Then he spotted the upper part of a mortar tube and the four men gathered around it. They had found a small depression in the land and had set up the mortar there. Because of the depression, he could see only the upper half of the men's bodies. They were out from the Kurds' position by five-hundred yards and over to Sean's right. Sean's shot would be around eight-hundred yards. He saw one of the men drop another round into the mortar tube. There would be another explosion in a few seconds. After the third explosion, Sean saw one of the men at the mortar lift a phone to his ear. They had a spotter amongst the Kurdish ranks giving them directions.

Sean lifted the heavy sniper rifle and rested it on one of the sandbags. He didn't know if the telescopic sight had been zeroed with the rifle. Nevertheless, he would find out very soon. He adjusted the scope for bullet drop at eight-hundred yards and placed the crosshairs on the back of one of the men at the mortar. He squeezed the trigger. The man didn't fall, but he looked to his right. The man's glance told Sean the bullet impact was to the right of his target. He readjusted the scope again to move the impact left. The next shot was close to the men and they all hunkered down. Obviously, Sean had a rifle that had not been zeroed to the scope. He would zero it before shooting at the men again.

Looking through the telescopic sight, Sean spotted a football-sized rock far to the left of the mortar crew. He put the crosshairs on the rock and fired. From the puff of sand he could tell the impact was low and to the right by four feet. He adjusted the crosshairs. The next shot was in-line with the rock but low. Again, he readjusted the scope again. He was getting close to zeroing the scope to the rifle. But he was having another problem. Because he was firing rapidly, he would be heating the barrel and a hot barrel would throw the shots off target. Another explosion indicated the mortars would soon be falling close to soldiers. Sean had to act and immediately. He again placed the crosshairs on the back of the man who had been charged with dropping rounds into the mortar tube. On impact the man fell across the mortar tube and then slipped to the ground. The mortar team knew someone had their sights on them and they would all soon be dead if they didn't clear out. The three grabbed their equipment and started running for Mosul. Sean considered shooting at the running men, but declined. The chances of hitting a target moving on an oblique route at that distance were slim.

With the cessation of the mortar explosions, Sean stood to stretch his legs and to return to his sleeping mat. The sun would not be rising for another five hours. Someone standing outside the sandbags shined a flashlight in his eyes. "Who fired that rifle?"

Sean recognized the voice of Captain Mirzo. Sean said, "I did, sir."

"Who told you to fire?"

Sean knew that Kurdish soldiers were prohibited from firing their weapons until given orders. Besides, he, wearing the insignia of a lieutenant, should not be firing a weapon at the enemy. Firing weapons was an enlisted man's task. Sean knew all of these rules. At the same time, he knew there would probably have been several dead Kurdish soldiers nearby had he not used the big rifle when he did. He said, "I shot at the enemy, sir. They packed up and returned to Mosul."

The captain said, "Give the rifle to the squad leader. He will find someone to do the shooting."

Sean knew that his actions were against all established protocols. He responded, "Yes, sir."

Sean had more thoughts he wanted to express, but he knew he should not be discussing these topics in front of the enlisted men. He knew that nobody will be firing the .50 cal rifles well without at least several days training. He would find the captain later and speak with him in private. At the moment he merely wanted to get more sleep before daylight.

37

Uday Sarraf

IMAM Uday Sarraf walked to the window on the second floor of the house in Mosul. He had heard bursts of gun fire in the distance, and he went to the window out of curiosity. Several blocks to the east a mixture of white and black smoke was rising from a large building. At first, the imam stood near the window in order to have a good view, but then he stepped back a few paces. It was never a good idea to stand at a window, presenting one's body as a target.

The property where he stood had belonged to a wealthy Shia merchant before ISIS invaded the city. The building was a beautiful property. There were paintings on the walls, oriental carpets throughout, a fountain. Unfortunately the merchant will no longer be able to enjoy the expensive objects that he had bought since his body was rotting in a field outside Mosul. The merchant's wife and daughters had likewise been taken away to unknown destinations. The imam wondered what the ISIS fighters were doing with the city's women. Yet, he was not inclined to inquire. It was perhaps best that a cleric remain uninformed on the matter of women. As Sarraf stared at the puffs of smoke in the distance his thought wandered back to his days in Baghdad. He wondered if he had made the right decision. In Baghdad he had a comfortable life whereas living near the field action, life was Spartan. Especially, the food was poor.

The mosque in Baghdad where Sarraf was imam was situated in a well-to-do suburb. For this reason, finances were never a problem. The faithful gave generously to support the mosque's programs. That all changed when the Americans invaded Iraq and introduced turmoil. The Iraqi economy was destroyed and lawlessness prevailed. For a time there was rampant looting, robberies, unemployment.

In Baghdad, Imam Sarraf had been known for his sermons. He knew the holy Koran intimately and often recited long passages that he knew by heart. He had a good speaking voice that many said was inspiring. Perhaps in part because of the widespread pestilence that followed the defeat of the Iraqi forces at the hands of the Americans, Sarraf's lectures had become more bellicose. He blamed non-believers for the troubles in Iraq. He became an advocate of aggressiveness and action. As the imam's rhetoric grew more rebellious, a number of Muslims who had been regularly attending his mosque stopped visiting the mosque. They believed their religion was a religion of peace, and they took exception to advocates of violence. Nevertheless, Sarraf developed a devoted following amongst those of a radical persuasion, and the numbers grew by the month. In time, the ISIS higher-up heard of Imam Sarraf, his sermons and his rhetoric.

It was inevitable that ISIS would be attracted to Imam Sarraf and vice-versa. When the call came, Saraff willingly responded. At first, ISIS used him as a spokesman to espouse the ISIS philosophy. He spoke several times a day on radio. He read from the Koran and became an apologist for ISIS policies and practices. However, during the battle for Mosul field casualties had risen. The ISIS higher-ups decided to have Imam Sarraf act as a field commander. They thought a man of his capabilities could inspire the troops to soldier on under adverse conditions. He always seemed to find the right words for any situation.

After backing away from the window, the imam returned to the desk that had been brought in for his use. As he sat reviewing papers on his desk, he heard the footsteps of someone climbing to the second floor. It could have been his cook, his valet or his clerk. It was the clerk and he asked, "Imam, Commander Nazari has an inquiry about captives. He says they have rounded up about two-hundred and fifty men. They are mostly Sunni and Shia but there are a few Christians and Yazidi too. They are being held in a building that had been a Shia school before the ISIS invasion. He wants to know what to do with them. Should I send him up to see you?"

The imam rubbed his beard as he thought.

The clerk added, "He says they left the women at their houses for the time being."

"Tell him to take all the men except the Sunni to a field outside the city and leave their bodies there to rot. Keep the Sunni men incarcerated for at least the immediate future."

The clerk bowed and returned down the stairs to relate the order. The ISIS commander waited at the foot of the stairs for direction. He expected the clerk would tell him that the imam would see him. Instead, the clerk told him, "The imam says to take all the men except the Sunnis outside the city and shoot them. Don't bother to bury them. Leave the bodies for the vultures."

Upon hearing what the clerk had to say, the commander blinked his eyes several times. He was not accustomed to receiving orders through a clerk. He started to respond with an acerbic response, but reconsidered. Clerics were sensitive to hearing questions after they had issued orders. It would be best to be polite under all condition. He told the clerk, "As directed, I will take care of the prisoners."

Commander Nazari told himself to exit the building before he said something that would get him into trouble. He turned quickly and, with pursed lips, walked to a waiting pick-up truck. Once seated, he snapped at the driver, "Back to the school. We have dirty work to do."

***

Upon arriving at the warehouse, commander Nazari called a junior officer to him and told him, "Load all the captive men except the Sunnis on trucks. Tell them they are going to Raqqa for religious instructions. They will think we hope to convert them to Sunnis. Be sure to bring enough soldiers and enough ammunition with you. A mile or two out of town shoot them. Don't bother to bury the bodies."

38

Battle Lines

AT dawn the cooks in the three kitchens were busy preparing breakfasts for the Kurdish soldiers. Sean, Karim and five other soldiers from their small compound made their way back to one of the kitchens for their meals. They carried their food back to the circle of sandbags and relieved the other soldiers who had been waiting their turn.

After Sean finished eating, he told Karim he was going to speak with Captain Mirzo. The other soldiers within the partially built defensive position resumed filling bags and piling them on top of the ones they had filled the previous day. Because the captain did not want a conspicuous gathering of sandbags that suggested the presence of an officer, he changed his headquarters to one of the other circles of sandbags. When Sean entered, the captain was sitting on a sandbag, eating breakfast. Sean stopped near the entrance, and waited for the captain to finish eating his breakfast. The captain saw Sean but didn't acknowledge him and continued eating. When he finished the last morsel of egg, he stood and walked to speak with a lieutenant who was in the compound with him. Returning to Sean, he curtly asked, "What is it?"

Sean said, "Sir, there were twenty of the .50 cal sniper rifles in the arms shipment I brought from America. Because the soldiers of the garrison were ordered here I didn't have time to complete the instructions on use of the rifles. Nevertheless, I could continue with instructions in the fields behind our battle line. Then our soldiers would be ready to use them if needed. If those rifles would be brought here, I could instruct, say, twenty-five men to be proficient with the guns and another twenty-five to be spotters. In two or three days of instructions, we could have twenty teams of snipers moderately proficient with the weapons."

Captain Mirzo stared at Sean without saying a word. Deep down, he believed he had reasons for not liking Sean, but he had to admit Sean might be right about the heavy-duty sniper rifles. Nobody knew what might develop from the current situation. Yet, those in command realized it was always better to have more firepower available. He said, "I know the rifles are still back in the garrison in Erbil. The subject was mentioned in one of our staff meetings before we came here. You might have a valid argument though. We could be in this static line for who knows how long. I've heard about the rifles, and I believe we would be well advised to have access to them. Nobody knows what might develop from the current situation. I'll speak to the major and see what we can do to get the rifles here."

Sean said, "If you decide to bring the rifles here, try to also bring along about four-hundred bricks, and mortar. I'll need those items for demonstrations."

An hour after Sean spoke with the captain, two trucks with forty armed soldiers departed for the garrison in Erbil. Their mission: Secure the heavy duty sniper rifles, four-hundred bricks and mortar and return promptly to the Kurdish defensive line east of Mosul. Mid-afternoon, the trucks returned with the retrieved cargo. Captain Mirzo came over to Sean and told him, "We have selected fifty soldiers for training with the heavy-duty sniper rifles. Four are women. As you had suggested, half will be shooters and half will be spotters. Tomorrow morning you will take them a kilometer behind our line and begin training on use of the weapons. Try to complete the training in three days."

***

The following day Sean went with the selected snipers to fields behind the Kurdish line. Under Sean's direction, a mason constructed a wall with the bricks. It measured five feet high and five courses deep. The first day, Sean reviewed techniques, practices, maintenance and ballistics. Instructions continued the second day. The afternoon of the second day, Sean did live demonstrations to show the capabilities of the rifle with the masonry walls that had been constructed. The third day, all of the shooters practiced shooting at targets between one-hundred yards and two miles. At the end of the third day, Sean believed all the teams were capable to some degree with the new rifles. The teams, together with the heavy-duty sniper rifles, returned to their units. On average, every fourth entrenchment along the defensive line was equipped with one of the .50 cal rifles.

***

The fifth day seemed like the previous four days along the Kurdish line. The sandbags at all of the circles had been piled to a height of about six feet. The Kurdish line was a challenge to ISIS that essentially said: Here we stand. We, the Kurds, are here to prevent your further movements toward our homeland. If you wish to have a fight, come out here and meet us. ISIS intended to accept the Kurdish challenge, but on their terms, not the Kurd's. When the sun was about half an hour from setting over the city of Mosul, ISIS opened up with a 155 mm howitzer. It was an American-built gun that ISIS possibly had acquired from the Iraqi army. Or, perhaps ISIS took possession of the gun when the Iraqis abandoned it. Then, too, an ISIS operative might have bought the gun from an Iraqi officer.

ISIS waited until near sundown because they knew that as the Kurds looked toward the gun emplacement the sun would be in their eyes. The howitzer was capable of firing several miles, and that is how the gun would normally be used. A truck pulled the howitzer to a position east of a row of building at the outskirts of Mosul. The ISIS gunners decided to shoot directly at the Kurds. Their spotter would be positioned within earshot of the men firing the weapon, and he would relay the impacts to the officer directing fire. In a matter of minutes, the gun was anchored and the muzzle repositioned to point at the Kurdish line.

The first round from the howitzer landed several hundred yards behind the Kurds' line. Immediately there was panic amongst the Kurdish troops. They realized they were in the open and highly susceptible to artillery fire. The entrenchments with the sandbags would protect the soldiers from rifle fire, but an artillery strike to or near a compound would be deadly. If some action were not taken soon, there would be severe Kurdish casualties. The second strike from the howitzer was one hundred yards from the first strike and more near the line of the Kurdish circles of sandbags. Everyone knew the next impact would be either in or very near one of the circles of sandbags. Suddenly the soldiers within the compound that was the apparent target grabbed their gear and ran along the line to find a safer place to stay.

Sean was quick to realize the Kurd's plight. Unless changes were made, and soon, the Kurds would be suffering casualties. He signaled for Karim to go along with him, and he ran to the compound where he thought he would find Captain Mirzo. When they realized the captain was not there, Karim asked the nearest soldier, "Where's the captain?"

The soldier said, "He went to meet with the major. They are three squads to the north."

Sean and Karim ran to the third installation where they found a group of officers standing outside the protection of the sandbags. The officers were intensely discussing their situation. When Captain Mirzo spotted Sean, he pointed to Sean while speaking to the other officers. Then he waved Sean and Karim over to their conference. When Sean came near, the captain asked Sean, "Is there a chance the heavy-duty rifles could be used to silence the howitzer?"

Sean said, "Yes, by all means. The rifles can shoot that far, although it is difficult to hit a specific target with a single shot. Nevertheless, if we had at least several teams firing multiple rounds, they would be bound to connect with the men operating the howitzer. That would stop their firing the gun. More important, they could prevent ISIS from moving the artillery piece to a safe location where we could not see them."

Immediately the major turned to the seven company commanders and instructed them to have the heavy-duty snipers commence firing at the men operating the howitzer. An artillery shell fell amidst one of the sand bag enclosures and blew the sandbags to small pieces. Fortunately, the occupants had run earlier to find protection within other enclosures. Within minutes, the reports from the .50 cal rifles could be heard up and down the battle line. Sean used his binoculars to watch the men operating the howitzer. Puffs of dust near the gun indicated where the .50 cal bullets were landing. Some strikes were as much as thirty feet from the gun. The artillery men glanced at the puffs now and then but mostly ignored the bullet strikes. As the minutes went by and the snipers readjusted their sights, the strikes came closer to the howitzer.

After some twenty rounds from the Kurd's heavy-duty rifles, the man loading artillery shells into the gun fell to the ground with his hand on his chest. One of the .50 cal bullets had found its target. The other men nearby stopped what they were doing to look around and then at one another. An order was apparently given, and the men resumed loading the howitzer. They fired another round. Shortly a second man, carrying a round to the rear of the howitzer, fell. Immediately the remained of the crew dropped what they were doing and ran toward the city, allowing the howitzer to remain unattended. The Kurds had won a reprieve although they realized it might be a short one.

39

Spoils of War

ISIS Commander Nazari had brought the men under his command to the warehouse that was serving as a gathering spot for an ISIS contingent. Standing in front of the group, he told them, "Men, you have fought well, and I am proud of you. Because of your bravery I can report that the City of Mosul is now under our control. Our forces have overcome all resistance. Congratulations for a battle well fought. Later we shall pray for the martyrs who were lost in the fight and who otherwise would be here with us today to celebrate our great victory. For now, it is time for us to rest and to become rejuvenated. It is also time to enjoy the spoils of war."

The men knew what their commander was about to tell them. They shouted and cheered. Nazari continued, "For the next several days, our group shall be going to the Yazidi neighborhood where there are no longer any men. I can tell you the Yazidi women have grown lonely and are in need of male companionship. I've been told they are especially fond of our courageous ISIS fighters and are desirous of meeting our men face-to-face."

Several of the men laughed, others cheered.

"You will leave your guns here. I don't want one of the unappreciative women picking up your weapon and sending you to heaven earlier than what you had planned. Besides, I may need you for more fights in the future. We will have several armed police with us to guard the streets. Be sure to watch for knives. Secure your rifles here and meet me outside."

When the last of the men came out of the building, they started walking toward the Yazidi section of town. Looking forward to the coming adventure, the men were in a jovial mood. Policemen, carrying rifles over their shoulders, walked behind the group. The police appeared happy for the soldiers walking before them. Once in the Yazidi neighborhood, groups of four men broke away from the larger group. The smaller groups each went to different houses. Commander Nazari went with three men to the home of the Tahir family. He knocked on the front door and stood back as though he actually expected someone to open the door. After waiting briefly, he nodded to one of the men. The man put a foot to the door and it sprang inward, tearing a piece of the jam with it.

Inside the Tahir family house, three women sat on a sofa in the living room. An older woman held her arms around the shoulders of two young girls. Commander Nazari walked to a spot in front of the older woman and said, "Didn't you hear me knocking?"

The woman looked at him, but did not respond. Nazari put his hands on his hips and repeated what he had said.

"I said: Didn't you hear me knocking?"

When the woman said nothing, he moved closer and slapped her first on her left cheek and then with a backhand on her right cheek. The younger girl screamed. The older woman said, "Please don't assault us. We did nothing to anyone. Your soldiers took our men and what little money we had. We have nothing. My granddaughters and I don't know what we will be doing for food."

Nazari said, "Old lady, you are wrong in two ways. First, you do have something of great value, namely two lovely girls. As far as the food problem goes, we are here to solve that problem too."

She said, "No, please. I beg you to let us alone."

Nazari told her, "I can't do that. You chose the wrong religion. You knew of the true religion, but decided to go your own way. You chose to be a nonbeliever. Now you must pay."

Nazari turned to his men and said, Moncef and Fahd, take the old hag to the police. She will be going to the slave auction. If she is lucky, a Sunni family may buy her for housework and cleaning. She immediately got up from the couch and knelt in front of Nazari with her hands folded. "Please, my granddaughters need me. They will be destitute without me."

The two young men took her by the arms and forcibly took her to the front door. Outside, Moncef told the nearest policemen, "This one's for the auction."

The policeman told her, "Old lady, go sit with the other women over there." He pointed to several women who were already sitting together on a street curb. All the women were holding handkerchiefs and sobbing. He told her, "If you get up before I tell you, I will shoot you. I enjoy shooting Yazidis. Now, get over there and quickly. I'll give you fair warning. I have a short temper."

Continuing to cry, she walked to the side of the road and sat along with the other women. Moncef and Fahd returned to the Tahir house. Inside the two granddaughters were holding handkerchiefs and sobbing. Intermittently, they were holding hands. Nazari tried to calm them. "Girls, we will not be harming you. Please, relax. Do you have some fruit juice for our brave fighters?"

The girls didn't answer. Nazari tried again, "Please, what are your names?"

When neither of the girls said anything, Nazari took a step toward the sofa. The girls had seen what happened to their grandmother when she failed to answer Nazari's questions. The oldest of the two said, "My name is Halima, and my sister's name is Aziza."

Nazari said, "That's better, Halima. If you do not have fruit juice, then fetch some water for your visitors. Show us some gratitude and hospitality. That would be the proper thing to do. I am sure you want to be friendly."

Halima disappeared to the rear of the dwelling and returned with a tray and four glasses of water. She gave each of the men a glass and then sat next to her younger sister. After the men had emptied their glasses, Nazari said, "Now it's time to get down to business. Halima, how old are you?"

Halima said, "I am eighteen and my sister is fifteen."

Nazari asked, "Are you both virgins?"

Halima looked at her sister and then responded quietly, "Yes."

Nazari looked at the men and winked. He asked, "Which of you would like to be first?"

Aziza stood and in a broken voice said, "I'll prepare the bed and call when I am ready."

Nazari said, "That's the spirit."

Aziza walked to a room at the rear of the building. Everyone was still as they waited for Aziza to call. But there was no call. Eventually, Nazari told the Moncef, "Go see what's taking her so long. Enjoy yourself."

Moncef walked to the room and opened the door. He then slammed the door. The men heard him say, "Shit."

He returned to the front room and said, "She slit her throat."

Halima screamed and clasped her hands in prayer. She began sobbing uncontrollably. Facing the men, Nazari said in a loud voice, "Enough. We tried to be polite and considerate, but these girls have not shown us the hospitality we deserve. So, we must do what we must do. Hussein, you go first."

Hussein said, "Commander, I appreciate the offer, but you are more deserving than me. Especially since she is a virgin, I think you should be first."

Nazari said, "Alright, we need to start somewhere. He took Halima by the hand, but she pulled away. She said, "No, please. I don't know how to do this."

He grabbed her by the wrist, pulled her away from the sofa, and wrestled her to the floor. She continued to struggle. She swung her fist and hit Nazari on the side of his face. She was not strong and Nazari hardly felt the blow. Moncef pulled a knife from his pocket, knelt near the girl and scraped the knife across her face, drawing blood. He moved the knife under her chin and, while pressing the point into her skin told her, "If you continue to struggle, I will kill you and leave your corpse with your sister's."

While Moncef held the knife under her chin, Nazari lifted her dress and removed her undergarment. She froze in position. Nazari entered her…again…again. She screamed again and again. After each of the four men has had his turn, they left Halima bleeding and exhausted on the floor of the small house. Back on the street, the men started laughing and joking with one another. Behind them, other small groups, likewise in a festive mood, were wandering along the street in the direction of the warehouse.

40

Special Mission

THE Kurds defensive line west of Mosul had been in-place going on four days. Except for the single mortar attack and the shots from the howitzer, ISIS had done nothing more about the Kurd's presence. Sean started to grow apprehensive. In the past, the ISIS fighters had proved they could be imaginative and well organized. At the same time, Sean thought the Kurds were in a precarious position. They were in the open and stationary. If ISIS could come up with more artillery, the Kurds will certainly suffer high casualties. It would be unwise to continue along a stationary line. The morning of the fourth day, Sean visited the captain of the group to which he had been assigned. When he found the captain he told him, "Sir, I believe we are making a mistake remaining along this stationary line. I suggest we should either attack ISIS in Mosul or devise another strategy. If ISIS can come up with more artillery pieces, they will decimate our ranks."

The captain drew a deep breath, let it out and told Sean, "I am inclined to agree with you. Staying in these static positions is only asking for trouble. I understand you have experience fighting the Islamists, so I guess I am not telling you anything you don't already know. Let's go talk with the major."

Together, Sean and Captain walked to the compound where the commander of the mission had located. Sean repeated to the major the same thoughts he had mentioned to Captain Mirzo. The major told Sean and the captain, "I cannot disagree with you. My orders were to move here and set up a defensive line west of Mosul, which we did. Yet, I am uncertain that those in Erbil fully understand the situation here. I believe, as you do, that our remaining as we are will only result in an unfortunate outcome."

The three looked at one another. The major stood and with hand motion indicated that his visitors should follow him outside the protection of the sandbags. He obviously did not want any of the soldiers within the compound to hear what he had to say. Once they were out of earshot from those within the circle of sandbags, the major, speaking in a low voice said, "Although we have a defensive posture here, we certainly are free to initiate offensive actions of any type we might devise. I should perhaps tell you we have received several messages from a friend within Mosul. He has a short wave radio and he has been updating us on ISIS movements within the city. So far he has been able to avoid capture. He reported that the ISIS fighters have been on R&R for several days now. Every morning groups of men have been visiting the Yazidi section to rape the women. He said they train up until ten in the morning and then several hundred of them meet to a warehouse in the Yazidi district. At ten, the men are free to visit houses in the area where they repeatedly rape Yazidi women. He suggested we could easily trap the enemy fighters in the warehouse."

Sean's asked, "Can we trust this person?"

The major said, "Actually, we can. One of our soldiers knows him personally. The contact says ISIS has been watching our line day and night. Nevertheless, he says there is an opening to the north. He says that if we want to bring men to assault the warehouse, he could signal us with a flashlight and guide us to a building where we can wait until dawn. He says forty men should be enough for the mission."

Sean said. "Perfect. Let me take forty men tonight and we will do it. We'll surround the warehouse and give ISIS a surprise."

The major told Captain Mirzo, "We must do something. Give the American four squads from your company. We'll tell our contact in Mosul to look for our men at four in the morning."

***

Early the morning of the fifth day, Sean, Karim and forty men stole away from the defensive line. Moving as quietly as possible they walked northward and well behind the Kurdish line. If there was a spy amongst the Kurds along the defensive line, as they suspected, they didn't want him to know about the clandestine movement. Several miles north, the group moved west to a position north of the city and waited there until four in the morning. At precisely four, a flashlight on the outskirts of the city blinked in their direction. With Sean in the lead, the group walked in a single file toward the light. It took half an hour to travel the distance to the source of the light. When they came to the man with the light he told Karim, "I live in a house two blocks from the warehouse. The house belonged to relatives of mine, but ISIS killed everyone who lived there. They don't know that I have been hiding there for several weeks in the Yazidi district. We will go there now and you can wait in the house until ten. Then, if God wills, you can surround the building and butcher the ISIS beasts the way they have butchered every Yazidi they could find. Except, of course, the poor women."

Continuing in single file, the group followed the man down alleys. Along the way, they passed piles of rubble that at one time had been homes. The smell of rotting bodies was overwhelming. Eventually the group came to a small building on an alley. Dawn was breaking. The man withdrew a key and opened a door to the building. The group entered, and the man said the group should rest because they will need their energy later.

A little after nine, the man came to Sean and told him to follow him. He said he will show Sean the warehouse. It was nearby. Karim joined Sean and the three exited the building. A short distance from the building, the man pointed to the warehouse. Men toting rifles were entering the building. The three took care to stay in the shadows and behind objects. The man said, "There is the warehouse. For several days now hundreds of men have been meeting there in the morning hours. They listen to instructions or orders of some kind and at about ten the men are allowed to exit for visits to the unfortunate Yazidi women. They bring food for the women and then they rape them. I suggest you attack just before ten so as to catch them in the building. You will need to cover all sides of the building or some will escape to come at you from behind."

Sean saw the building's walls were constructed of bricks, and that presented a problem. The Kurds could surround the building, but the ISIS fighters could shoot from the windows of the building. Unless the Kurds could find protection behind buildings or substantial objects in the neighborhood, they would be exposed to rifle fire from those windows. Yet, they had a great opportunity to inflict significant pain upon their enemy if they could figure out a way to pen them up in the warehouse. If they would have brought the .50 cal rifles, they could have put them to good use to shoot through the masonry walls. However, the rifles were too heavy to carry on their mission.

The contact told Sean, "Now that you have seen the warehouse, you can plan your attack. We must return to the others. If a policeman sees us, he may shoot us on sight."

The three set out to return along the path they had taken. After one block, they had to cross a street in order to return to the safe house. Before entering the street, the contact peered from behind a building that sat on the street. Not seeing anyone, he motioned for Sean and Karim to follow him. Half way across, a policeman stepped out from a passageway between two houses. When he saw the three men, he shouted for them to stop. The contact started running and after two buildings, hurried into a small house that faced the alley. After Sean and Karim followed, he closed and bolted the door. The contact told Sean, "If he enters you must kill him as soon as he enters. Otherwise he will immediately shoot all three of us."

Both Sean and Karim withdrew their handguns in case the policeman burst into the room. Shortly they heard the policeman try the door and then continue along the alley. After half an hour the contact looked up and down the alley but said he saw no one. They ran to the safe house and made it inside without seeing the policeman. It was time for the attack on the warehouse.

41

Crossing the T

SEAN addressed the assembled group of forty men within the small safe house where they waited near the targeted warehouse in Mosul. He assigned each of the squads to a specific side of the building they were about to attack. At ten minutes before the hour of ten o'clock, the forty men exited the safe house and walked toward the warehouse. Two local men spotted the group of soldiers and ran off down a street. When Sean and his group were near their objective, the squads broke off and circled wide to take up positions around the building. Sean, Karim and the contact remained with the nearest squad. They entered a house with windows that faced the warehouse. After waiting for all four squads to report they were in position, Sean told a sniper to fire an incendiary round at the roof of the warehouse.

The first shot failed to ignite the roof. The sound of the first shot was a signal for the other three squads to commence their attack. Shortly all four squads were shooting at the roof. Two of the rounds succeeded in setting the roof on fire. Soon the roof would be ablaze and whoever was within the building would be fleeing to escape the fire and smoke. While the flame on the roof was building, the squad at the rear of the warehouse spotted men at windows in the warehouse and opened fire. Shortly, a group of five men, carrying rifles, bolted out the main door of the warehouse. The squad near Sean cut them down in a burst of rounds. The Yazidi contact rose to his feet and stood at the open window. He shouted in the direction of the warehouse, "Eat lead you sons of harlots. We have more surprises for you. Just wait." He was jubilant, his hatred deep. A bullet whistled past his ear and he moved away from the window. Those within the warehouse would realize it was unsafe to exit.

As the fire on the roof started to spread, Sean knew he was running out of time. ISIS had thousands of men within Mosul, and once they knew of the attack on the warehouse, they would be marshalling forces to come to the rescue of those caught in the warehouse. While Sean watched the roof burning, snipers from each of the squads periodically fired rounds at the building. Most of the rounds were intended to keep ISIS from using the windows either to shoot or observe. The roof was taking too long to collapse.

Suddenly, someone shouted, "There's a truck coming up the street." Several men rushed to a window in the west side of the house to see the cause of the concern. After a pause another man shouted, "He has a large caliber gun and he's pointing it at this house."

Sean shouted, "Everyone out the back."

No sooner had the last man made it out of the house when the ISIS gunner started shooting. Bullets penetrated the front wall of the house and went out through the rear wall. When the shooter stopped, there were over a hundred holes in the front wall. Had Sean and the group remained, most of them would have certainly been killed. The gun on the truck was fitted with a steel shield that protected the gunner from fire that would be in the direction where the gun was aimed. However, the gunner had no protection from riflemen to his left or right. That was how a sniper in one of the squads surrounding the warehouse found his target. First, he took out the gunner and then the driver. As a precaution, he also put a bullet in two of the truck's tires.

Sean realized there would soon be additional ISIS fighters coming to the warehouse, possibly more than his band of forty men could successfully fight. The mission was not panning out as expected. Should he call the other three squads and do a hasty retreat? As he was considering his options, the roof collapsed and immediately the ISIS men started rushing from the building. Most were running out the front door, but some were jumping from windows at the sides and rear of the building. None got more than a hundred feet before riflemen in one of the squads cut them down. It was a turkey shoot. In a matter of minutes, there were over a hundred bodies spread on the ground surrounding the burning warehouse. Four of the bodies were those of Commander Nazari and three of his men, Moncef, Fahd, and Hussein. Those men would no longer be molesting the Yazidi women. In a manner of speaking, Sean and his band had crossed their enemy's "T." It was an old naval term that essentially describes a maneuver whereby one naval group successfully inflicts severe damage to an enemy while suffering little or no damage.

Sean had accomplished his mission, and it was time to retreat. They had capitalized on the Yazidi's intel. However, his group of guerrillas was not equipped to fight the large body of ISIS combatants that he knew would soon be coming up the street. He called the leaders of the other three squads and told them to rendezvous at the safe house. They would be going double time to the north to meet two trucks that were on the way to carry them back to the Kurdish line.

When all four squads were present, the Yazidi contact hurried them in reverse along the same path they had taken in the dark that morning. At the outskirts, two trucks were waiting for the men. After all the men were aboard except Sean and the Yazidi contact, Sean asked the man, "Are you coming along with us? It would be dangerous for you to remain here."

The Yazidi told him, "No, I am staying here. I want to help to kill more of these ISIS bastards. I have my short wave radio and I will keep your side informed of the situation over here. I can find enough food in the empty houses and gardens. If ISIS catches me, well, I have nothing to live for anyway. I no longer care. My loved ones are either dead or have disappeared. God knows where they might be, if they are still alive. Good luck to you. I will be in touch with your side. I hope that we meet again under happier circumstances. Now, please go."

Sean shook hands and wished him, "Good luck."

The drivers of the two trucks accelerated along dusty roads, returning along a circuitous route to the Kurdish defensive line.

42

Considerations

IMAM Uday Sarraf's clerk climbed the stairs with the news and gently tapped on the door. The imam did not favor loud noises or excited people. When he heard an almost inaudible "come in" the clerk gently opened the door. The imam was kneeling on his prayer rug. Obviously he had been in the midst of prayers. In a tone that could be considered somewhat angry, he asked, "Yes?"

The clerk told him, "Imam, insurgents have trapped a number of our soldiers in a building not far from here. They set the building afire and killed our men when they tried to escape. Commander Nazari was with them."

The clerk could have mentioned to the imam that over a hundred and fifty of them were killed, but he knew the imam did not like to hear disappointing news.

For this reason, he always tried to make disappointing reports seem like inconsequential happenings. He always embellished good news.

The clerk thought the imam might inquire about the insurgents or what countermeasures were being pursued, but he showed no interest in such matters. He reflected for a moment before resuming his prayers. As he bent to touch his head to the floor, in a low voice he said to no one in particular, "How lucky they were to die in such a manner."

No longer surprised by the imam's indifference, the clerk gently closed the door and retreated to his desk on the first floor.

***

When Sean arrived at the Kurdish defensive line along with the band of guerrillas, he reported directly to the major in command of the operation. He told him, "Sir, I can report we had a successful mission. We did not have time to make an accurate body count, but I estimate we killed well over a hundred of the enemy. Perhaps more. We thought they would be sending a large force soon, so we backed away while we could. I might add we were fortunate to suffer no casualties."

"You did well, lieutenant. My congratulations."

Sean said, "One more matter, if you don't mind, sir?"

"Of course."

"It is my opinion that we are vulnerable in this static situation. Our attack on the warehouse will most likely prompt ISIS to retaliate. If they find more artillery, they will position their howitzers around the city and have their fire directed by forward observers. We will have no escape out here in the open and they will slowly decimate our lines. I suggest we mobilize and enter the city to take on ISIS. Either that or we return to Erbil to devise another strategy."

The major said, "I agree with your thinking. However, I must tell you I received an important message this morning from Erbil. The government in Baghdad has informed the Kurdish authorities in Erbil that they do not want the Kurds attacking ISIS in Mosul. They told us we must leave the area and return to Erbil. The Iraqi Army is going to attack Mosul as soon as they can mobilize. Under the circumstances, we have no alternative but to comply with the mandate from Baghdad. As soon as we have fed the men their lunch, we will be boarding the trucks and returning to Erbil."

Sean was surprised by the news, but, at the same time, relieved to learn the Kurds will no longer be sitting ducks in their vulnerable positions.

43

Back in Erbil

THE Kurds allowed the sandbagged constructions to remain in-place as they prepared to depart for Erbil. The officers were desirous of moving away before ISIS might launch an attack. One hour after lunch the cooks pitched the mess tents, and the soldiers boarded the trucks that had been moved up from the rear. Two hours later the trucks entered through the gates at the garrison in Erbil. The next day the army returned to their routine of soldiering. Two days after their return to Erbil, Sean continued with the classes he had started the previous week.

Jabir al-Ateri had remained in Erbil while the Kurdish soldiers had moved to the outskirts of Mosul. When Sean returned, he continued stalking Sean, watching him from a distance and hoping for an opportunity to carry out the assassination. Eventually,

Jabir realized that Sean had forsaken running. He started to believe that Sean had become more cautious since the day he almost shot him in the park. Jabir would be obliged to find another way of getting at the American. On occasion Jabir walked through the hotel lobby and glanced into the restaurant. He failed to see an opportunity to complete the task he had in mind. The two guards were dedicated in their protection of their charge, and were continually vigilant.

The assignment in Kurdistan had become a headache to Jabir. He began to regret having volunteered his services and accepting the assignment. Above all, he did not wish to be captured. He had heard of the torture practices of the Iraqi police. Although he knew nothing of the Kurdish police, he did not wish to find out first-hand. He knew some of the Kurdish police held a deep hatred for Iraqis. Any attempt to kill the American must be done in a manner that would allow Jabir a fair possibility of escape. The situation presented difficult challenges. His handler told Jabir a "skilled assassin" was being sent to Erbil to assist him in "completing the task." The handler said the man would arrive in several days. *Good,* Jabir thought, *Let the newcomer risk capture and torture by the Kurdish police.*

Two days after the call, Jabir heard a knock at his hotel room door. Jabir let the man into the room. The would-be assassin said, "I am Nawaz," as if his fame would have preceded him. In a tone that suggested an order and not a request, the newcomer told Jabir to order him a meal.

Nawaz was a head higher than Jabir with long, strong arms. A neck like a bull. His fierce countenance and demeanor suggested he might enjoy administering pain and cruelty. His stare was defiant, his beard dark and thick. In his left hand he always held a string of prayer beads. He proudly displayed a square-shaped scar on his forehead. With a degree of pain, he had acquired the mark by repeatedly rapping his head on the floor while praying to Allah. Jabir knew he was going to dislike the man, perhaps intensely.

Nawaz didn't bother to shake hands. Jabir realized the man viewed him as a subordinate rather than an equal. He would need to be tolerant as best he could under the circumstances. Jabir placed an order with room service for one and told Nawaz he would be going for a stroll. He said he needed some fresh air. What he did not mention was that he needed to get away from the rude visitor who had invaded the room.

The first evening, Nawaz stayed in the hotel room reading the Koran. Since finishing his meal, he said nothing to Jabir or Salim, acting as though they were not present in the same room. Later, Nawaz undressed and crawled into one of the two beds, letting Jabir and his driver to resolve their sleeping arrangements. Salim said he didn't mind, he would sleep on the floor.

Rising early the next morning, Nawaz shook Jabir's shoulder while telling him, "Let's go for breakfast. I'm hungry."

All three dressed in silence. Jabir continued to resent such derogatory treatment. He had accomplished much for the cause and he didn't like being treated as a shirker. Yet, he did his best to avoid showing his resentment. He preferred to avoid a confrontation with the beast. He merely said, "I know of a restaurant two blocks away. I suggest we go there. We avoid the food at this hotel."

Speaking as though he were making the decision, Nawaz said, "That will do for today."

On the way to the restaurant, and likewise while they were eating, nobody said a word. At the restaurant, Nawaz, staring at the table top, said, "I want you to tell me about this American, and where we may find him. Also, why you have not taken care of him, although you have been here more than a week."

While Nawaz sat with his eyes looking down, Jabir related his recent efforts in Erbil and the difficulties he had encountered in his attempts to gain access to the American. He mentioned the near encounter in the park although with embellishments. Later that morning, Nawaz, Jabir and the driver parked near the Altin, where they watched the American and his two guards leave the hotel and enter a sedan. As usual they followed the sedan to the garrison where they watched the vehicle disappear into the well protected compound. See, thought Jabir, hiding a smirk. Let's see you figure out a way to get to our target, Mr. Skilled Assassin.

44

In the Souk

TWO days before his scheduled departure from Erbil, Sean told Karim, "Friday will be my last day in Kurdistan. I was thinking I might like to buy a souvenir of my stay here. Do you have any recommendations?"

"Sir, we could visit the souk in downtown Erbil. There you may find all sorts of items for sale–anything from motor oil to fine diamonds."

Karim paused to think before continuing. "In the souk a number of jewelry artisans display lovely items for sale. If you have a lady friend in mind, you might find hand-made jewelry that would greatly impress her. A number of shops also have hand-woven tapestries of all sizes and colors. Other merchants offer paintings and engraved metal vases. Osman and I would be pleased to take you there if you wish. You can spend hours in the souk because it's a large place with numerous merchants."

Sean said, "Sounds perfect. Tomorrow, I could do a class in the morning and in the afternoon we could go to the souk."

"Yes, sir, we could do that," Karim said. "Osman and I will go with you. Osman will stay with the automobile to guard it while you and I shop in the souk."

The following day, Sean, Osman and Karim traveled to downtown Erbil. Outside the souk, Osman parked away from the main entrance and in a remote section of the lot. Positioned well away from other vehicles, Osman would see anyone approaching the sedan. He remained with the vehicle to guard it while Sean and Karim headed into the souk.

A directory inside the entrance to the souk listed numerous vendors and a great variety of goods for sale. Immediately inside the entrance, most of the vendors sold small appliances and electronics. Farther along, clothing vendors displayed their merchandise. At the first corner, Karim said, "If you wish to shop for jewelry we could go to the right here. Most of the better jewelry shops are down this aisle. Some of them sell only gold jewelry while others sell less expensive items."

Sean said, "Good idea. Lead the way."

Karim led Sean to the shop where, he said, years in the past, he had bought a gift for his wife. Inside, Sean spotted a gold necklace with a pendant that had been formed into the shape of a flower. Pointing to the piece, Sean asked, "How much?" Karim translated the response. "Three hundred thousand dinars. That would be about two hundred and fifty dollars."

Sean said, "I like it," while reaching for his wallet.

Karim moved to block the vendor's view and reached over and put his hand on Sean's forearm. He told Sean to put his wallet back in his pocket. "The price he gave is only a starting price. He does not really expect to be paid that amount under any circumstances. What he truly expects is for us to argue and haggle with him for a time before we come to an agreement on a price. All the while he will be trying to determine your true level of interest. I'll tell him you like the necklace although you had seen a similar one in town for two hundred thousand dinars. I suggest we talk with him for a few minutes. That would be the more polite way of doing business."

Sean said, "You know best."

Karim told the jeweler, "My friend said the necklace is truly beautiful. He was wondering if you made it."

The jeweler responded, "Yes, I make all of the jewelry you see in my display cases. For many years I was an apprentice to a gifted jeweler. He taught me the art. The man passed away years ago, and I bought all of his tools. May he rest in peace. I should mention the flower in the necklace you are looking at is a cornflower, which is native to Kurdistan. I spent many hours on that one piece alone, and I might add every bit of the necklace is twenty-two karat gold."

Karim repeated what the jeweler said and he also said to Sean, "He's proud of his work, and he says the gold is twenty-two karat, which is no doubt true. In the Western countries, I'm told, gold jewelry is typically made of seventeen and eighteen karat gold."

Sean said, "It's lovely. I'm sure my girlfriend would like it."

Karim said to the jeweler, "My friend said he likes the necklace. However, he has seen a similar one for much less in another store. The craftsmanship of the other necklace is not as good as the one you have here. As you know, some people do not appreciate finely crafted jewelry, so perhaps your quality workmanship is not all that important to everyone. Would you take two-hundred thousand dinars?"

The jeweler said, "I cannot. I must pay rent in the souk, and I need at least a small profit. Although my wife and I eat very little, still we must eat."

The merchant paused to take in a deep breath before resuming his pitch.

"I would like to see your friend have this lovely gift for his lady friend. She would certainly treasure the piece, and, I presume, graciously show her appreciation. I can sell it today for only two hundred and seventy-five thousand dinars and not a dinar less. And that price is only for the moment."

Karim said to Sean, "The man is offering a price of two hundred and seventy-five thousand dinars. I suggest we offer two hundred and thirty-five thousand dinars. If he refuses, and he will, we will move to the door as thought we intend to leave the shop. If he is serious, he will have a counteroffer. If not, we can either visit another jeweler or return later. If you would say something to me while appearing concerned about the price that would help our cause."

Sean continued with the charade. Grimacing, he said, "I would say you are better at this game than me."

Karim responded, "Yes, I believe he would not understand. I think we have fooled him."

Karim said to the jeweler, "My friend says he will buy the one in town. It's less expensive and his lady friend probably will not notice the difference in the quality."

"Sorry. If you prefer the other necklace, perhaps you should buy it. From what you tell me it sounds like a bargain."

Karim said, "Good day, sir."

The jeweler responded, "Good day to you. Please come back another day."

Sean had passed through the door and Karim was about to follow when the jeweler called out, "Two hundred and fifty, then."

Karim asked Sean, "What about two hundred and forty?"

Sean said, "Sure."

Karim said, "Two hundred and thirty-five."

"Two hundred and forty."

"All right. It's a deal."

Sean and Karim returned to the counter where Sean paid the agreed-to sum. The jeweler gift-wrapped the necklace and in a separate box also gave Sean a small porcelain flower. Sean put the two small packages in a front pocket of his trousers.

Sean and Karim continued meandering the aisles of the souk. Outside one of the stores that sold carpets and tapestries, Sean said to Karim, "I might be interested in seeing what this merchant has to offer."

Karim said, "If you wish, sir. Remember, though, that the price of any item will be elevated if you show interest. I suggest you examine several items while showing a lack of serious interest in any particular one. You will save money that way. These merchants are keen at detecting an interest, and they are out to collect the highest price they can for their goods."

***

Triumphant, Nawaz turned to face Jabir, "You see our patience has paid off. The jewelry section was unsuitable for our plot. The police are never far from the area. Sometimes they are dressed as plain-clothed and they intermingle with the shoppers. Now, if I can find the American behind some carpets, I will slip my stiletto into his kidney. He will scream with pain and he will bleed to death in a few minutes. Then we can go and have a relaxing lunch. I will say that something fell on the man and injured him. I shall say I am going for medical help. Our business will be done and I can return home. Stay out of my way and meet me later at the car. Don't be late. If you are not there I won't wait for you."

***

Sean spotted a tapestry on the merchant's wall that caught his attention. The scene depicted a sunset over a forested mountain. Karim explained the tapestry represented a scene west of Erbil, and he added it would be an excellent memento of Sean's stay in Kurdistan. Sean concurred and asked the merchant to see the item. While fetching the tapestry from the wall, the shop's owner told Karim that it was made of lamb's wool and that an employee in his shop had woven the piece. He said she was a talented artist, and is unmatched in her artistic ability. Her husband had died a few years ago and she works to feed two small children and herself.

The merchant handed the piece to Karim, who held it at chest-high level so that Sean could have a view of it up close. Sean's interest grew. Contrary to Karim's prior advice, Sean commented, "It's lovely."

While holding the piece, Karim, forever alert, noticed a lone man disappear behind hanging carpets located a little beyond Sean. Karim signaled Sean and repositioned himself so he could watch for the man to reappear. When the man next came into view he had one hand in a pocket and he was walking with purpose toward Sean's back. Karim shifted to a spot beside Sean and then suddenly threw the tapestry into the would-be assassin's face. He shouted, "Knife."

Sean whirled about as Karim grabbed the man's left forearm. The assailant struggled to free his arm from Karim's grip and to clear himself of the tapestry. Sean saw the right hand with the stiletto and immediately grabbed the attacker's right wrist. His army training had programmed him to deal with the situation in which he suddenly found himself. He first pulled the man's arm forward and away from his body. Next, Sean quickly yanked the arm down and up hard behind the attacker's back. A distinct snap suggested the move had dislocated the shoulder. The man howled.

Karim kicked one of the Nawaz's legs and he went down on his back. To keep the man distracted, Karim slammed a swift boot into his rib cage. The man moaned and rolled to one side in agony, his arm limp and useless. He seemed to have difficulty breathing. Neither Sean nor Karim paid any attention to the knife as it lay on the floor several feet from the assailant. The tapestry fell away from the man's face, revealing a thick-necked brute with a dark black beard.

Karim picked up the tapestry from the floor and brushed away dirt. He calmly carried it to the merchant and asked the price. Unnerved by the disturbance, he said it was on sale for one hundred and fifty thousand dinars. Karim related the price to Sean, who withdrew the amount from his wallet. While the assailant writhed on the floor, the merchant hurriedly wrapped the tapestry. Karim retrieved the stiletto and handed it to the merchant, telling him, "The police might like to have this."

Sean told Karim that he had seen enough of the souk. "Let's go to the hotel. It's almost supper time." Much as they might look with disdain at litter along the roadside, they both turned for one last look at the man on the floor. In the parking lot, Osman was waiting for them while listening to music on the sedan's radio.

45

Settlement

AT the bar in the Altin Hotel, not far from the restaurant where Sean and his guards sat, Jabir finished his third bourbon. The alcohol gave encouragement. According to his plan, he would carry out the assassination and in the resulting confusion escape through the kitchen to the alley behind the building. His driver waited in their automobile at the end of the alley. This time he felt confident he would succeed. He no longer had to contend with Nawaz, his bluster or his insulting talk. Jabir knew he was good at what he did and he thought he would exceed all expectations. In particular, he would demonstrate to those who had sent Nawaz that he, Jabir, was the more capable of the two.

Jabir came to the hotel armed with a subtle yet efficient killing implement that had been perfected by the KGB. The device contained a sharp needle at the bottom, which could be used to inject a small grain of ricin into the targeted victim. The Russian politicos had perfected the device for terminating their enemies in public without causing a scene. Once the grain had been injected, the victim was doomed. Nobody had an antidote, and the victim would expire within a few days.

Karim and Osman had met Sean for their usual supper routine, and each sat at a different table although near one another. Osman sat where he could see Sean and Karim, as well as the main entrance to the restaurant. Karim sat facing the other two as well as the approach from the kitchen. In that configuration Osman could see anyone approaching Sean or Karim, and likewise, Karim could see anyone approaching Sean or Osman.

Osman, Karim, and Sean had just started their meals when Osman coughed. Karim immediately set his knife and fork on the table and turned toward the entrance. He stood when he saw a man approaching the table where Sean sat. At the warning sounds, Sean twisted around to see what was going on. Immediately he recognized the face of the man who had tried to kill him in the Parisian restaurant. At the same instant, Sean realized it was the same man who was waiting on the bench in the park. The intruder moved forward with a determined step.

As Jabir approached Sean, he withdrew what appeared to be a ballpoint pen from his shirt pocket. Karim, uncertain of the visitor's intentions, called out to Sean, "Watch out, Sean," as he moved between the this is your voice, keep it in; delete re-peated text.

stranger and Sean. The stranger forged ahead, stiff-armed Karim and knocked him backward over a table.

Osman realized the seriousness of the situation and bolted toward the attacker. Sean was there first. When Sean spotted the pen in the man's right hand, he knew he had to be careful. One jab and he would be doomed. Normal street-fighting tactics may not be sufficient. The assailant lunged at Sean, swinging the dangerous pen in a right-handed roundhouse. Sean sidestepped while grabbing the man's right wrist. He realized he had to restrain the attacker's right hand with the pen. The young man struggled with determination. While Sean held fast to the man's right forearm, the man's left fist swung wide and into the side of Sean's head, momentarily stunning Sean. Still, Sean held securely to Jabir's wrist. A voice inside his head told him it was do or die.

Osman came up to the assailant and grabbed his left arm while positioning his right foot behind the man. Sean noted Osman's signal and pushed the man backward over Osman's leg, tumbling Jabir to the floor. As they went down together, Sean kept hold of the man's right wrist. Osman likewise held tight to the man's left arm, pinning it to the floor.

The man twisted his arm with the pen and pointed it toward Sean, as though he still had a chance to finish his target. Osman kept the man's left arm out of the struggle. It was Sean's two arms against one. Slowly, Sean twisted the assassin's arm and aimed the pen toward the assailant's chest. The needle went in to its full depth. The man knew the unavoidable consequences and gave up the fight.

Sean remained at the restaurant while Osman and Karim tied Jabir's hands and feet with twine they borrowed from cooks in the kitchen. They dragged the would-be killer out of the restaurant. In the parking lot, they threw their captive in the trunk of their sedan. Because Osman and Karim were military personnel on duty at the time of the attack, they saw no reason to contact the police. The army represented the higher authority. They had captured an enemy combatant. They drove to the garrison, where they locked their captive in the stockade. At the most, he would live another three days, and those days would not be pleasant. The jailers might give him water and perhaps a little food until the end. They, too, had heard of the brutality of which the ISIS fighters were so proud. The Kurds were not inclined to turn a cheek. It was not one of their guiding principles.

Shaken from the two assassination attempts, Sean returned to the hotel. For a time he paced around the small room, trying to settle his nerves. He didn't want to resort to alcohol. He tried reading which also didn't help. Out of frustration, he slipped on a jacket and went out the front entrance of the hotel.

Sean wandered the streets of Erbil, musing. Strange, he thought, how his opposite on the enemy's team had followed him from Paris to Erbil. In a way he shared a common trait with the man. They both had a persistent devotion to duty and, it seemed, only a modest fear of danger. Without giving thought to where he might be going, Sean found himself in a neighborhood occupied by people of a lower income. The poor of the city reminded him of the neighborhood he knew in Donora. Both peoples were trying as best they could to survive and maybe find a modicum of happiness along life's path. As he passed by a house, he heard a woman singing behind a wall. She sang in a melodious and happy tone. At one point two small boys came running from a property, one chasing the other. Sean wondered if the boys had fathers to watch out for them and to guide them. If so, Sean would have envied them. The promenade relaxed Sean's tense muscles and settled his nerves. Karim and Osman would be back to the hotel and wondering where their charge had gone.

Karim was seated in the hotel lobby when he saw Sean enter. He stood and walked over to meet Sean. "Sir, are you all right? We were concerned."

"I'm fine. I merely went for a little fresh air," Sean said.

Although Karim knew walking the poorer streets of Erbil alone could be hazardous, he didn't lecture. Changing the subject, he said, "We missed dinner. If you like, sir, the three of us can go for the meal we intended to have hours ago."

Sean said, "That's a great idea. I've developed an appetite. Where's Osman?"

"Osman is waiting outside your room while I waited in the lobby. I'll call him."

When Osman came to the lobby, the three went to the hotel restaurant for supper. Contrary to their past habit, all three sat at the same table. The mood was somber, given the two attempts at Sean in one day. To lighten the mood, Sean asked, “I wonder how many more are out there?”

“Not to worry,” Karim answered. “However many there may be, we are prepared for them.”

Sean smiled at his guards. “I like your spunk. Had it not been for you two, I would not be sitting here now.”

When Sean returned to his room from the restaurant, his body needed a rest and his eyes were becoming heavy. Perhaps later he would get up and again try reading. He crawled into bed and fell asleep almost immediately. He began to dream.

Marielle and he were strolling along the Champs Élysées. People were out enjoying the pleasant weather and the sights. As they strolled along holding hands, Marielle suggested they play a game. They would take turns. One point earned for every correct prediction that a person approaching along the sidewalk was a foreigner, one point detracted for every wrong prediction. As the people passed by, they would determine if they were French or otherwise by listening to their language. Sean was captivated by Marielle’s carefree laughter and the way she teased him. In a short period of time, Marielle had four points to Sean’s negative two. Sean couldn’t understand how her predictions were so accurate. She explained her rationale. When a native Frenchman walks, she said, it’s easy to see he has determination to move from one location to another. Besides, most French persons on this avenue probably had been here before and they would not be taking in the sights. Foreigners, were different. They were not so dedicated to arriving at a particular destination. As they moved along, they gestured and observed. Americans are easy to spot. They talk a lot.

Suddenly Marielle stopped as she stared ahead. A man came up to Marielle and kissed her on the cheek. She excitedly exclaimed, "Camille, I thought you had moved away." The man answered, "No, it's just that I've been busy and traveling." Marielle turned to Sean and said, "I enjoyed seeing you again, Sean." The man took her hand, and the pair stepped away. Without turning around, she held her hand high to wave her fingers behind her in a goodbye gesture.

Sean bolted up in bed, wide awake. He felt as though a heavy wet blanket had fallen on him. He felt desperately lonely. The clock beside his bed read nine o'clock. Marielle would still be up. He reached for his phone. When she answered, he said, "I've been thinking of you."

"Likewise."

"Are we still on for a vacation?"

"Yes, I'm looking forward to time away from the hospital. When Mother was ill I couldn't take time off because I had to tend to her every day."

"I can be in Paris on Monday. How would that fit in with your schedule at the hospital?"

"Monday will be fine. I told my supervisor I was thinking of taking time off. Should I meet you at the airport?"

"No, I don't have my airline ticket yet. When I arrive, I'll take the Metro to your apartment. I'll let you know more later."

Toward the end of the second week, Sean went to visit Rojen.

The colonel said, "According to reports, our men are learning all they need to know from your classes. Thank you for your assistance. Now that we are nearing the end of your stay, is there anything I can do for you?"

"No, thank you. Your men are very dedicated, and they showed great interest in the classes. I think it all went well."

"Yes, the classes indeed went well," Rojen said. "I spoke to some of the junior officers and they all had only complimentary reports."

Pleased, Sean said, "This Friday should be the last class. I expect that your cadre can easily train the remainder of your men on the weapons. I'll be in Erbil over the weekend. If you need me for any reason, please call me at the hotel."

Rojen thanked Sean again for his "tremendous assistance" and they shook hands.

Karim and Osman escorted Sean to the Erbil International Airport, where he had reservations on a flight to Paris. Before Sean passed through security he thanked the two men and, in true Kurdish fashion, gave each a bear hug.

Osman wished Sean "As-Salaam." Karim added, "God speed."

46

Marielle

SEAN climbed the stairs to Marielle's apartment holding a bouquet of roses in one hand and his travel bag in the other. Waiting at her open door, she spread her arms wide waiting for an embrace. She wore black silk slacks, a pale green blouse, small gold earrings, heels, and a light blush on her cheeks. Taking care to avoid jabbing her with rose thorns, Sean wrapped one arm around her and they kissed. He stood back for a full view of his friend and lover from past years.

"Marielle, I didn't think a woman could be so alluring."

"You are exaggerating again. I'm not paying any attention to your fabrications. Anyway, welcome to Paris, world traveler. I want to hear about your adventures. Come inside."

Arm-in-arm they entered the condo, and Marielle closed the door.

"Have you eaten?" she asked him.

"Not for a time."

"How about a salad, a couple of eggs, and a baguette?"

"Next to you that would be the most beautiful thing I would see today."

"I'll put something together. Have a seat and put the telly on awhile."

Marielle arranged the roses in a vase, added water, and bent to inhale their aroma.

"The flowers are lovely. Thank you."

She said she would be only a moment and disappeared into the kitchen. Sean heard the sound of a cork being pulled from a bottle of wine. She returned with a tray of cheese, two wine glasses, and a bottle of Bordeaux. She set the tray on a coffee table near Sean.

Sean responded, "*Tu es plus gentille.*"

"So our traveling American has been practicing his French?"

"*Oui, exactement.*"

"*Tres bien.*"

Marielle brought the promised *repast*, and sat next to Sean. While he ate, she poured wine into both glasses. Lifting one glass, she wished Sean, "*Santé.*"

Sean took a few bites and turned to her. In profile, he thought Marielle to be more attractive yet. He began to hate himself for not having written all those years and for the strange way he behaved the last time he had seen her. In retrospect he came to realize his letters to her could not have done any damage. He had acted foolishly by failing to continue their correspondence in past years. When he finished eating, Marielle stood and carried the dirty plates to the kitchen. Sean watched her every step. The satiny slacks accentuated her firm, gorgeous *derrière*. She returned and sat beside Sean.

Holding her wine glass, she asked, "Tell me! Where were you, anyway? Or was your mission a secret that you cannot discuss?"

"In a way you are correct. I'm not supposed to talk about any details. I can tell you, though, I was in Iraq, helping our French and American friends fighting barbaric religious fanatics. These were people who wanted to kill all of us because we don't believe what they believe. More than that would bore you."

"I doubt that it would. In any event, I am glad you made it back."

"I almost didn't make it back. Maybe someday I'll tell you everything." He hesitated before continuing. "How about vacation plans and maybe a little travel?"

"Yes, by all means. Let's do it. We could see more sights in Paris, and in the provinces too."

Marielle peered at Sean over her half-empty wine glass. He hadn't taken more than a sip. He wondered: Was she trying to get him drunk, or was she drinking out of nervousness? He took a generous swallow in an effort to catch up with Marielle. He said to her, "That's an exceptionally good wine."

"Yes, I thought so too. I bought it last week. It cost a little more than what I usually pay, but..."

She stopped mid-sentence, and took a sip from her glass. "We can talk about travel and vacations tomorrow," she said. "I believe the best vacations are the ones without any big plans made in advance. You know: Just follow one's inclinations a day at a time."

Marielle sat her glass on the coffee table. "It seems I lost track of time. How long ago did you leave the Army?" she asked.

"Three years ago this past March. I was in for a stint of six years."

"If I am correct, your visit to me here in Paris was five years ago."

Sean felt guilty and ashamed. Although they had a hot romance years ago, it suddenly ended the day he disappeared across the Atlantic. Sean repositioned himself on the sofa to face Marielle.

"Marielle, I've done many foolish things in my past. Because you are a very attractive and alluring woman, I assumed that after I returned to the States you would soon find the love of your life. I knew you were devoted to your sick mother and she would be keeping you in Paris for a time–perhaps for a long time. Although I liked Paris, I never would have been able to find employment here. I would have been unable to survive in Paris. I thought the best favor I could do for you was to fade out of your life."

Marielle took a tissue to her eye. "You are kind and considerate. Actually, I did date men after our affair. I went with one particular man for two years. His name was Jacques. Marriage was not in the cards, though. We can discuss that in more detail another time. Jacques and I agreed on a friendly parting. He is now married. One Christmas he sent me a picture of his two daughters. Lovely children."

They continued talking throughout the remainder of the evening. The discussions traversed a wide range of subjects, from French politics to American involvement in the part of Iraq they both knew. When the Bordeaux was finished, Marielle went to the kitchen. Shortly she reappeared with a bottle of Chablis and a plate of warm, stuffed mushrooms. She declared the occasion to be special and one that called for more wine than usual. Their conversation during the second bottle became more spirited and varied. Around midnight Marielle expressed the opinion that Sean must be tired from his world traveling, and accordingly he should go to bed. She punctuated her announcement.

"You may sleep in mother's room."

Marielle stood and wagged an index finger at Sean like a schoolteacher scolding a naughty first grader.

"What am I talking about? Let's review history for the record. One evening I am going home from the hospital with a co-worker, discussing the hospital where we work. We were minding our own business, having a civil conversation. By chance, and entirely by chance, I glanced over to the tables at a local bistro as we were passing by. Who do I happen to see standing there? An American I knew once in the distant past. An American who was in the neighborhood. An old boyfriend who didn't bother to come knocking on my door to say hello or to ask how are you, Marielle. No, I had to roust him out from amongst the drinkers and revelers at a neighborhood hangout. Without much enthusiasm he tells me, 'Oh, hi, Marielle, nice seeing you again.' This is what I am talking about. So we need to get to know each other all over again. No, there will be no sex tonight at Marielle's condominium."

Being neither sentimental nor romantic by nature, Sean was at a loss for words. She had speared him through the heart with her valid accusations, and he knew he deserved the reprimand. He swallowed and closed his eyes. When he opened his eyes, he spoke in a soft, apologetic voice.

"You are entirely correct. I was wrong, and stupid would also apply. I thought knocking on your door would not have been the right thing to do. Today, I sorely regret it."

"Come along. Brush your teeth and then I'll tuck you in bed. Tomorrow we shall continue our conversation."

Marielle took Sean by the hand and led him to the washroom. When he finished brushing his teeth, she took him to her mother's former bedroom. She watched as he undressed to his underwear. When he got in bed, she pulled the sheets up to his neck and planted one on his forehead. She winked once, and he responded with another wink. She softly closed the door behind her.

***

In the morning the smell of brewing coffee in the condo caused Sean to stir. He turned on his side, and when he opened his eyes he realized he was in an unfamiliar bedroom. Rays of light streamed through a window framed with ruffled curtains. The walls were pastel–colored. At first he thought he might be in a dream; the real events of the previous day gradually drifted back. The travel from Kurdistan, the flight, Marielle, the wine, a kiss on the forehead at bedtime. The events all seemed surreal and different from the daily routine he had come to know as a bachelor living in rural Pennsylvania. He rolled the covers aside and stood, running his hand through his hair. He shook his head in an effort to clear the fog away. In the kitchen he found Marielle fussing with a skillet, her back to Sean. She wore shorts, a T-shirt, and Adidas running shoes.

Sean said, "Good morning."

At the sound of Sean's voice, Marielle jumped. "Oh, you startled me. Good morning. I am not accustomed to having a man in the house."

Sean came up behind her and kissed her on the neck while squeezing her behind.

Marielle asked, "Do you like crepes? How about a mushroom crepe? I bought fresh mushrooms yesterday."

"A crepe would be great. Yes, I like mushrooms."

Marielle served the crepes and coffee at a small table in the kitchen. As Sean sat, he asked, "Going running this morning?"

"Yes, I'll be gone for a little less than an hour. Relax. Take a shower."

While Marielle was running, Sean checked his emails. Wally had sent him an encrypted email.

I found the right path and I transferred the thirty from the SOB back to your second account. Did another ten for good measure. …..W

When Marielle returned from her run, Sean handed her the two small gifts he had purchased in Erbil. He told her to open the larger one first. When she saw the gold necklace, her mouth dropped. She said, "Oh, Sean, it's lovely. Thank you."

He told her the gift was a souvenir of Erbil. He helped her put it on, and told her it was becoming on her. She went to a mirror to see for herself. Upon opening the second box and expressing a second "thank you." She set the small porcelain flower on a table in her living room.

Later in the morning Sean and Marielle planned their excursion for the afternoon. Sean said he would like to go to the Louvre again. He hadn't seen everything there. Marielle said she always enjoyed going there, so the first afternoon they visited the Louvre.

That evening they ate at a restaurant where one of Marielle's cousins was a waiter. When the cousin saw Marielle, he walked over and they embraced. Marielle introduced her American friend. The cousin whispered that Marielle and her friend should avoid the beef and fish. The lamb was fresh and tasty. Although a little expensive, it was worth a try.

On their way back to Marielle's condominium Sean and Marielle stopped at a wine store. Sean said he was buying. On Marielle's recommendation, Sean selected a 2003 Chardonnay. He said he also liked Chablis, and Marielle recommended a 2005 vintage. With the two wine bottles they returned to Marielle's condo. That evening they watched a movie on TV, sitting side-by-side and sipping wine. Marielle found a station with English subtitles. Sean said that he was learning French, but that the language in the movies was too rapid for his brain to register the meaning of the words. At midnight, Marielle said, "I think it's bedtime. I've come to know you well enough by tonight, so sex is a possibility at Marielle's condo tonight. It depends."

Sean was taken aback. He didn't know what Marielle meant by "it depends."

"Marielle, I haven't had a chance to visit a pharmacy since I arrived in Paris. I think you know what I mean. I suppose they are all closed now. Tomorrow I'll make a trip."

"A trip won't be necessary. Remember I mentioned my former boyfriend Jacques?"

"Yes."

"Jacques made it clear that he hoped to have children. He said not many, maybe one or two. As you know, the French do not believe in large families. Jacques was due to inherit a sizeable farm one day, and he hoped to pass it along to children. When I knew his true wishes I had to be honest with him. One night I started crying, and I had difficulty stopping. Between tears I told Jacques that I was incapable of being a mother. In previous years I had a serious infection, and I had to have a body part removed. Jacques said he had to think of practical considerations. We drifted apart. In short, you need not visit the pharmacy."

Sean wrapped his arms around Marielle and held her tight. "Marielle, I'm truly sorry."

He took her by the hand and they walked to her bedroom where Sean helped her remove her blouse and slacks. Smiling shyly, she crawled into bed, waiting for Sean to join her. That night there was more than a little sex at Marielle's condominium. Sean said he was only trying to make up for lost years.

Throughout the first week Marielle and Sean visited sights around Paris. Sean was enthralled. Interesting sights during the day, delicious meals, wine in the evening and…Marielle. Monday and Tuesday of the second week they took a tourists' bus trip to the Touraine region to visit castles that were once the country estates of the kings. On a Tuesday evening, they returned to the condo and were sitting on the sofa, as had become their habit. Sean reached over and took Marielle's hand.

"I must think of returning home. I cannot continue living in fantasy-land indefinitely."

Marielle appeared sad. "I understand. I expect you have responsibilities in America."

He said, "Marielle, if I were to return to America without you, I would miss you dearly. My life would be hollow without you. Why don't you come with me?"

Marielle sat up straight. "Sean, I've grown very fond of you. I believe it might be called love in the near future. But, me go to America? I don't know. I'm Parisian. I've lived in Paris all my life. I have relatives here." She paused. "Although it's true I rarely see any of them. We all more or less go our own way. I would need time to think about it."

"Sure, I understand. Think about it. I thought I would leave Friday."

"Sean, you surprised me. I never expected that kind of an invitation."

She frowned. "What would I do with the condo?"

She pressed a hand to her check, thinking. "I suppose I could rent it, though. Apartments in this neighborhood command a good price. I always thought I might like to see America. A change would do me good. My passport is still valid."

Epilog

KURDISH police in Erbil tried to determine the identity of the man they had in custody–the man who had tried to kill another man in the carpet and tapestry shop in the souk. The man gave a false identity to the police, but they were not misled. In an effort to identify their prisoner, they sent a photo of their prisoner to various police departments around Iraq. Soon the police in Bagdad identified him as a notorious thug by the name of Nawaz Hadid. They sent a van to bring him back to Bagdad for "aggressive questioning." His interrogators questioned Nawaz until they were convinced he had no more information to provide, and then they sent him to the hangman for the war crimes he had committed at the behest of the ISIS fanatics.

After the Kurds evacuated their positions east of Mosul, the Iraqi Army moved to those same positions before launching an assault on the city. The ISIS soldiers fought well with what they had at their disposal, but the Iraqi Army was too large and too well equipped for their adversary. Although the fighting was savage at times, eventually the Iraqis forces took control of the city. Men of the Iraqi Army were appalled to find large numbers of young minority women living in homes without a male guardian.

Halima, the young Yazidi woman who had been raped repeatedly by the ISIS men survived. One afternoon when she was in her living room talking with a neighbor girl, someone knocked on her door. Naturally apprehensive since the ISIS invasion, she looked through a front window to see who was there. To her great delight, she saw her grandmother, thin and frail, standing at the door. She rushed to the door and threw her arms around her grandmother. The elderly woman explained that Iraqi Army personnel had forced the Sunni families to release their slaves.

The Yazidi contact who had the short wave radio, and who had kept the Kurds informed of the ISIS movements, survived the ISIS occupation of Mosul. After the Iraqi Army rousted the last of the ISIS soldiers from Mosul, he went to live with a cousin near the Iranian border. He said he no longer wished to live in Mosul. The sights of the city brought back too many sad memories.

After some thought on the matter, Marielle decided a change might be a good idea. She concluded nothing was keeping her in France so she went with Sean to America. When Sean first brought her to the trailer park where he lived, she was crestfallen. The scene was starkly different from the environs she enjoyed in Paris. The area lacked bistros where one might stop for a fresh croissant, coffee, or a glass of wine. The few restaurants nearby offered marginal fare that lacked imagination. Detecting Marielle's disappointment, Sean let her know that he was planning changes. The payment the agency had sent him for his help with their "project" would allow him to make several upgrades.

Sean had no trouble selling his gun shop. The new owner was a man who owned a similar store in a town fifteen miles east of McDougal's Firearms. Thinking of opening a gun shop in a large city, Sean considered the Washington DC area. He and Marielle spent days driving their new Toyota Camry around looking for a suitable property. Eventually they settled on a building in the town of McLean, Virginia. The building had been the home of a liquor store that went bust. Sean commissioned a Pennsylvania Amish cabinetmaker to build display cases and gun racks for the new shop. With help from Marielle and Wally, Sean transferred inventory from the shop in Pennsylvania to the property in McLean. When the work was finished, he staged a grand opening and was duly impressed with the prospective clientele of the area.

Sean bought a condominium in town, thinking Marielle would feel more at home and safer in a condo than in a house. Marielle selected all "French country" furniture for the new living quarters. Sean told her to buy top-of-the-line goods and not to worry about prices.

Because of increased traffic at the new gun shop, Sean hired a part-time salesman. Few hunters lived in the McLean area, although many of the locals had a strong interest in shooting and handguns. And the locals didn't quibble about price, as they did in Pennsylvania.

Marielle settled into her new life in Virginia. At first, she enjoyed a life of leisure and having nothing special to do. In time though, she became bored staying at home while Sean was occupied with the shop. Eventually, she told Sean she wanted something to do during the day. However, she did not care to do nursing anymore. While shopping in McLean she noticed there were no crepe shops in town. She suggested that a crepe shop might prosper in the town, and she enjoyed preparing crepes.

Together, Sean and Marielle considered several prospective sites for a crepe shop. They settled on a small section of a strip mall that had previously been a Chinese restaurant. They christened the shop "Marielle's Creperie." A waitress was hired so Marielle could concentrate on the cooking. Marielle wanted every crepe to be just right. The shop's hours were seven in the morning to two in the afternoon. She didn't think people would be hungry for crepes in the evening hours. Besides, she wanted her evenings free to be home with Sean. She loved her new life in America, and the following year she sold the condo in Paris. Sean insisted she open an account in her name and transfer the money from the condo to it. That money, he said, was hers alone. He wanted no part of it.

Matthew Barton called Sean one evening when he and Marielle were home reading. He repeated effusive compliments regarding Sean's accomplishments in Iraq. He said he was calling to offer Sean another assignment. He added that he believed Sean would like this one because it was "up his alley." Sean looked over to Marielle and told Matthew he was "not interested." He also mentioned that, nevertheless, he appreciated the call.

The next day Sean called Matthew from his shop. He said he wondered if Matthew could tell him a few more details of the proposed assignment. He was "just curious." Would the assignment involve travel overseas? Did it involve gun running again? Would he be alone or working with others?

Acknowledgements

Front cover photograph by
Aleshyn Andrei
Belarus

Developmental editing by
Carol Gaskin
Editorial Alchemy

The Author

Joseph E. Fleckenstein, an engineering graduate of Carnegie-Mellon University, grew up in Pittsburgh, Pennsylvania. Today he lives in eastern Pennsylvania with his wife Ana. Over the years, he made his living as an electrical engineer involved in the design of electrical power generating plants. He is the inventor of seven US patents and a number of foreign patents.

For recreation, Fleckenstein enjoys hunting, skiing, reading and, especially, writing. He has published over 36 items, most of which were short stories.

More particulars are available at the author's website, www.WriterJEF.com.

Watch for Fleckenstein's next book, a collection of short stories titled "A Family Matter and Other Stories."

CPSIA information can be obtained
at www.ICGtesting.com
Printed in the USA
BVHW070858060919
557728BV00001B/38/P

9 781532 398599